Australian Contemporary
Romance

Loving Fenella

LENA WEST

Gymea Publishing

Published by Gymea Publishing

https://www.facebook.com/LenaWestAuthor/

www.lenawestauthor.com

ISBN-13: 978-0-6482110-4-4

Disclaimer

This story is a work of fiction.

Names, characters, places and incidents are the product of the author's imagination and are used fictitiously. Any resemblance to events, locales or actual persons, living or dead, is entirely coincidental.

Some actual locations may be referenced in passing.

Table of Contents

Lena West

Dedication

To Darryl, who has supported my writing journey from the
beginning

1

Fenella sat half-way up the beach, sketchpad on her knees and a pencil loosely clasped between idle fingers.

This late in the afternoon the dotterels she'd been sketching as they ran back and forth along sand exposed by the low tide had all disappeared, but the concept for a new painting was firing her imagination. She sat where she was and let the idea develop. Aphrodite emerging from the sea, only something about the image didn't quite gel.

At first, she imagined the figure rising from the water was part of her vision, until she realised it was a man, not the goddess of her imagination.

Yes. Of course!

Exultant, she thanked her Muse for providing her with an ideal model.

Her image would be male. A young Poseidon laying aside his aquatic duties of the day to disport himself among his temple maidens as evening spreads its mantle of darkness.

Yes! That was it!

Galvanised, Fenella straightened, focusing intently on the figure of a man striding through the frothy backwash. She carefully studied the play of impressive muscles and the exact carriage of the head flung proudly back on the strong corded neck, as if paying silent homage to the dying sun's vibrant glory.

There was neither time nor light enough for sketching, so she concentrated eyes, heart and soul on memorising details; absorbing the essence of her god emerging from the sea's embrace. Water droplets, turned to sparks of fire by the setting sun, scattered around him. Confetti strewn by invisible attendant sprites.

Across the wet, hard-packed sand below the high tide line he strode.

Nearer and nearer he came, and still the image of a pagan god held true. The summer sun's last fiery rays haloed him, burnishing well-defined muscles, and filling the hollows of his body with inky shadows. The last tiny runnels of water trickling down his arms were transmuted into liquid gold.

For Fenella, the moment was utterly magical, and she prayed for the skill to translate her living god onto canvas. Seen at close range, as well as his body, his high-cheeked Nordic face dominated by an authoritative nose, provided the perfect model for the painting she would create, and she locked it into her memory, finding the contrast between sensually curved lips and imperious chin particularly apt.

But her super-intense survey had drawn her subject's attention. His steps slowed, and as he drew level he swung his head to stare down at her from an impressive height. Lips tightened, and a frown creased his broad forehead, snapping Fenella out of her trance-like concentration with a start.

This man was no model posing for a life class! He was real; and a total stranger. An apparently annoyed stranger!

Mortified, Fenella cringed. Before she could tear her gaze away, their eyes clashed. Locked. Mouth suddenly dry, pulse racing, she wanted to jump to her feet and run, only her limbs froze, holding her in thrall until, chin tilted imperiously, he dismissively turned from her, continuing on his way up the beach.

With a whoosh, Fenella released the breath she hadn't been aware of holding, and slumped forward, head on her knees. Goosebumps pebbled her flesh and a shiver sent a chill up her spine.

~~~~~

Initially, Greg had been unaware of the presence of another person on the beach. It wasn't till some disturbing quality in the woman's concentrated gaze raised the hair on the back of his neck, that he glanced her way.

A broad-brimmed sunhat pulled low to shade her face, and a loose, long-sleeved shirt effectively hid her identity. Only a pair of long, slender legs hinted at youthfulness. She was staring fixedly at him and something about her roused his curiosity.
~~~~~

Involuntarily, he almost went directly up to her, his eyes held by the power of her intent gaze, when it occurred to him she was probably just a star-struck fan.

Bloody hell! One of his reasons for moving to this backwater coastal town was to escape being continually in the limelight, and get to live a normal life again. Normality was especially important now that Aimee lived with him. He turned away impatiently and quickened his pace, heading for home.

~~~~~

Freed at last from the trance in which she'd been locked, Fenella giggled weakly. It was a pity he wasn't anyone she knew, a friend she could ask to pose, but he was a stranger. A summer visitor she guessed, whom she was unlikely to see again. Which meant she'd have to rely on her memory and augment it with imagination.

Perhaps it was best anyway, that her god remain in the realms of fantasy. Anticipation lifted her lips in a smile as she gathered her bits and pieces and set off briskly in the opposite direction along the beach, gradually blending into the rapidly falling darkness and becoming one with the night.

Eager to commit her god from the sea to canvas, she was almost running by the time she reached home. An apple munched absent-mindedly while she cleared space in her studio for the new project sufficed for dinner, as, under the lash of a now urgently demanding muse, Fenella worked through the night. Still on a creative high although limp with exhaustion, she at last lay down her brush and stood back to study the emerging picture.
~~~~~

Good, she thought. It was more than good. Possibly, when completed, it would be the best she'd ever painted. To the left of the central figure she'd sketched in a small, white temple high up on the headland.

Beside a boat drawn up on the sand to the right, two elderly fishermen, who bore a more than passing resemblance to Matt Sykes and his mate Johnno Maguire, sat mending nets, heads bowed respectfully as their god strode by.

As for the god himself, he was magnificent. Lustily male, proudly majestic, yet young and eager, a gleam lighting his eyes. A pagan deity, brow bound with finely wrought gold and a workman-like trident trailing carelessly from one hand. His smile's sensuous curves hinted at pitiless omnipotence.

In spite of her exhilaration, Fenella shivered. Even incomplete it was obvious her subject was more than a mortal man. He was truly the god she'd envisaged.

A mortal man had provided the inspiration though. A man who lingered in her mind as she lay down to snatch an hour or two's rest. The dreamy thought crossed her mind that yes, if he ever crossed her trail again, she would recognise him. For sure. And...

But that was too foolish to even contemplate.

2

Much too short a time later Fenella awoke to find Zilla, her faithful canine companion, demanding to be let out. Awake now, whether she wanted to be or not, she ruefully pulled on athletic shorts and top, slipped into a comfortable pair of down-at-heel joggers, and set off for her regular morning run along the beach; faithful pooch frisking in and out of the water close by. On the way home, they detoured via the shops to pick up a newspaper.

"You know, Fenella, I reckon that little kid over there is lost." Shirley Morton, the tall, thin, grey haired proprietor of the Topaz Sands Newsagent, the only shop open this early in the morning, nodded towards a tearful, scruffy blonde moppet in the beach-side carpark across the street. "I know most of the kids, at least by sight, but she's not one I recognise," she added, her pensive tone a toss-up between motherly concern for the child's welfare, and the exasperation felt by many of the locals towards the hordes of holiday visitors upon whose trade the seaside community's prosperity depended.

"A recent arrival, I guess."

"You may be right, Shirl," Fenella answered thoughtfully, catching her bottom lip between her teeth. After a moment's further consideration, she offered corroboration of Shirley's theory.

"She looks like the kid who was collecting shells while I was jogging. Probably she can't remember which house her family's renting."

Fenella flashed a quick grin. A tall, shapely brunette with an abundance of wild, fly-away curls tied carelessly at her nape, and a scattering of freckles gracing a regally straight nose, she pursed generous lips in a whistled command to the fox terrier nosing curiously about in the gutter.

"Come on Zilla. Off we go to the rescue. Bye Shirl, catch you later."

Fenella ambled across the street, approaching the distressed child quite casually. Zilla, who adored all children, ran ahead, making a bee-line for the little girl as Fenella had guessed she would. Startled by the wet nose investigating her knee, the child jumped back with a squeal.

"My cue," murmured Fenella under her breath.

"It's okay Sweetheart," she called, using the friendly, no-nonsense voice that was familiar to every child at the local primary school. "Zilla won't bite. She's just asking you to be friends. Let her sniff your hand a moment, then you can give her a pat."

By the time she finished speaking, she had come up with the child and was scrutinising her closely.

She was most definitely not a local, Fenella confirmed to herself, noting the unfamiliar dainty features and china-blue eyes framed by long, straight, pale gold tresses.

She also noted the crumpled, misbuttoned blouse. The child had dressed in a hurry, and without adult assistance by the look of it.

"Out for a walk on the beach before the others are up, are you Sweetheart?" Fenella smiled encouragingly as the child, regaining her composure by the second, bent to pat the ever-willing Zilla.

Chin trembling uncertainly again, the moppet eyed Fenella cautiously.

"I'm not allowed to talk to strangers," she whispered.

"That's an excellent rule," Fenella agreed, "and normally I don't talk to strangers either. You never know what sort of dreadful people they might be, do you?" The little girl nodded, round eyed and wary. "The thing is though, Sweetheart," Fenella continued, "I was watching you, and I got the feeling you're lost. If that's so, Zilla and I would like to help you."

The equal proportions of fear and hope that suffused the small face confirmed her own and Shirley's assessment, although Fenella still took care not to rush matters.

"How about we introduce ourselves?" she suggested. Seeking to establish her bona fides, she waved to Shirley, still standing in the shop doorway. "That lady over there in the shop knows Zilla and I really well," she informed the child.

When Shirley waved right back, the little girl exclaimed in relief.

"Oh! She does know you. And look! There's a Safety House sign in her shop window."

"That's right," Fenella answered lightly. "Mrs Morton and I are old friends." The woman and child shared a smile and Fenella continued with her introductions.

"My name is Fenella and I live right here in Topaz Sands," she said, bending down to stroke the friendly terrier. "This little lady is my dog, Zilla. If you offer nicely, she'll shake hands with you," Fenella coaxed.

"Okay." The child offered her hand, laughing out loud when Zilla promptly sat down and politely held up a paw.

"I don't know where my house is," the little girl confided a few moments later, bottom lip wobbling dangerously. "I went down the steps onto the beach, but when I came up again everything looked different. My house should be right near the steps." There was a catch in the plaintive voice as its owner gazed up and down the street in bewilderment. "Do you know where I live, Fenella?" she asked hopefully.

"There are two sets of beach steps, Sweetheart," Fenella explained calmly. "Lots of people get mixed up at first if they come up the wrong ones. How about I show you the others. Do you know what your house looks like? Let's see if we can find it," she said.

When the child nodded affirmatively. Fenella held out her hand and the girl placed her much smaller one in it.

"My house is a pretty blue one," she informed her new friend. "It has a deck, so you can look at the beach. There's a great big pine tree in front, but I forget the number."

The little face crumpled momentarily and her hand clasped Fenella's more securely.

"We just got here yesterday, and I don't remember it yet."

"I think I do know your house Sweetheart. Let's go and see, shall we? Your mummy might be getting worried about you by now."

"I haven't got a mummy any more. My Mummy went to live in Heaven."

Delicate pink lips quivered piteously then assumed an ominous pout.

"Daddy and Linda won't be worried though," she added, "they're still asleep in bed. I looked."

Fenella glanced sharply at her small companion. Deciding against making any comment, she merely gave the small hand a comforting squeeze. They walked along silently for a while until the child spoke again.

"Why do you call me sweetheart all the time?" she asked, curiously.

"Because you look like a real little sweetheart," Fenella answered with a warm smile, "and because I don't know your proper name. You forgot to tell me."

"Oh. I'm sorry Fenella. I'm Aimee," the little girl answered politely. "I used to be Aimee Stone when I lived with my Mummy," she confided, "but now Daddy says my name is really Aimee Kendall. Sometimes I get mixed up."

Poor moppet. Fenella's heart went out to this kid who was so obviously missing her mother and was unsettled by recent dramatic changes in her life.

A right turn, then a left, brought them onto The Promenade; a street lined on both sides with mature Norfolk Pines. The eastern side was taken up by big modern houses overlooking the beach. On its western side, more modest houses were interspersed with two and three-story blocks of holiday flats. This was where most of the transient population of Topaz Sands lived.

Part way along was a flight of wooden steps giving beach access to the occupants of this section of the town. Just past the steps Aimee stopped and tugged at Fenella's hand, bouncing up and down in her excitement.

"There it is, Fenella! That's my house," squealed Aimee. "See, there's Daddy's car in the driveway, 'cause he couldn't get it in the garage yesterday 'cause of all the boxes."

Fenella cast an idly admiring eye over the electric blue BMW.

Daddy has expensive tastes, she thought, comparing it with her humble, but eminently serviceable yellow Pulsar.

At that moment feet pounded up the steps from the beach.

"Daddy! Daddy! Were you looking for me?"

As Aimee called out, icy fingers played up Fenella's spine, her breath hitching in her throat. She'd just spent most of the night mentally basking in this man's company, committing his image to canvas.

A dull flush swept across her cheeks, dissipating almost as quickly to leave her white and dizzy.

A rich baritone shouting its owner's relief brought her back into the present.

"Aimee! Aimee, thank God you're safe."

A blond man, tall and deep-chested with an impressive set of biceps, jostled past Fenella.

Falling to his knees, he scooped the child up against his broad chest.

"Oh, Aimee love. You gave me such a scare when I woke up and found you gone." He gave the little girl a gentle shake. "Don't ever do that to me again, will you honey?" he begged, rising to his feet and swinging his daughter up onto his hip.

"I won't Daddy," Aimee promised solemnly, her small arms strangling him in a fierce hug. Leaning back in her father's arms she explained. "I only went to look for shells on the beach, Daddy. See."

She dug into the pockets of her shorts to produce a handful of shells. "Aren't they pretty?"

Nodding agreement, her father opened his mouth to speak. Aimee, sensing she was about to be reprimanded, got in first with her excuse.

"But you know Daddy, when I came back it was the wrong steps, and I didn't know where our house was. But it was okay," she reassured him, "Fenella showed me."

Remembering her manners, she turned to introduce her rescuer. "This is Fenella, Daddy, and that's her dog, Zilla. Zilla can shake hands," she added, as if that would make everything alright again.

Aimee's father tore his distracted gaze from his child, subjecting Fenella to a piercing scrutiny from a pair of the bluest eyes she had ever encountered. Acute, discerning eyes, deeply set beneath a broad, high forehead topped with a mop of thick, honey-gold waves. A determined chin added a touch of sternness to the whole.

A man to be reckoned with, Fenella judged.

A man used to getting his own way.

But only a man, she reminded herself, *not a god*. Especially not her god. Although yes, she'd recognised him instantly, just as she'd known she would. Last night had been too dark to discern the colour of his water-slicked hair, but there was no mistaking those features or that imposing height and build.

Amazingly, Aimee's father was both a flesh and blood man and her god from the sea.

Something unashamedly female which had been dormant for way too long quivered painfully to life within her.

Boldly, refusing to be intimidated, Fenella returned his assessing gaze. *If he can look, then so can I,* she thought recklessly. He was certainly worth a second look. A disconcerting warmth began stealing its way into her intimate core.

Mortified, she became excruciatingly aware of her ancient, sweat-stained running clothes and windblown hair scruffed back any old how, with only a rubber band to restrain its unruliness.

Hardly an alluring image for meeting a god, she reflected, smothering her belated vanity with ego-saving amusement.

As if he cares, she mentally chided herself.

All he's concerned about is his daughter; and rightly so. Besides, since when have I made impressing a man one of my priorities?

Since you saw this one, her subconscious whispered right back.

Automatically, Fenella accepted the hand he thrust in her direction, responding with equal firmness to his handshake.

She liked his strong grip. Liked, also, the intimate warmth of feeling her slim fingers enfolded within his large hand.

Liking altogether too much about this chance-met stranger, Fenella strove to maintain a cool, self-possessed control, and not to dissolve into a state of incoherent adoration like a silly over-impressionable teenager.

"Greg Kendall." Aimee's father introduced himself tersely.

His clipped tones snapped Fenella back to reality. Thank goodness he was apparently unaware of her inner turmoil. She breathed a little easier.

"Thanks for taking care of young Aimee, here." He ran his free hand distractedly through already rumpled locks Fenella's fingers itched to smooth into place. "We only arrived yesterday, and haven't had time to set the ground rules yet. Like not wandering off to the beach alone."

He grinned at Aimee and tousled her hair to take any sting out of his words. Her heart skipping a beat at the sudden lift to her own spirits in response to that infectious grin, Fenella smiled right along with him.

She had liked him as a stern father; but the engaging boyishness of his grin melted her all the way through to her bones.

This Greg Kendall was too sexy for words. Or for her peace of mind.

Bemused, Fenella snapped her wandering thoughts to attention and caught up with the conversation. The havoc wrought by his rich, toe-curling voice was threatening to completely upset her entire nervous system. Taking a deep breath, she forced herself to focus.

"It was an awful shock to wake up and find her missing," Greg shuddered graphically. "I've been scouring the beach for her, and was about to start on the streets when I heard her voice."

The sympathetic reply hovering on Fenella's lips was forestalled by a strident exclamation issuing from the mouth of an angry young woman rapidly approaching from the blue house. Her precise grooming, this early, and in such anxious circumstances, contrasted sharply with the rough and ready presentation of the other three.

"You're a very naughty little girl, Aimee," she shrilled. "You should know better than to run off by yourself. Daddy and I were very upset," she concluded, a frown marring her immaculately made up face.

A dreadful, hollow nausea curdled Fenella's stomach.

Now, when she was almost panting with lust for Aimee's father, she recalled the child's reference to Linda. Linda, who shared her Daddy's bed.

Saved in the nick of time from making a fool of herself over the man; a married man at that, which was even worse; Fenella turned curiously to the new arrival, studying the immaculately presented blonde who abruptly attempted to disguise her temper with hastily assumed sweetness.

"You're lucky Daddy found you so quickly, Aimee dear," she trilled, replacing the frown with a smile that didn't quite reach her eyes.

The child obviously dealt with to her satisfaction, she eagerly refocused her attentions upon her husband, oozing well-practised sensuality in his direction. A woman thoroughly used to the effect her charms had on the male psyche, she twined both hands round Greg Kendall's arm; her back turned with deliberate rudeness, excluding Fenella.

"Now that our naughty little miss is safe and sound, let's go inside, Darling," she urged sweetly. "I'll have breakfast ready in a jiffy."

Walking purposefully towards the gate, she propelled the other two Kendalls along with her.

"Thanks again, Ms... er..." Greg Kendall smiled an apology over his shoulder as he allowed himself to be led away.

"Bye Fenella. Bye Zilla."

Aimee turned, waving an enthusiastic farewell from the safety of her father's arms.

So much for that, Fenella shrugged. In her opinion the petulant beauty had been far more annoyed than worried over her step-daughter's escapade.

Her chastisements had been cold, lacking the warm overtones of loving concern so evident in the father's.

Poor Aimee, Fenella thought, returning the child's wave. However, the Kendalls were no concern of hers, even though Greg Kendall was the first man in way too long to stir lustful yearnings within her. Impatiently, she thrust them from her mind, running lightly down the nearby steps onto the beach.

On the way home to her belated breakfast, Fenella remembered to stop by the newsagency again to reassure Shirley Morton about the child's safety.

"A family by the name of Kendall," she recounted. "The mother's dead and Aimee lives with her father, Greg Kendall. Now why does that name ring a bell?"

"I can give you one reason why," Shirley chuckled. She plucked a paperback from the nearby stand of best sellers, *A Death Too Far* by Gregory R Kendall. Turning it over she showed the author's photo on the back cover.

"But that's him, Shirl!" Fenella squeaked. Taking the book from Shirley, she scanned the blurb and the brief author biography. "So Aimee's father is a writer, Shirley. I've read his books, and they're not bad. The latest one is being made into a movie. Exalted company we're getting in Topaz Sands these days." She grinned slyly at the older woman.

"You'll have to arrange a book signing if he's here long enough, Shirl."

Fenella was impressed in spite of herself. No wonder the dratted man had such an imperious air, she thought. She hadn't been overly taken with his Linda, though.

For Aimee's sake, she hoped she'd been mistaken in her assessment of the woman she assumed to be the child's stepmother.

3

The very next day while enjoying her early morning run on the beach, Zilla at heel as usual, Fenella encountered Aimee again. This time the child was a small, lonely figure standing on the bottom rail of the blue house's observation deck, gazing wistfully down at the beach.

"Fenella! Hello Fenella!" she called, waving excitedly. "Can I come down on the beach to play with Zilla? Daddy says I can't go on my own, but I won't be on my own 'cause you're there," she cajoled, her logic tickling Fenella's ready sense of humour.

Aimee was a truly engaging child, but Fenella was more than a match for even the most engaging of childish wiles.

"Better not, Aimee love," Fenella called back. "I don't think that's what your daddy meant, do you?"

Aimee pouted.

"Your daddy meant you should be with him or Linda, didn't he?"

She waited for Aimee's grudging assent, then, sure the child would stay put, called out a cheerful goodbye and resumed her interrupted run.

This early morning hour was the time Fenella loved best on the beach, when the air was still and crisp, retaining the night time coolness. The muted colours of waves and sand held a pearly glow that would rapidly dissipate as the sun climbed higher. Here, for a brief time, she felt at one with the universe.

The serene benediction of ocean and sky had played a crucial role in her healing and she returned each morning to renew her spirits and gird her soul against the rigours of the day ahead. Running on the beach was more than exercise for Fenella Wilkins.

A lot more.

Usually there were few people about, allowing her the exhilaration of feeling she owned the whole beach. Zilla enjoyed their run too. During the busy summer season this was the only time Fenella could let her off her leash to run freely, splashing in and out of the waves hissing onto the sand as she chased the elusive gulls. Later in the day there were too many people about for her to bring her dog onto the beach.

Aimee was on the deck every morning after that, and the exchange of friendly good mornings between the two of them quickly became an integral part of Fenella's run.

Repelled by Linda's rudeness and Greg Kendall's celebrity status, not to mention his marital status, she avoided the Kendalls by keeping to the other end of the beach later in the day.

It would have been fun to spend a little time with Aimee, to whom she had taken an instant liking, but Fenella was loath to intrude where she felt certain she'd not be welcome.

Also, unless they had business with them, the locals, among whom she counted herself, steered clear of the summer visitors; keeping themselves to themselves.

Thus, it wasn't until the middle of Sunday morning that Fenella found herself face to face with the Kendall family again.

Her easel set up in a sheltered corner of the beach, she was engrossed in capturing the antics of a group of children building a sandcastle nearby. She had painted the beach and its habitués many times, entranced by its ever-changing moods which never failed to provide her with inspiration.

Long ago she'd learned to block from her consciousness the attentions of inquisitive onlookers, so at first, was unaware of the family strolling towards her. It was Aimee, recognising her with a delighted shriek, who first intruded on her concentration.

"Fenella! Hi, Fenella!" Aimee called.

Pulling free of her father's hand she dashed ahead, coming to an abrupt stop at Fenella's side.

"What are you doing?" She stared curiously at Fenella's work in progress. "Are you an artist, Fenella? I never met an artist before."

"Hello Aimee." Fenella smiled at the child then turned her head towards the two adults following her more sedately. "Hello Mrs Kendall. Mr Kendall," she added, cool tone contradicting the rebellious thrill the sight of the tall, broad-shouldered man evoked.

Working on her sea god painting had caused her thoughts to stray in his direction too often for comfort since their brief meeting. Vainly, she had striven to convince herself it was merely his fame which attracted her. Face to face, she was forced to admit the compelling aura was an integral part of the man himself. Regardless of his occupation or company, Greg Kendall would always command attention; particularly female attention.

Coolly aloof today, he merely nodded casually in reply to her greeting.

"Her name's not Mrs Kendall, silly."

Aimee giggled, her comment releasing Fenella from introspection. She glanced down, meeting the sparkling gaze of the eagerly upturned little face.

"Linda's just Daddy's girlfriend," Aimee announced.

An angry flush stained the young woman's classically beautiful features.

Greg Kendall, frowning at his daughter's rude dismissal of the woman on his arm, stepped forward. "Let me introduce you two ladies to each other. Linda Beck, my *fiancée*," he elucidated crisply, emphasising the title ever so slightly, "and Fenella ... I'm sorry, I didn't catch your name in all the excitement the other day."

The incomplete introduction was concluded with the impatient air of one unused to finding himself at even so minor a disadvantage.

He stared at Fenella, silently commanding her to provide the missing information.

"Wilkins," she complied mildly. "Fenella Wilkins. Nice to meet you Ms Beck."

Although it wasn't nice at all.

And neither was Linda Beck.

With a cool social smile Fenella offered her hand only to have it disdainfully ignored by the supercilious Ms Beck. Smile fading, Fenella's eyes coldly raked Linda Beck from head to foot, one expressive eyebrow raised as she slowly lowered her hand, refusing to be put out of countenance.

It was Greg Kendall, not his fiancée, who flushed angrily this time. The ensuing awkward silence was broken by Aimee's innocent treble.

"Look at Fenella's painting, Daddy. It's really good," she urged, leaning trustingly against Fenella's shoulder. Greg, lips easing from their tight grimace at his fiancée's lack of manners, obediently moved closer to look. His slightly bored, casual glance sharpened, and he peered more intently at the nearly completed watercolour.

"The kid's right." He ruffled his daughter's hair. "This is very good. You're quite a talented artist, Fenella Wilkins. Do you exhibit your work anywhere?"

"Only locally so far, Mr Kendall," Fenella replied, warmed by his compliment. "Some of my work sells through the 'Lotus Flower Gallery' here in Topaz. I also do children's book illustrations," she added proudly, eager to impress on this highly successful man that she too, was successful in her chosen field; her work not to be lightly dismissed.

Greg eyed her with grudging respect. He appeared about to speak again when Linda Beck, jealous of his attention to another woman, slipped her arm through his to possessively drag him off once again.

"Come along, Darling," she urged, "Ms Wilkins must be wanting to get on with her work. And you did promise Aimee an icecream, remember?"

"Bye Fenella. See you around," Greg threw casually over his shoulder. With a self-deprecating grin that endeared him to Fenella all over again, he allowed himself to be led away.

"Bye Fenella," Aimee accompanied her words with a wet, child's kiss on Fenella's cheek, surprising her, then ran to snatch up her father's hand in both of hers.

So, Linda was only his fiancée, not his wife.

Yet.

Fenella grimly disparaged herself for her conflicting reactions to that snippet of information. *Is fiancée a euphemism for girlfriend, or does Greg Kendall actually intend to marry that abominable woman?*

Either way he wasn't free.

Chiding herself for her curiosity, she refocused her concentration on the painting resting on its easel.

Greg Kendall was undoubtedly the most attractive man she'd seen in ages, maybe ever, but he was nothing to her; and could be nothing to her as long as he remained encumbered by a fiancée.

Fenella Wilkins did not poach other women's men.

So, get used to it, she instructed herself.

The following morning the deck of the blue house stood bare and empty. A sharp pang of loss surprised Fenella. Surely she hadn't allowed herself to grow as fond of the child as all that! It would be folly to become closely involved with this particular child. Greg Kendall's imposing image flashed into her mind only to be ruthlessly expunged. As she jogged towards the southern end of the beach, where her own modest cottage was tucked into a sheltered nook below the headland, Fenella wondered if Aimee's absence meant the Kendalls, holiday over, had departed.

All the better if they had.

Greg Kendall had made way too strong an impact on her for her peace of mind. She wouldn't miss Linda Beck though. Not with her high and mighty airs. It was a pity a sweet kid like Aimee was doomed to suffer such an unsympathetic woman as her stepmother. Fenella was afraid that that one wouldn't turn out to be a happy relationship.

Shrugging, she dismissed the Kendall ménage from her thoughts. They were no concern of hers and she could do nothing anyway, she reminded herself. And that was the unhappy truth!

She steadfastly refused to listen to the inner voice that insisted otherwise.

4

So much for having seen the last of the Kendalls!

Irony briefly darkened Fenella's usually cheerful features, and her heart performed unwelcome flip-flops in spite of all her stern lectures to herself on the subject.

Even relegating the now completed sea god to the spare bedroom and turning him to face the wall, hadn't helped in her attempt to banish his model from her treacherous heart.

Upon entering the newsagent, she had instantly spied Greg Kendall's blond head towering above a chattering group of customers. No matter how unwanted, anticipation added an unconscious swing to her walk and an extra sparkle to her warm brown eyes which set their golden depths dancing.

While not a conventionally pretty woman, her glowing vitality and keen interest in everyone and everything around her endowed Fenella with an attractive vibrancy that inevitably drew the eye and lingered in the memory as mere prettiness never could.

"I see you took my suggestion to heart, Shirl," she murmured in a laughing aside. Leaning back against the counter Fenella watched Greg Kendall good-humouredly autographing books; his easy charm to the fore, winning him as many fans as his novels did.

"It's so good of him." Shirley, more pink-cheeked than usual, fluttered restlessly. "Julie Munroe recognised him." Guilty eyes slide towards a prominently displayed poster advertising the latest Gregory R Kendall novel.

"She asked him to autograph the book she'd just bought. Next thing I knew a couple of others followed suit. Word passed around pretty quickly after that."

Culpability written all over her face, Shirley glanced at Greg, then quickly away, causing Fenella to wonder with good natured cynicism how much her friend had helped that word along.

"Greg's been busy signing books for about half an hour now," Shirley continued. "I even had to fetch more of his novels from the storeroom to meet the demand."

Confident Fenella would appreciate her perspicacity, Shirley smirked, not even pretending false innocence.

"Just as well I ordered in more last week."

Fenella well knew an astute business woman lurked beneath Shirley Morton's dithery exterior. In reality, she was sharp as a filleting knife, and extremely efficient. Undoubtedly, she had been hoping for an opportunity like this; hence the order for more Gregory R Kendall thrillers last week.

At Fenella's uninhibited peal of laughter, Greg glanced up from his task.

Blue eyes clashed with brown, sending a skitter of breath-catching awareness tickling up Fenella's spine. She stood a little straighter, a faint tinge of pink warming the tan of her cheeks.

"Fenella Wilkins!" Greg beamed a well-practised, million-watt smile at her across the head of the last of his fans who waited patiently for his attention.

"We meet again. Most fortuitously, I might add, since I was about to go searching for you."

Fenella snapped shut a mouth that had dropped open in surprise.

"Don't rush away, will you," Greg continued. "I want to talk to you about a painting."

"Okay." Fenella's nonchalant demeanour belied the excitement fizzing in her blood. Her heart had skipped a beat when he announced he was looking for her, but she grimly ordered it to behave. Her painting, not her self, was all that interested Greg Kendall.

And that's just the way I prefer it, she told herself mendaciously.

"Hi, Fenella." A small, moist hand curled snugly into hers and Fenella tore her eyes away from the father to meet the daughter's joyful grin with an equally cheerful one of her own.

"Hello Aimee love. What's that you've got?" Fenella asked.

"Mrs Morton said I could pick out a book for myself. I like this one. It's all about a beach like Topaz Sands." Aimee held up the picture book for Fenella's inspection.

"It is Topaz, Sweetheart, only it's got a different name in the story. That's one of the books I painted the pictures for. See, there's my name on the cover – 'Illustrated by Fen Wilkins' it says."

"Daddy, look at this!" Aimee squealed as Greg escaped at last from his fan club to join Fenella where she still leant against Shirley's counter. "This is Fenella's book! See, that's her name, right there." Her chubby finger carefully traced Fenella's name on the cover.

"So I see." Greg flashed another of his dangerous, spine-tingling smiles in Fenella's direction. This one with an added tinge of genuine respect for her achievements.

"Why don't you ask Fenella to write in it for you, Honey."

With a wicked glint, he handed Fenella the expensive gold fountain pen he had used to autograph his own books. As Fenella accepted it, their fingers brushed accidentally. Abruptly, Fenella bent her head over Aimee's book to hide the betraying blush his touch had startled out of her. Head still bowed, she sought a suitably innocuous topic of conversation.

"If I'd known you were doing a book signing this afternoon, I'd have brought along my own collection," she teased. Emboldened by the steadiness of her voice, she braved his eyes for a challenging moment before kneeling down to speak to his daughter eye to eye.

"There you are, Aimee. 'For my friend, Aimee Kendall, whom I met at Topaz Sands.'," Fenella read carefully, pointing to each word as she came to it.

"This last bit is my name, Fen Wilkins, the same as on the front. Underneath is today's date. The squiggly little fish underneath is my special sign. If you look carefully you'll find it hiding somewhere in every one of my pictures."

"Thank you, Fenella." Aimee circled Fenella's neck with both arms and planted another of her sweet, wet kisses on her friend's cheek.

"A pleasure, Sweetheart."

Fenella kissed the child back then straightened, catching the quickly disguised grimace of annoyance with which Greg had observed their affectionate exchange. She stiffened, a martial glint in her eyes as she returned his pen; careful that this time there was no physical contact.

Did he have a problem with Aimee's fondness for her?

"I don't have as large a fan club as you, Mr Kendall," Fenella addressed him drily, "so I make the most of my meagre opportunities. Besides, Aimee and I are mates. Aren't we?" She winked at the child, who giggled and attempted to wink back while swinging from her two-handed clasp on Fenella's arm.

What the hell? Greg thought sourly, his air of bonhomie slipping for a second. Denying his instinctive liking for Fenella, a liking he obscurely felt carried with it a nebulous danger, he covered his confusion with an assumed annoyance.

No wonder Linda was jealous.

No matter how hard she tried, Aimee rejected all her efforts to be friends; yet here she was, all over this woman they didn't know from Eve.

Fiercely protective of his child, he resolved there and then to find out a whole lot more about Fenella Wilkins. It was his duty as a parent, after all.

If she turned out to be an undesirable acquaintance for Aimee, then this friendship would be ruthlessly nipped in the bud. Wiping away the fleeting frown, he directed his most winning smile towards the audacious young woman standing before him.

"I'll just settle my business with Mrs Morton." He flashed his potent smile briefly towards the older woman then switched it back to Fenella. "Then, perhaps you'll join Aimee and myself next door. We can discuss that painting over a coffee," he suggested, seductive voice deliberately inviting.

Fenella, thoroughly distrustful of both smile and tone as she hadn't been of his frowns, reminded herself that business was business and nodded her acquiescence.

5

Seated comfortably at one of the pavement tables of the cafe next door, Fenella took an appreciative sip of her iced coffee. Charlie Beck, the proprietor, made absolutely the best iced coffees in New South Wales.

"Now, Mr Kendall," crisply business-like, Fenella wasted no time in getting straight to the point. "What's this about a painting?"

"The name's Greg, Fenella." He switched on that high voltage smile again; the one that made Fenella go weak at the knees in spite of her intuitive belief that its purpose was deliberately manipulative. "No need for formality, is there?"

Fenella nodded agreeably at the questioning lift of his brow. Satisfied, he continued.

"As for the painting, I liked what you were doing down on the beach, so I took a look in the 'Lotus Flower' to see what else you'd done. Bought one of your beach scenes for Aimee's bedroom. The chap who sold it to me pointed out some more of your work, those child studies."

He looked up, then continued. "He said you sometimes accept commissions. I'd like to order a couple of Aimee for her two grandmothers. For Mother's Day, if you can get them done in time."

"Mother's Day is four months off. I shouldn't have a problem with that," Fenella agreed.

"I'd like several sittings, though, if I'm to make a decent job of them. Do you have enough time before your holiday is over? I can work from photos if not, but I prefer to paint from life when I can."

By fixing her mind firmly on business, Fenella discovered she could subdue her inconvenient, unwelcome reaction to Greg's charm. Studied charm at that, unless she was grossly mistaken; and she didn't believe she was.

Although why he should bother turning it on for her, she couldn't imagine. Probably habit.

She recalled another too charming man who could never resist adding yet another conquest to his tally. She did not remember him with kindness. Consequently, she was chary of trusting this man smiling so confidently at her across the table.

"Oh, we're not on holiday, are we Aimee?" Greg informed Fenella. A quick grin for his daughter, then with an insouciant air he added, "We're locals too. Here to stay."

"Yes," Aimee corroborated importantly, parroting something she'd obviously heard more than once. "A flat in the middle of the city is no place to bring up a child."

"Too true," Fenella murmured, feeling slightly nauseous as her emotions underwent sinking dread and joyous uplift simultaneously.

There was to be no easy let out then; she would have to learn to live with this disturbing man's continued intrusion into her secure haven.

"I'd often thought about living at the beach," Greg elaborated, unaware of the turmoil his innocent words had stirred up in Fenella's breast. "Having Aimee come to live with me provided the necessary motivation to take the plunge. Topaz Sands is close enough to Sydney for business, and small enough to have retained its appeal in spite of the inevitable development," he continued, looking rather smug at his own cleverness.

"The local school was the clincher. I don't want my kid spending hours on school buses. Here, she's only got a few blocks to walk every day. Perfect."

Greg leaned back in his chair, inordinately pleased with himself at scoring a point against this woman who was beginning to get under his skin rather annoyingly. He was disconcerted, therefore, when his explanation was met by Fenella's rich, infectious laugh, and raised that commanding brow again.

"Oh Lord." Fenella chuckled again. "School. Is this moppet going to school here in Topaz?" The laugh was seriously at odds with the nausea once again churning in her gut.

"Umm. I'm going to be in kindergarten class, Fenella." It was Aimee who answered, eliciting yet another weak chuckle. "Why are you laughing?"

"Yeah," huffed Greg, "What's so funny about my daughter attending the local school?"

An honest disapproving glare replaced the calculated seductive gleam in his eyes.

"That's just me feeling happy, Sweetheart," Fenella excused her laughter diplomatically.

"You and I are going to see a whole lot of each other Aimee. When you start school, I'm going to be your teacher. I teach the kindergarten class at Topaz Sands Central School."

"Ooh, that'll be fun. Daddy, Fenella's going to be my teacher," Aimee giggled.

"I thought you were an artist," Greg exclaimed, sounding aggrieved. "What's all this about being a teacher?"

Unreasonably, he felt as if he'd been made the victim of a bad joke.

Just when he thought he had Fenella Wilkins pegged as a potentially undesirable acquaintance, a footloose bohemian, here she was claiming to belong to a profession which demanded the utmost respectability!

"I'm both." Fenella answered his complaint, and Greg frowned, as if doubting her words.

"Teaching takes top priority, for now. Painting's for holidays and spare time. At least it is until I become sufficiently well known to make a full time living at it. But you know, I love teaching; so I guess I have the best of both worlds." Contented with her lot, Fenella had spoken from the heart.

It took Greg a few moments to fully assimilate this information. Adjusting rapidly, he turned seriously to his daughter.

"With Fenella as your teacher there's no need for all those nervous worries of yours, Pet. But you know, you won't be able to call Fenella by her name once you're at school," he warned. "Perhaps you'd better start calling her Ms Wilkins right away, so you don't forget."

Worry shadowed the child's face, so, in spite of what she believed were Aimee's father's good intentions, Fenella hastened to reassure her.

"No rush, Sweetheart," she soothed. "When you're with the other children it'll come naturally enough. Now, back to business." She turned to Greg before the conversation became any more personal.

"Greg, why don't you or Ms Beck drop Aimee in at my house each morning. I'll do some preliminary sketches, then we'll get to work on those portraits." Fenella felt more comfortable now they were talking business again. "I'll walk her home at lunchtime. If you can let me have several sessions I think I can get at least one of your pictures completed before school begins."

"Linda's in Sydney."

Fenella made a surprised murmur.

"She's a photographic model," Greg explained impatiently, "and has contracts to fulfil. She'll spend as much time as possible here with us, travelling down to Sydney when she's working. I'll bring Aimee."

Concluding, his lips tightened, although what there was to make him angry Fenella couldn't see.

Did this egotistical man object to the woman in his life having a career, or had some other, more personal peeve, caused his anger? She would be the first to admit Linda Beck wasn't her cup of tea, but the woman had the right to a life and career of her own, even if she was about to become Mrs Gregory R Kendall.

Strike two against Greg Kendall.

Fenella's warm, easy-going friendliness, having already suffered a setback born of her earlier suspicions, cooled another degree or two as her feminist hackles rose on Linda's behalf.

If she could score enough demerits against the dratted man, perhaps she'd successfully inure herself to his charm.

Ignoring Greg's inexplicable moodiness, Fenella completed her arrangements and briskly took her leave, still firmly determined to ignore the attraction he held for her; an attraction that persisted in rebelling against her vigorous efforts to smother it.

Fenella had learned the hard way that handsome, charming men weren't to be trusted. She had no intention of making any kind of a fool of herself over another one.

One who just happened to be engaged to the incomparable Linda Beck.

If she spent too much time chatting to Greg Kendall though, her resolution would be in acute danger. When they met in future she would have to take care to steel herself against that wickedly dangerous charm of his.

She had been badly burned by one charismatic charmer and she'd be damned if she'd lay herself open to being hurt again by this one. Even supposing he'd be sufficiently interested in her to bother.

Remember the beauteous Linda, Fenella warned herself.

6

"You know, Fenella, I wish I had lots of money." Aimee's wistful comment broke the companionable silence. Even Zilla, tired out by Aimee's energetic games in the back garden, was dozing while Fenella lay the foundations of her first portrait. Absorbed in her work, Fenella barely registered Aimee's words.

"Umm," she murmured absently. "Why's that Sweetheart?"

Encouraged, her young friend confided earnestly.

"It's Daddy's birthday next week and I know he'd really like one of your paintings of me for himself. He said he should have asked you to do three, Fenella; so I know he'd like one. He said he'd have to make do with a photo of me instead."

"So, why do you wish you had lots of money?" Her attention caught by this interesting snippet of information to add to her mental file on Greg Kendall, Fenella was curious. In spite of her determination not to get involved with him.

"'Cause, if I had lots of money, I could pay you to make a special painting of me for Daddy's birthday, of course."

Forlorn blue eyes gazed up at Fenella as Aimee explained her problem.

"Only the man in the gall'ry said your pictures cost hundreds of dollars, and I've only got twenty dollars and fifty-five cents. I know, 'cause Daddy helped me count it last night. That's not enough, is it?" she concluded, a faint tinge of optimism permeating her doleful tones.

Fenella put down her brush, giving the matter her serious consideration.

"Well, no. It isn't," she confirmed after a moment's thought. "Not if you want a proper painting like the ones I'm doing for your grandmothers. But you know, Aimee, I do pencil sketches like these," she waved her hand at the preliminary drawings strewn across her worktable, which depicted Aimee in a dozen different poses and moods, "for a lot less. They only cost five dollars each at the school fete."

"Five dollars is less than twenty, isn't it Fenella? I've got enough money for a little drawing, haven't I?" With an enthusiastic bounce, Aimee ran over to leaf through the sketches.

"I rather like this one, don't you?"

Joining her, Fenella picked up a delightful drawing of Aimee glancing up, an impish, mischievous grin lighting up her face.

"How about I do a bit more work on it. Do you think your daddy would like it?"

Aimee nodded happily and ran back to rummage in the backpack of toys and books she'd brought with her, returning with a fat, clinking purse which she upended on the table.

"Help me count five dollars, please Fenella," she demanded.

Fenella had no wish to take the child's money; she would willingly give her the drawing for nothing. However, she recognised a fiercely independent streak in the girl. Paying for her father's gift was clearly important to Aimee, so Fenella helped her count the money.

"Grandma gave me extra pocket money to buy Daddy a nice present," Aimee confided. They counted five bundles of coins and she pushed them carefully across the table to Fenella.

"There," she said. "That's for you for the drawing." Hopefully she added, "Have you got a frame to put it in?"

"No, but I'm sure Mrs Morton has some in her shop. Shall we pop in and see when I walk you home?" Problem solved, Aimee eagerly agreed.

Putting aside the portrait, Fenella worked on the drawing until satisfied with her efforts, then slid it into a folder and called Aimee to gather up her things.

Their foray into the newsagent proving successful, the drawing was fitted into place there and then in the black wooden frame Aimee had carefully selected. Shirley gift wrapped it in dark blue tissue paper and finished it off with a scrap of tartan ribbon left over from Christmas.

"All done," she announced cheerfully. "Now all you need is a card and it's ready to give to your Daddy. You've even got some money left over." She popped the package into a plastic bag and helped the girl stow it securely inside her backpack.

"I'll make a card," Aimee decided. "We learned how at preschool. You'll help me tomorrow, won't you Fenella?"

Fenella agreed. Her business completed, Aimee thanked Shirley and the pair of conspirators continued on their way. Singing her favourite song about three little fishies, Aimee danced and swung off Fenella's hand, totally satisfied with her morning's achievements.

Until she spied the red sports car parked in the driveway of her home.

Abruptly, the gay little song died on her lips and her feet began to drag. A scowl darkened the cherubic features.

"Linda's back."

Fenella, inordinately disappointed herself, was nonetheless taken aback at Aimee's overt lack of welcome for her father's fiancée. Normally an open, affectionate child, she hadn't been aware that Aimee actively disliked Linda Beck. Although she should have suspected.

During the three mornings they'd spent together, Aimee had not once mentioned Linda, while chatting freely about any number of other people; especially her father.

For herself, Fenella knew she should welcome the other woman's return.

She should.

It would lessen the danger of making an abysmal fool of herself.

Only she couldn't.

Greg Kendall was bad for her; but, like a fish to the baited hook, she found herself irresistibly drawn.

Their brief twice daily meetings over Aimee's sittings, spiced by an element of sensual danger, had become the highlights of Fenella's days. Refusing to pander to Greg's arrogant assumption of masculine superiority, she had fallen into the habit of playing devil's advocate to his every opinion.

Their brief conversations had rapidly assumed the form of sparring debate with Greg continually challenging her, demanding she back up her sweeping assertions with cogent arguments.

It had been a long time since Fenella had enjoyed herself so much in a man's company. I need to get out more, if that's all it takes, she scoffed, immediately deciding to make the effort to get out of Topaz Sands into the wider world more often. She realised she had begun to stultify in her safe, idyllic haven.

At a deeper, purely emotional level, Greg Kendall also challenged her. That was where the true danger lay. It had become more and more difficult to remember why she shouldn't surrender herself to the pleasure of his company.

So it ought to be a good thing his fiancée was back.

Linda's return spelt the end of those bitter-sweet tete-a-tetes with Greg Kendall.

Meshing neatly with Fenella's gloomy cogitations, it was Linda herself who opened the door, gathering the reluctant child into a perfunctory embrace; careful at the same time not to smear her make-up.

"Aimee, darling, it's so good to be home again. I've missed you such a lot," she intoned in a cloyingly sweet voice.

Apparently, she was totally uncaring that she received no reciprocal response from the child. Turning to Fenella, she thanked her coldly for escorting Aimee.

"I'll be bringing her tomorrow," she added pointedly. "Her father is far too busy writing to be bothered with tiresome errands." She whisked Aimee inside, closing the door in Fenella's face.

Well, that puts me in my place, doesn't it, a disgruntled Fenella observed. It was one thing to enumerate the advantages to Linda's return and quite another to come face to face with the unpleasant reality of it.

7

The following day Fenella was one of a dozen or more Topaz residents whose mail included a buff envelope containing an invitation to a party at the Kendall house on Friday night.

An Australia Day party, she noted, reading it again, even though Friday was not quite the twenty-sixth of January. There was no mention that it was also Greg Kendall's birthday. I wonder how old he is, Fenella mused.

Curiosity moved her to take down one of his novels from her overflowing bookshelves. Working from the year of birth listed in the biography, she calculated that he must be thirty-four on Friday.

"A good age for a man, I reckon, Zilla. In his prime. Still young, yet mature enough to have seen the back of his youthful follies." Guiltily, she turned her thoughts away from the fact that thirty-four was thoroughly compatible with her own twenty-seven years.

The invitations generated considerable interest among those locals fortunate enough to be asked.

The general consensus appeared to be, as Charlie Peck from the cafe put it, "The young fella oughta be given a chance to show what he's made of, and we can always do with a good party."

Since Greg was obviously making an effort to get to know his neighbours and become part of the Topaz Sands permanent community, his mailbox filled with acceptances from people set on having a good time. Joking around, they drew up a list of things Australian to offer him as host gifts at his Australia Day bash, the result of which was, that on Friday night Greg's coffee table disappeared under offerings of lamingtons, Anzac biscuits, meat pies and Aussie brands of beer and wine. Pride of place went to a huge jar of vegemite tied with green and gold ribbons.

Greg, the most amicable of hosts, swapped joke for joke and added the unexpected largesse to the trays of sophisticated canapes Linda had ordered from a catering firm, and offered them around.

"Thanks young fella," twinkled white-bearded Matt Sykes who still hired out his boat with himself as skipper, for the odd day's fishing. Provided he liked the look of the hirer. "There's nothing to beat a pie and a cold beer to wash it down."

"My sentiments exactly. Here, Greg, leave those pies for us. That mob over there don't need 'em."

Jason Kendall, Greg's younger brother, dragged up a chair and settled in beside Matt.

Soon, they were joined by several other like-minded souls and fishing yarns, where the catches grew progressively larger, became the order of the day.

The Kendall's, Greg, Jason and their parents, were blending in seamlessly with the local contingent.

"Greg seems a decent enough sort, but I can't say I think much of that toffee-nosed fiancée of his." As usual it was Charlie, muttering in Shirley's ear, who voiced what everyone was thinking.

"Did you notice how she was all sweetness and light while he introduced her, then couldn't get back to those posh Sydney friends of hers fast enough."

Shirley had; as had a number of others.

Chatting quietly with Mrs Kendall, Fenella overheard her drawing of Aimee, prominently displayed on the mantel nearby, being discussed. Already annoyed by the snub Linda had dealt to her friends, her anger flared anew when that same familiar voice chipped in scornfully.

"That ridiculous bit of kitsch! I just hope Greg didn't get taken in and pay through the nose for it. These so-called artists think they can charge anything and get away with it, in spite of their pathetic lack of talent."

Linda Beck's distinctive metallic tone had been slightly raised. So that she herself couldn't help hearing, Fenella felt certain.

"Oh!" Mrs Kendall, who had also heard the spiteful put-down, protested quietly. "I'm so sorry dear. I don't know how she could say something so blatantly untrue! She knows perfectly well that that picture was a gift from Aimee and that Greg is absolutely delighted with it."

She continued earnestly, "Rest assured, Fenella, everyone who sees your work recognises that you are *very* gifted."

Fenella shrugged, pretending an indifference she certainly didn't feel.

"Linda seems to have taken me in dislike," she understated with deceptive calmness. "But since it's entirely mutual, I guess I don't have grounds to complain."

She flashed a brilliant couldn't-care-less smile at the older woman and changed the subject.

"Aimee's really looking forward to starting school, isn't she," she commented, aware that her granddaughter was a sure-fire topic to deflect the other woman's attention.

"Isn't she just," Mrs Kendall replied, equally eager to put the unpleasant episode behind them. "Also to having you for her teacher. She was chattering on about you and that little dog of yours half the afternoon."

Ah! Enlightenment dawned. *So that's what got Linda's knickers in a twist tonight.*

Startled, she jumped when a hard, masculine arm slid sinuously round her waist, unaware that someone else who had overheard her being insulted had decided to play knight errant.

"Hi Mum," Jason Kendall said over her shoulder. "I'm stealing Fenella. Come on woman, let's dance." Jason continued his banter as he led her outside onto the deck where a number of guests were dancing to recorded music.

"You know," he confided with mock intimacy, "I've always wanted to dance in the moonlight with a beautiful girl."

"Oh, what a pity you chose me then, Jason, since I'm neither a girl nor beautiful. And besides, the floodlights have drowned out the moon." Gaily, Fenella laughed up at him, only too willing to escape from Linda's vicinity and join the group of lively young people dancing on the deck.

I like Jason Kendall, she decided shortly. Younger than herself, he was full of cheerful nonsense, immediately making her feel as if she'd known him forever. Rather like one of her own brothers *He's very good company*, she mused silently. *Actually, he's much nicer than Greg, who's so intent on hiding behind that wall of polished urbanity that most of the time it's difficult to see the real man.*

The tentative friendship that had blossomed between them had suffered an early frostbite upon Linda's return, Greg reverting to his earlier aloofness.

Fenella was inordinately hurt by his easy discarding of her friendship, even though she knew it was better this way.

Less perilous to her heart.

Fenella and Jason were enjoying themselves hugely in a lively exchange of outrageously flirtatious banter that culminated in a stagy embrace when the music ended. As the next song began Greg Kendall cut in smoothly on his brother.

"My turn," he announced, curtly dismissing his younger sibling. Dancing her away, Greg turned an unsmiling countenance on Fenella. A hot, dangerous glitter lit up stormy blue eyes.

"You and Jason seem to have hit it off remarkably well, considering you've only just met," he snapped.

He felt uncomfortable with an anger he didn't understand but couldn't deny. An anger instantly aroused by the sight of Fenella so obviously enjoying herself in his brother's arms.

"Are you always such a quick worker when it comes to picking up strange men?" His lips tightened and he added harshly, "Jason's far too young for you, Fenella. Chuck him back before any harm's done."

Fenella threw back her head, her spontaneous peal of laughter changing his expression from scowling command to red-faced anger.

"Greg Kendall," she gasped, "you have got to be joking." Only the sight of his totally serious demeanour caused her chuckles to die a quickly strangled death. Her volatile temper roused by his unwarranted interference, her voice reflected her emotion. "Are you by any chance warning me off your brother? Because if you are, you're wasting your time. I choose my friends where I please, and I like Jason. I think you could say we understand each other pretty well, even though we've only just met. And Greg? No. I. Will. Not reject his friendship, just like that, on your say-so!"

"I mean it Fenella," Greg hissed between clenched teeth, goaded to unwise rage by Fenella's defiance. "You stay away from Jason. There must be plenty of other men you can amuse yourself with. You don't need to get your claws into a youngster like him."

Any lingering inclination to laugh was quite doused by Greg's hurtful, absurd accusation.

Fenella smiled thinly up at him, flashing brown eyes belying her travesty of a social smile, her own quick temper coming to the boil at his unjust character assassination.

Greg's arm tightened cruelly, crushing her soft curves against the hard muscles of his unyielding frame. Further incensed by this manhandling, especially since his every touch kindled a tingling excitement that fizzed and bubbled through her bloodstream, Fenella retaliated.

Planting her feet solidly on the deck, she forced their swaying bodies to a halt beside the sliding glass doors leading back into the house.

Although she displayed a bright, false smile to the world, Fenella was now fairly seething.

The normally sparkling gold lights in the velvet depths of her brown eyes blazed with fury.

First, she had had to suffer Linda's spiteful ambush, and now this hurtful direct verbal assault from Greg, whom she'd believed knew her better!

Fenella had had it with Greg Bloody Kendall and his insufferable fiancée!

If he thought he could get away with accusing her of being some kind of unprincipled femme fatale, then he could think again! She'd show him a thing or two!

Throwing caution and common sense to the wind, Fenella deliberately allowed her tense body to relax and mould itself to Greg's so that not even a matchstick could be squeezed between them.

Standing on tiptoe, she threaded gently caressing fingers through his thick gold locks, tugged his head down, and planted a deep, open-mouthed kiss fair and square on those deliciously inviting full lips.

She gave free rein to the simmering desire she'd been denying ever since she'd learned he had a fiancée.

Moving her hips sinuously against Greg's suddenly rigid body, she let her tongue enter his mouth, stroking sensitive flesh. Savouring the rich, masculine flavours comprising a taste that was distinctively Greg Kendall's; the heady tang of expensive after shave drowning her senses.

Fenella's seducing lips commanded his to respond.

Hands, at first poised to thrust Fenella away from him, altered their intent, Greg gliding them from her shoulders to her hips, trailing fire in their wake. He gripped her firmly and hauled her even closer against the hard planes of his body. Despite himself, Greg found himself responding to the blatant sexuality of Fenella's attack.

Now Fenella's was not the only tongue stroking and thrusting deeply; her hands not the only hands fondling and caressing as they explored unfamiliar territory. Greg's had joined the heady dance.

Angry with himself for responding, unable to prevent himself from doing so, Greg lost control of the situation.

Now his mouth ground savagely against the tender lips clinging to his; his male hardness imprinted itself against yielding female flesh. Fenella's fake seduction mutated as Greg punished her for her temerity.

Except that Fenella was too lost in the pleasure of being in Greg Kendall's arms, sharing this long desired kiss, to know she was being punished.

Pulse racing wildly, she felt herself on the verge of total surrender when a piercing wolf-whistle snapped her out of her enthralment.

"Attaboy Greg! Way to go Fen," hooted Jason, bringing her thudding back to earth.

Into the centre of an interested crowd at Greg Kendall's party.

During the few seconds it took to disentangle herself from an equally dismayed, and furiously angry, Greg Kendall, Fenella fought and won a desperate battle for her temporarily misplaced self-possession.

Still shaky, but once again in command of herself, Fenella returned to the attack. It took a major effort, but she managed to flutter her lashes theatrically and purr appreciatively up into Greg's gratifyingly flushed face.

"Ooh yes! You could be right about Jason, Darling. He may be too young for me. But *you* certainly aren't. What a pity you're engaged; we might have had some fun together otherwise."

Riding high on a wave of pure defiance, Fenella patted Greg's cheek derisively. A limpid, sultry sweep of expressive brown eyes subjected him to a leisurely survey from head to foot; and back again.

Almost at the end of her endurance, Fenella turned to step through the door and came face to face with Linda Beck, her beautiful features contorted into murderous rage.

"You want to watch that man of yours, Linda dear," Fenella advised sweetly, pre-empting the other woman's incipient outburst.

Two for the price of one, Fenella thought savagely. Linda could only stare, mouth agape, momentarily speechless.

"He's really hot stuff, isn't he?" she continued with malicious sweetness.

There! she thought, anger still sweeping her recklessly along on its crest, *I might as well give her good reason to hate me. And damn Greg Kendall and that holier than thou attitude of his to hell!*

The cynosure of all eyes that hadn't gravitated towards Linda and Greg, Fenella, a triumphant exultation defying anyone to detect the bleak devastation it hid, sailed across the room and out the front door. Bare seconds later, scalding tears began trickling unchecked down her cheeks.

✳✳✳✳✳

High heels tapped out a brisk staccato rhythm on the footpath when suddenly another pair of feet came thudding after her.

"Hey, slow down there, Fen," Jason panted. "Boy, did you shake up the party! I thought for a minute Linda might throw that bloody great diamond back in poor old Greg's face. Pity she didn't. Would have been the best thing she could have done for the whole family. Don't know what came over that brother of mine, asking that cold-hearted piece to marry him. He's usually got more sense."

Jason stole a quick peek at Fenella's stricken, tear stained face and continued to prattle on while keeping pace with her. Righteous anger no longer sustaining her, Fenella was appalled at her own shocking behaviour.

I've really done it this time, she thought, sick with shame.

It was bad enough to make such an exhibition of herself in front of the Kendalls and all their out of town friends; but her own friends had been there too, watching while she made an absolute and utter fool of herself. She'd be lucky if she ever managed to hold her head up in Topaz Sands again. Underneath all that an even deeper fear had sprung into existence during that explosive kiss.

Fenella was afraid she had moved beyond lust, and fallen in love with Greg Kendall.

If that wasn't a recipe for disaster, she didn't know what was!

Silent and almost forgotten, Jason still matched her stride for stride when she raced up the path to her own door. Fighting back the tears surging in the emotional backwash of her earlier rage, Fenella was shaking so badly she dropped her key.

Jason scooped it up and unlocked the door. He switched on the lights and urged her inside, closing the door behind himself, taking in her badly shaken state with a discerning, sideways glance.

"Where do you keep the grog?" Following her unsteady finger, he flung open cupboards, discovering a half bottle of brandy left over from her Christmas baking. Snatching a glass from the shelf, he poured a generous slug.

"Sit down, Fen, before you fall down", he ordered brusquely. "Now, get this inside you."

He handed over the brandy glass and stood over her till she'd drained it, shuddering as the undiluted spirit burned its way down her throat.

Retreating to the kitchen, he put the kettle on. By the time he returned with two steaming mugs of tea, Fenella had mopped her face and steadied the shakes. Desperately striving for normality, she attempted to make a joke of it all.

"That was some show I put on, wasn't it?" She essayed a laugh that didn't quite come off, and gave up the pathetic attempt. "I'm a damned idiot, losing my temper and making an ass of myself," she added bitterly. "Not my usual style, Jason, I assure you."

"Never thought it was. I was watching you both while you were dancing. Don't know what Greg said to you, only that he was in a right paddy already. Next thing you were too. I heard the lovely Linda though, a bit earlier, and from the look on Mum's face, the two of you heard her too. So Fenella, between her and Greg, I don't blame you for losing it."

Jason laughed, a deep-bellied guffaw. "You gave old Greg as good as he got, you know. By my reckoning Fen, you came off best in that encounter. At least you were able to smile as you made your dramatic exit. They were left standing there glaring at each other, both as black as thunder."

Jason's generous partisanship kindled a little warmth in the bottom of Fenella's frozen heart.

He might have something else to say though, she thought, if he knew the truth she had so recently discovered about herself and her feelings for his older brother.

"Do you mind if I hang out with you for a bit?" he asked sheepishly. "Before I left I added my poor mite to stir the pot even more; so I doubt if I'm likely to be very popular back there tonight. I'm not going back till everyone's gone to bed and I can sneak in quietly."

Restlessly, Jason prowled around the room, peering out into the darkness and fingering books and knick-knacks.

He's almost as upset and nervous as me, Fenella realised. *If he goes back too soon, he's afraid he'll end up in an unforgivable row with a brother he obviously loves.* She wondered if anything else lay behind the unhappiness now clearly discernible on the face so much like his brother's. Surely there was more to it than tonight's debacle.

In the end, they made popcorn and ate it watching an old comedy movie Fenella had in her DVD collection.

Two unrepentant outcasts laughing at corny one-liners; giving each other much needed moral support.

✳✳✳✳✳

Jason failed dismally in his attempt to sneak in unobserved. Self-deprecation leant a pseudo comedic tone to the account he gave Fenella the next morning when he called in on his way out of town.

"Unfortunately, Greg was still up, clearing away some of the mess."

Jason grimaced. "He tore into me for making a show of myself – his words – with you, and walking out on his party, thereby making him look a fool." This was a greatly expurgated version of the actual encounter.

"Well of course I couldn't resist pointing out that he'd managed that quite satisfactorily without any help at all from me. Quite reasonably, I thought." Jason sniggered. "As you can imagine Fen, that went down like a lead balloon."

An understatement if ever there was one! In actual fact, the brothers had had a ding dong row, almost coming to blows as Fenella's character and morals were scurrilously maligned by one and vociferously defended by the other.

It had ended inconclusively with their father sticking his head round his bedroom door. "I wish you two would bloody well shut up and let the rest of us get some sleep!" he'd testily demanded.

In the morning Greg had still been glowering moodily while Linda fussed over him, oozing sweet sympathy.

"Watching them together turned my stomach, so I put them both straight on one or two more points, then decided I couldn't stand a whole weekend of the pair of them. That's it, Fen. I'm off. Back to Sydney. Just popped in to say goodbye to my partner in crime and give you an updated sit-rep. Meeting you turned out to be the only good thing to come of this trip. Pity. I'd particularly wanted to have a serious talk with old Greg."

Fenella glanced up in time to catch a forlorn expression flit across Jason's mobile features before his cheerful mask was resumed.

"No chance of that now." A jaunty grin almost convinced her she'd misread that fleeting glimpse of painful regret. "Don't know when I'll be back, Fen, but I'll look you up then."

A quick bear hug from the young giant who topped even his brother's impressive inches, and Fenella was left alone on her doorstep. Guiltily, she hoped she hadn't been the unwitting cause of a serious falling out between the brothers.

8

Dreading meeting anyone, friend or foe, Fenella kept to her own quarters for the rest of the holiday long weekend, moodily pottering about except for her early morning runs with Zilla. By midday Monday, still restlessly unable to concentrate on anything, she finally rebelled against her self-imposed confinement.

This was her last weekend before school commenced for the year; and the surf was up.

Wriggling into her purple and gold wetsuit, Fenella hefted her surfboard and trotted down to the beach. Layne Beachley she wasn't, however, since her arrival in Topaz Sands she had acquired the rudiments of the sport, becoming a keen amateur adherent.

Two hours later the tide had turned, the surf flattening out. Serious surfers were leaving the water to the children paddling at its edge. Soothed as usual by the timeless rhythms of the great Pacific Ocean and the undemanding fellowship of her fellow board riders, Fenella's equilibrium was close to restored.

There was a spring in her step and a relaxed, smiling face was uplifted to the glorious sunny afternoon. The boys who'd shared her last wave called an easy farewell when she tucked her board under her arm and strode purposefully down the beach towards home.

Her upbeat mood was shattered by the hard, uncompromising, and all too familiar voice that hailed her.

"Fenella Wilkins!"

Greg Kendall descended the last few steps of the beach access below his house and sauntered to where she'd reluctantly halted at his imperious call.

Icy blue eyes stared out from a dour countenance, scanning her with slow deliberation. Lingering scathingly on the pert swell of skimpily covered, bikini-clad breasts exposed to his view by the unzipped wetsuit. Eyes that didn't miss the involuntary tightening of nipples when mentally stripped of their scant camouflage.

"I hope you're proud of your achievements on Friday night," he accused bitingly. "You successfully managed to cause an estrangement between Jason and myself; something that's never been done before, least of all by a *woman!*"

His sneering denunciation turned that last word into a vile epithet.

"To top off your performance you only just failed to provoke a fight between Linda and I. Unfortunately for your nasty little scheme, she had too much good sense to fall into your trap.

Nasty little scheme!

Fenella's shame at her body's initial reaction to Greg's challenging masculinity was forgotten.

Forgotten also was how her mouth had dried, her stomach dropped and her pulse raced on merely hearing his voice. She forgot, even, that she loved the infuriating man, albeit against her better judgement.

The flush born of embarrassment bloomed hotly, ripened by unadulterated fury that hardened the warm golden lights in her deep brown eyes into cold, killing lasers. Rage, first ignited on Friday night, rekindled instantly at this new and equally gratuitous insult.

Fenella drew a deep, steadying breath, and, with a supreme effort, harnessed her anger, wielding it as a weapon against her tormentor. Scathing look was returned to sender, as Fenella refused to be cowed.

"You'd be well advised to take a closer look at your own behaviour before you start assigning blame," she drawled coldly. Precisely. "Jason and I are both of an age to please ourselves in what we do; and whatever we choose to do, it's none of your damn business, Greg Kendall. Until you butted in making your filthy, unfounded accusations we were simply two people enjoying each other's company at a party. Incidentally, the whole thing started when he witnessed your dearly beloved fiancée's libellous attack on me over that drawing of Aimee's and set out to cheer me up."

Fenella paused to see if he had any comment to make regarding that. He didn't; merely tightening his lips, and, if possible, scowling even more blackly.

"Jason and I discovered we like each other. A lot." That was laying it on a bit thickly, only he deserved it, didn't he? "We clicked; the way some people do. Although maybe you never let yourself respond naturally enough to anyone to have experienced such instant rapport."

Greg winced slightly as that shaft struck home.

"After you stuck your oar in where you weren't wanted, causing me to lose my temper and behave badly," Fenella's voice rose a decibel or two as, ruthlessly, she continued her tirade, silencing Greg when he showed signs of being about to speak, "Jason was gentleman enough to see me safely home. We had a nice evening together, away from your poisonous company."

Fenella paused, chest heaving.

"Any estrangement between the two of you is entirely the product of your own actions, Mr High-And-Mighty Kendall! As for the fight with your sweet Linda, you brought that on yourself too, when you started picking on me."

Unable to think of any more accusations to lash him with, Fenella's denunciation ground to a halt.

"Goodbye Mr Kendall. Don't bother apologising, because if you do I'll refuse to accept it."

Head high, Fenella swept off without waiting for his reaction. As she swung round Greg was forced to jump back to avoid being clobbered by her surfboard. He tripped, landing on his backside in the loose sand. By the time he picked himself up Fenella had stalked off out of range.

"Damn!"

He castigated himself, uncomfortably aware Fenella had spoken the truth.

Jason had told him much the same, only in more pungent language.

When he'd seen Fenella, he'd impulsively set off to clear the air between them.

Only, the sight of her sauntering along without a care in the world, while he'd spent the last few days in a state of seething, self-disgusted misery, had been too much for his already fragile temper.

The devil inside him had escaped his control, exacerbating an already appalling situation.

He was all too well aware of his own culpability in provoking the incident at the party - he should have waited to tackle her in private — yet it irked him unbearably to have that self-possessed virago stridently point it out to him.

Good intentions long forgotten, Greg Kendall bathed his lacerated ego in angry listings of Fenella Wilkins's shortcomings.

Muttering to himself, he took off in the other direction, to walk himself into a pleasanter frame of mind.

That unspeakable witch had been getting under his skin rather too often lately. It was time he put her firmly in her place once and for all.

If he only knew where that place was.

A mental image of Fenella stretched out between his sheets flitted into his mind unbidden.

Along with the memory of their iniquitous kiss. Beneath his anger, he'd enjoyed it; enjoyed it too much for his peace of mind.

Linda, he thought guiltily. The woman to whom he'd pledged his love and loyalty deserved better of him than that, by God.

In future he'd see to it that he kept well clear of that damned infernal temptress!

✱✱✱✱✱

Carried along on the floodtide of her anger, Fenella made it all the way home before the inevitable backlash to such an excess of corrosive emotion set in. A smattering of bitter tears mixed their salt with that of the ocean as she showered after her carefree afternoon in the water. But by the time she'd dried and dressed her resolve had stiffened.

Twice now, Greg Kendall had reduced her to tears. In love with him or not, that was two times too many.

Following the cruel disillusion that marked the collapse of her marriage to Paul Fremont, Fenella had dragged herself out of the bottomless slough of depression into which she'd fallen, swearing never again to permit any man to wield such power over her.

For four years she had adhered steadfastly to her private vow. Her unsought and unwanted love for Greg Kendall exposed her to the stark probability of a repeat performance of that dreadful anguish unless she took immediate action to avert it.

What you'll do, woman, she strictly ordered her reflection in the steamy bathroom mirror, *is keep right out of his way.*

No more fights either, regardless of the provocation. No more anything. Simply turn your back and walk away from the damned man. If he had had something to offer me, he may have been worth the risk. Because of Linda, he doesn't; and isn't. So forget him. Forget this one-sided travesty of love and sooner or later it'll die a natural death.

Defiantly, she stared at the woman in the mirror, daring her to answer back.

When she didn't, Fenella turned slowly away, back straight, eyes refusing to let further teardrops fall.

"Sooner, I hope," she whispered, concluding the self-counselling.

Unfortunately, the first object her gaze settled on when she emerged from the bathroom, was an unfinished portrait of Aimee Kendall. The first of the two ordered by Aimee's father was already completed. The second, this one, almost so. Freshly bolstered confidence wavered momentarily until she marshalled her courage, reminding herself sternly that she was a professional.

A commission was a commission, and however unwelcome it now was, she was under an obligation to fulfil it.

"Okay, then," she muttered. "I'll finish the damned thing, and as soon as the paint dries he can collect the pair of them. Then there'll be no further need to see him."

Except for Aimee. Fragile spirits plummeted again. With Aimee in her class at school, she was doomed to at least occasional contact.

No matter, Fenella reassured herself. At school the career woman persona of a busy teacher should be a sufficiently adequate shield against any personal altercations. She hoped.

Picking up her brush, Fenella centred her concentration on the canvas, ejecting all else from her mind through sheer willpower.

9

Nothing further disturbed Fenella's precarious peace of mind or challenged her resolution to steer clear of Greg Kendall. She hadn't caught so much as a fleeting glimpse of the man; and thanked providence for the welcome respite.

When enrolment day for the kindergarten class rolled around, Aimee had been accompanied by both her father and Linda; clinging possessively to his arm as usual. Office formalities completed, they merely kissed the child goodbye at the door and let her enter the classroom alone. Fenella, busily occupied with a tearful mother and child, had time for no more than a brief smile and word of welcome for Aimee, and a direction to join a nearby group activity.

Staring impassively across Aimee's head at the smartly dressed, well-matched couple hovering in the doorway had strained Fenella's poise without shattering it.

Greg's equally impassive stare had somehow helped, although she heaved a sigh of relief when he nodded curtly and strode off.

The last she had seen of them had been Linda Beck tossing her head with a triumphant smirk as she hurried to keep pace with him. From then on, whichever of them walked Aimee to school, they never deigned to come past the front gate.

Which suits me just fine, Fenella thought soberly. Life was easier for her if Greg Kendall shared her disinclination for further face to face encounters.

Her last niggling worry was laid to rest when Jason phoned to report that he had received a handsome apology from his brother.

"He seemed keen to patch things up and so was I," Jason informed her, downplaying his relief at the reconciliation. "I met him half-way Fen, so now you can stop worrying about coming between us."

"Oh, Jason. That *is* good news," a deeply relieved Fenella had responded. Perhaps her outburst had done some good, if it had been her words that caused Greg to rethink his position. On the strength of it, phone call concluded, she reached for a pen and jotted a polite, business-like note to tell Greg his pictures were ready. Whistling for Zilla, she clipped the foxy's lead on and took her for a late walk, dropping the note in the Kendall's mailbox on the way.

The following afternoon, Greg Kendall was sitting on her front steps when she arrived home from work. Stony faced, he wordlessly stood aside, allowing her to unlock the door.

"I guess you've come for the paintings," Fenella said, her voice flat and lifeless. If he couldn't manage a simple hello, she felt perfectly justified in omitting it also.

Greg followed her inside, his impassive gaze examining the eclectic collection of mismatched furniture, bric-a-brac, bright fabrics, plants and shells which she had blended into a stylish, comfortable decor.

Fenella ignored him.

Putting her basket tidily beside her desk, she stooped to greet Zilla who came scampering through the dog-flap in the kitchen door. Only when the affectionate little dog subsided happily onto her mat, did Fenella return her attention to her guest, directing him into her bright, airy studio.

The two paintings, each with a distinctly different pose, rested side by side on their easels, awaiting Greg's inspection. Still without a word, he subjected each to a careful scrutiny, picking them up and turning them towards the light before declaring himself satisfied.

"I may have reservations regarding your character, Fenella," he uttered harshly, "however I do acknowledge your talent. These are excellent. Mum and Mrs Stone will be thrilled with them." He pulled a chequebook from his pocket and wrote a cheque for fee they had previously settled upon.

"Thank you." Fenella, her voice stiff from repressed hurt, exchanged the cheque for a receipt. "Now that you've approved them, I'll wrap them for you."

Greg stood silently while Fenella wrapped the two paintings, first in tissue paper, then covering it with strong brown paper tied with string. Handing them to him, their fingers brushed, shooting a frisson of tingling sensations up her arm.

Hurriedly she dropped her hand and stepped back, finally raising defiant brown eyes to his face when Greg continued to stand there, silent and unmoving, in the middle of her studio.

Mouth opening as if about to speak, he shook his head in denial of the unspoken words. Frowning, emotion clouding the clear blue of his eyes, Greg stood lost in dark thoughts. Fenella was left unaware that he'd regretted his cruel repudiation of her as soon as the words had left his mouth. He'd glimpsed the pain she hadn't been quick enough to hide, and, gratuitous cruelty being repugnant to him, shame had prompted him to immediately retract them.

Reluctant to risk another slanging match, and confused by his dangerous urge to offer comfort, he'd had second thoughts.

Let it stand, he told himself. *The woman already knows I have serious doubts about her, so what does it matter, anyway?* He turned brusquely towards the door.

"Goodbye Fenella," he slung over his shoulder from half-way down the path, and was out the gate before she reached the door to close it behind him.

Fenella expelled a pent-up breath, collapsing onto the sofa; knees giving way now that the hazardous encounter was safely in the past.

"Well, that wasn't so bad," she told Zilla, relieved to have got off relatively unscathed. That nasty crack he'd made had merely confirmed to her that she'd made a wise decision when she set herself to stop loving him.

The man didn't deserve to be loved. Not in the way she knew herself to be capable of loving.

****

The days fell into a regular pattern of work, hours on the beach surfing and jogging, and painting. Occasional glimpses of Greg Kendall, usually at a safe distance, allowed Fenella to become inured to his presence. *Rather like being desensitised to treat an allergy,* she thought, hoping the treatment worked as well on love.

The time came when she felt proudly capable of meeting him anywhere with casual aplomb.

A pattern emerged also in Aimee's behaviour, which disturbed Fenella sufficiently that she began documenting it.

Whenever her father was absent, leaving Linda in full charge of Aimee, the little girl would become subdued and withdrawn; a state which was in sharp contrast to her giggling high spirits when it was Linda who was absent.

That the child did not like her prospective stepmother was one thing; that she appeared to be afraid of her was quite another.

Increasingly disturbed, Fenella was unsure what she should do. No way could she approach Greg Kendall on a matter of such extreme delicacy. Not with their personal history.

"Unless you see some definite signs of abuse, wait and see," advised Mrs Crammond, the school principal to whom Fenella took her concerns.

"It may yet turn out to be a storm in a tea cup. Anyway, you never know, Fen, the fiancée might get a better offer and toss him over. Problem solved."

More seriously, she concluded the interview.

"Watch out for the child, Fen, and keep me posted; especially if there are any developments I need to be aware of. I'll trust your judgement."

Ensuring that school was a safe, happy haven for her if she was truly as unhappy at home as it appeared she sometimes was, Fenella continued to watch over Aimee.

Several days after this discussion, Mrs Crammond put her head round the door of Fenella's classroom one afternoon.

"Excuse me, Fenella. Could I see you for a moment?" she requested, waiting till they were alone before continuing.

"I've had a phone call from Aimee Kendall's father," she began. "That Linda Beck you were telling me of left for Sydney this morning. He's been away for a few days himself. Due back this afternoon; supposedly in time to meet Aimee after school."

Fenella, who already knew all this, nodded to Mrs Crammond to continue.

"The problem is, he's been held up and can't get back till sometime after four. There's no-one home for Aimee, and he's in a panic over what to do. I told him there's always someone working late, so I'd see that she's supervised till he arrives. Can you handle it Fen, or should I ask someone else?"

"No problem. I've got plenty to keep me busy here. Aimee can stay with me," Fenella assured her.

Although after hours child care wasn't the responsibility of either of them, neither objected in a genuine emergency.

Thus it was, that when Greg Kendall rushed into her classroom closer to five o'clock than four, it was to discover Aimee playing with building blocks on the floor while Fenella was busy at her computer.

"Daddy!" squealed Aimee, the first to notice her father's arrival. "You're very late, you know," she scolded as he swung her up for a hug and a kiss.

"I know, Aimee love. I'm really sorry." He repeated his apology to Fenella. "I really am terribly sorry to inconvenience you, Fenella. The extra meeting was both totally unanticipated and unavoidable. I appreciate your stepping into the breach; I truly do. Especially in view of our past run-ins."

He had the grace to blush slightly, Fenella noted with satisfaction.

His willingness to face the truth impressed her, and her tender heart ached at the harassed, uncertain expression replacing his normal confidence. Without warning she felt past grudges being wiped out and had to steel herself not to rush over and smooth his troubled brow.

She had no right to offer such comfort.

"Aimee's been no trouble at all, have you Sweetheart?" Fenella sought to do with words what she couldn't do physically. "I was only too happy to help out in an emergency." She directed Aimee to tidy away the blocks and purposefully motioned Greg outside; out of the child's hearing.

"That's just it, though. It shouldn't have been an emergency. As a parent, Greg, it's your responsibility to be prepared in advance for scheduling glitches and other changes of plan.

She eyed him warily.

"You should have someone else you can call on, besides yourself and Linda. Just in case. For busy people like the two of you, hold-ups like today's are always going to be on the cards."

"Damn it all, Fenella." Greg ran his hand distractedly through his hair. "Don't you think I haven't been kicking myself all the way back from Sydney? The trouble is, I don't know anyone to ask, or I would have, instead of dumping my problems on the school. And you. This is the first time my plans have gone skew-whiff." Fenella nodded her understanding.

"I've been thinking it over," she glanced apprehensively at the anxious man facing her

"Please don't be annoyed at my presumption, Greg. You've only been Aimee's guardian for a short while, so you're still new to all this. I'm only trying to help. For Aimee's sake," she placed a placatory hand lightly upon his arm, then stepped back to a safe distance.

At her words Greg's accustomed arrogance had stirred briefly. Now he relaxed and told her to go on.

"I've compiled a list of local women who might be willing to do some occasional child minding for you. Mrs Peterson would probably suit you best. She has an excellent reputation."

Unfolding the sheet of paper she took from her pocket, Fenella pointed to the name and address at the top of her list.

"Whoever you employ though Greg, be sure you let the school know so we can add her name to Aimee's authorised contact list."

Greg reluctantly took the paper from Fenella.

It really irked him to ask a favour of her considering their past acrimony, but surprisingly, he discovered that he truly believed she was the best one to help with his daughter. Despite having thought otherwise, his discreet inquiries around the town had afforded nothing but glowing accolades for her character. Matt Sykes had expressed it both admirably and succinctly.

"No-one more reliable than Fen, although mind you, the girl's got a bit of a temper when something gets her dander up."

This had been confided with sly grin, insinuating that Greg had done just that. Maybe he had; she'd sure got under his skin. In the resulting contretemps, it was possible they had both overreacted. He couldn't help thinking it was long past time to mend fences.

Fenella's generosity over Aimee confirmed that resolution.

Goggling in amazement Fenella watched a flush warm Greg's cheeks for the second time as he diffidently made his offer.

"I don't suppose you'd consider the job yourself, Fenella? Aimee likes you and you're here on the spot." Stunned by his offer, Fenella struggled for words. Misinterpreting her silence, Greg hurriedly upped the ante.

"I know we've had our differences," he began, fumbling awkwardly for words that would not ignite Fenella's capricious temper.

"My sincere apologies for my part. It's simply that I can't get out of the habit of being responsible for Jason," he explained, ignoring the weakness of his excuse; trying instead to convince Fenella of his sincerity.

"Mum was busy helping Dad get his business established, so it became my job to keep tabs on the kid. Old habits die hard, I guess." Shrugging, he dropped the delicate subject of his brother. "Anyway, everyone tells me how lucky Aimee is to have you for her teacher, and I can see for myself how good you are with her. Do you think we can bury the hatchet and start over?"

A magnanimous apology from the man she simultaneously loved and loathed. Coming on top of the job offer it totally disarmed Fenella. Loathing disappeared like morning mist leaving only the loving.

This time it was her turn to flush a becoming shade of rose. Words tumbled over each other in her haste to agree with him.

"So true," she gasped. "More than time, provided the hatchet isn't buried in my skull."

She attempted a light giggle, seeking to relieve her tension. Events were progressing so fast she felt in danger of losing her grip. "Really Greg, I agree wholeheartedly. I hate being at odds with anyone. Being friends will be so much more comfortable."

She wasn't altogether sure of that; prayed her words wouldn't come back to bite her.

"So how about it?" he prompted. "Will you be Aimee's emergency carer?"

"I would if I could, Greg. Only quite often I'm not here. Conducting in-service training on the new art syllabus will be occupying a lot of my afternoons this year. Not just here, other schools in the region as well. I'm sorry." She spread her hands helplessly.

"Try Mrs Peterson Greg."

Thanking her again, both for minding Aimee this time and for her advice, he took his leave. The defeated slump to his shoulders when he led his daughter out to the car tore at Fenella's sensibilities.

In her heart she wished she could have done more to help. In her head she thanked providence that a genuine excuse existed to prevent her from throwing herself into harm's way. Finally, she had come to terms with her hopeless one-way love. It would be foolish indeed to expose herself to undue temptation. The new detente would be short lived if she spent too much time in Greg Kendall's heady company.

Nevertheless, it felt good to have cleared the air between them.

10

On Saturday morning Fenella wasn't altogether surprised to see that Aimee had a companion at her station on the deck. At school on Friday Aimee had sidled up beside her. Tucking her hand into Fenella's she had whispered her news.

"Uncle Jason's coming tonight Ms Wilkins." She giggled, then shared the rest of the message her Uncle Jason had confided to her.

"He called you his best girl. 'You tell my best girl, Fenella Wilkins, that I'm coming to see her,' he said. Is Uncle Jason your boyfriend Ms Wilkins?" Aimee asked, agog with curiosity.

Fenella laughed.

"Not at all Sweetheart, although we are friends. Good friends, I hope. You tell your Uncle Jason his best girl's looking forward to seeing him, too."

She accompanied her message with a conspiratorial wink which had the young messenger giggling again, covering her delighted grin with both chubby hands. The happy sound wrenched at Fenella's heart.

Linda Beck had been at home for over a week, and she hadn't heard much of it in all that time. Still giggling, Aimee ventured another question.

"Is that a joke Ms Wilkins?"

"That it is Aimee," she smiled. "Your Uncle Jason's a cheeky devil, isn't he? So I'm being cheeky right back at him."

✱✱✱✱✱

Fenella recalled that conversation when she saw the tall, blond man alongside Aimee's diminutive figure on the deck.

For a moment, with the sun in her eyes, she'd thought it was Greg, the brothers being so much alike. Until he waved and called out to her and immediately she realised her mistake.

"Hold on Fen, Aimee and I are coming down." Obediently Fenella waved back and slowed to a halt, waiting till her two friends arrived on the beach.

As if Greg would even be out of bed yet, she scoffed to herself. Aimee's artless prattle had revealed that her daddy wasn't an early riser.

"Daddy stays up too late writing his books," she'd complained. "And then he's always running late in the morning."

Jason greeted her with one of his characteristic bearhugs, lifting her off her feet and twirling her around as if she were as much of a lightweight as his niece. Hamming it up, he growled in mock indignation. "I'm a cheeky devil, am I? Well, here's something even cheekier." With that he planted a smacking kiss on Fenella's laughing mouth.

Winking down at a delighted Aimee, he set Fenella back on her feet. Holding hands the three of them strolled on down the beach, Zilla gambolling around Aimee's legs; looking for all the world like a happy little family enjoying an early morning ramble.

That's how they appeared to Greg Kendall. Awake early for once and looking to see where Jason and Aimee had got to, he caught the kiss. Why it should cause him pain, he didn't know. But it did.

After making a date to swim together later in the day, Jason and Aimee left Fenella at the southern exit from the beach and returned home to breakfast.

Jason spent a good part of the morning playing about with his niece; teasing her about school and her friends while he did so. In the process he discovered more about the child's doings than Greg ever had with his careful questions. His momentary jealousy of his younger brother's easy rapport with Aimee gave way to an unaccustomed feeling of bleak inadequacy. He loved Aimee, but this parenting business wasn't as easy as it looked. Lately, he was sometimes assailed by grave doubts about his ability to make a success of it. Making the situation worse, Linda appeared to be having even more difficulty with the job than he was.

Poor Aimee, if we can't get our act together soon.

During his short visits with Aimee while her mother was still alive, they had got along well, he'd thought, the child enjoying the treats that always accompanied those occasions. However, since his ex-wife, Marcia's death, Aimee had been deeply despondent and unhappy for some time.

He had finally begun to build a solid relationship with her, believing he had won her love and trust at last, only to have her become quiet and withdrawn all over again.

He was sure she loved him. She was always so eager to spend time with him, only she no longer confided in him as she had earlier begun to. If only he knew what was troubling her. Several times he had been tempted to turn to Fenella for advice, only Linda's confident assertion that Aimee was merely going through a difficult phase had lulled his concern.

Watching his daughter with Jason he wasn't so sure. Next time he saw his mother, he decided he would have a serious heart-to-heart with her.

Safer all round than talking to Fenella. Consulting Fenella felt vaguely disloyal to Linda.

Meanwhile, he'd tag along with Jason and glean what he could from the easy camaraderie the younger man shared with the child.

Include Fenella Wilkins in that exalted company, he added to his gloomy thoughts, witnessing his daughter's exuberant welcome for her friend when Fenella joined them for the promised swim.

Fenella's confident stride had faltered when she saw that Jason and Aimee were accompanied by Aimee's father.

Although she shouldn't have been surprised, she realised, since she had often seen Greg on the beach with his daughter on the weekends. Invariably, she took care to keep the length of the beach between them on those occasions and Greg had never sought her out.

What really did surprise her though, was to see Linda Beck, her luscious curves temptingly displayed in a tiny red string bikini, artfully arranged on a beach mat, drawing lascivious glances from every man wandering by.

Fenella cast a disparaging glance at her conservative maillot, a wry grimace twisting her lips. Even though she possessed an eminently satisfactory figure, next to Linda Beck's voluptuous endowment she felt at a distinct disadvantage.

"Can I have a go on your boogie board Fenella?" Aimee had been enviously eyeing the bright yellow board under Fenella's arm. Some of her school friends had boogie boards and she had been longing to try one.

"That's up to your Daddy, Aimee. If either he or your Uncle Jason would like to show you how to use it, of course you may borrow it."

This was why she had picked up the board used by her nephews on their visits. She was positive Aimee would get just as much fun out of it as they did. Speculatively she eyed the two blond giants.

"How are your boogie boarding skills Old Man? Up to giving the kid a lesson?" Jason taunted.

"Probably rustier than yours," Greg retorted, "but here goes nothing. How about it Aimee? Do you reckon the two of us can figure it out together?"

"You're being silly Daddy. Susie," her best friend at school, "says it's real easy."

Father and daughter shared a laugh. With a word of thanks to Fenella, Greg clasped Aimee's hand, hefted the board under his other arm, and waded into the shallows.

"They look as if they can cope," Jason observed. "Let's you and I go do some body surfing." He grabbed Fenella's hand and raced her, laughing with pleasure, through the foamy backwash until the water was deep enough to swim out to where the waves were cresting.

Lips tightening in inexplicable annoyance as he watched Jason take Fenella's hand and run with her into the breakers, Greg was once again assailed by the disquieting pain he had felt that morning.

It was concern for his brother, he told himself. Nothing more than that. He even more than half believed it.

Half an hour later, after several good rides, Fenella waded ashore where Greg still encouraged Aimee to master the boogie board in the shallow waves.

"If you'd like a turn surfing with Jason, I'll keep an eye on Aimee for you," she offered.

Greg glanced up, warmed by her consideration. He peered up the beach to where Linda lay sunning herself on her mat, but he knew she didn't enjoy the water, and wouldn't appreciate the board riding lesson or body surfing.

"Thanks Fenella," he accepted. "Don't mind if I do." Waving to Aimee, he swam out to join his brother. When the men returned Fenella and Aimee, floppy sunhats covering both salt tangled heads, were engrossed in building a gigantic sandcastle. Instantly Jason joined in, sure of his welcome.

Watching enviously for a minute or two and offering several unsolicited pieces of advice on their architectural techniques, Greg ambled off to throw himself down on a towel at his fiancée's side.

Linda appeared to be rather left out of things here on the beach. He would have preferred to join the construction crew building castles in the sand with Aimee. *And Fenella?* He wondered.

Conscious stricken, he decided he owed it to Linda to keep her company for a while. Almost asleep, he was roused some time later.

"Come on Lazybones. How about we kick the soccer ball around for a bit? Fen and I will take on you, Aimee and Linda."

Tossing aside the magazine he'd dozed off over, Greg scrambled to his feet, an anticipatory gleam in his eye. Opening his mouth to accept the invitation, he was forestalled. Linda sat up extending a daintily manicured hand to him to help her up. Her brittle laugh tinkled mockingly as she wrapped both arms enticingly around Greg's waist and gazed adoringly into his eyes.

"You and Fenella can please yourselves of course, Jason, but if Greg and I want to get all hot and sweaty there are far more enjoyable *adult* ways to do it than playing children's games." Simpering, she added a coy rider. "And we know just about all of them, don't we Darling?"

Preening under Greg's admiring, albeit self-conscious gaze, hair and make-up as immaculate as when she'd left the house, Linda cast a scornful glance over Fenella's bedraggled tresses and sand caked legs.

"It's time we were going in anyway, before we burn to a crisp," she purred, leaning into Greg's body as if she intended to seduce him right there and then, in front of them.

Fenella seethed.

"Well you two go ahead and amuse yourselves with your *adult* games, then." Jason's sardonic laugh raised an angry flush on Greg's cheeks. "I'll help out by taking Aimee to Fen's place for an hour or two; keeping her out of your hair."

With that, Jason scooped up his own and Aimee's towels and sandals and stalked off, annoyance in every line of his too-straight back. "Come on girls," he ordered, "grab your gear and let's go."

There was nothing left for Greg to do except to gather up the remaining scatter of possessions and trail tamely after Linda.

This time Fenella wasn't the woman towards whom his tightly leashed anger was directed. Although in some mysterious way he couldn't fathom, Greg blamed her for the discordant end to a pleasant morning.

11

Apparently, Jason had made his peace with his brother yet again, Fenella surmised when she observed the Kendall brothers and Linda Beck enter the dining room of the Mermaid Tavern that evening. The two husky, charismatic young titans and their elegantly beautiful companion created quite a stir in the casual atmosphere of the Mermaid.

Cynically, Fenella was enjoying the show when Jason caught her eye across the room, waving and calling a cheery hello. Linda and Greg, following his gaze, accorded her equally chilly stares, carefully seating themselves with their backs to her, deliberately snubbing her. Confused and a little bit hurt by the way Greg blew first hot, then cold, Fenella shrugged and returned to the conversation at her own table.

If that's the way he wants it, she told herself, defiant in spite of her hurt, *there'll be no argument from me.*

Shortly after she felt arms circle her from behind as Jason dropped a friendly kiss onto her temple.

"Hi Fen. That's for the audience," he muttered sotto voce and grinned, indicating his brother standing at the bar, watching them in the mirror, thin lipped and disapproving. Fenella's raised brow elicited no response other than another of Jason's infectious, lop-sided grins. Shelving her questions, she introduced him to her friends, three other teachers with whom she was enjoying a girls' night out.

"I hope you're all staying for the dancing." Jason playfully ogled the party of women. "I'm bent on having fun, and figure that's more likely with you ladies than with my brother and his fiancée." He made a moue of distaste at the thought of an evening spent playing gooseberry.

Enthusiastically he was assured that they did indeed intend to dance the night away. It wasn't every day the Mermaid had a decent band.

"Save me some dances then, ladies," Jason begged, returning to his own table.

Jason fit right in with Fenella's friends when he rejoined her party after dinner. Finding themselves temporarily alone, he allowed the conversation to become personal.

"Old Greg was a bit put out when I said I was joining you girls. Reckoned I only came to visit him to chase after you." This was accompanied by a devilish snigger.

"Pity he doesn't like you better Fen."

Fenella thought so too. She had believed they'd reached a better understanding. Now it seemed she'd been mistaken. Jason was lost in morose thoughts of his own for a moment.

"Actually," he confided with embarrassing candour, "aside from seeing you Fen, I keep hoping that one day I'll see that dumb brother of mine wake up to himself and give the wicked witch over there her marching orders."

He grimaced. Then, unable to hold his feelings in any longer, he spoke out impulsively.

"She's all wrong for him, if only he could see it," he despaired. "Greg needs someone warm and caring who's not afraid to stand up to him and tell it like it is. Someone like you Fen."

Fenella's heart thudded in painful agreement. Hopefully the dim lighting was dark enough to cover her fluctuating colour. Apparently, it was, as Jason ploughed on, unburdening himself.

"Linda's even worse for Aimee, poor little brat. She's a sweet kid, only Linda really doesn't like kids at all. Those pretty maternal posturings are an act she puts on for Greg. He can't see, or maybe doesn't want to see. Either way, Linda's making poor little Aimee's life a misery." Exasperated, he huffed out a huge sigh.

Jason's words and the bitter, derisive grimace accompanying them, tore at Fenella's sensitive heartstrings.

If only she didn't share his misgivings.

If only she didn't share his hopes.

There was nothing she'd like better than to win Greg Kendall's love and take care of him and his beautiful little girl forever. She'd make a decent job of it too, she was confident of that. If ever the opportunity came her way. Unhappy reality stared her in the face in the person of Linda Beck.

She shook her head, resigning herself all over again to the stark truth. She was deluding herself, believing she could stop loving Greg. Real love couldn't be turned on and off as if it were a tap.

"Ah hell, Fen." Jason ran his hands distractedly through his hair in a gesture which reminded Fenella of Greg on those rare occasions when he was unsure of himself.

"What's the use! He'll never listen to me. He thinks I'm just a kid who's still wet behind the ears."

The music changed to a livelier tempo and Jason cast aside his sombre mood. Hauling Fenella to her feet he twirled her round and round the dance floor, improvising elaborate steps as he went; until she was incapable of any purposeful thought beyond the immediate moment.

"Enough Jason. Have mercy on me," Fenella gasped. Laughing from the pleasure engendered by the music and their energetic exercise, she collapsed against his chest. Encircling arms supporting each other, they left the floor. A stolen glance showed Fenella that Greg Kendall was again staring at them, rigid with condemnation.

Refusing to allow him to spoil her pleasure, she turned her back on him, becoming the vivacious centre of a crowd of young people, drawing more eyes than his; though none so censorious.

"Nice to see our youngsters having a bit of innocent fun, eh Shirl?" commented Charlie Peck, sedately waltzing Shirley Morton past the group copying Jason as he demonstrated what he claimed to be the latest dance craze in the Sydney nightclubs.

"Young Kendall's less stiff-necked than his brother. Though mind you, Shirl, I think that could be down to that uppity fiancée of his. Greg's pretty easy-going if she's not hanging off his arm."

Charlie's comments summed up the opinions arrived at by quite a few members of the Topaz Sands community.

Several more times in the next half hour Fenella's eyes accidentally clashed with Greg's; the sight of his disapproving scowl annoying her anew.

Trying hard to ignore him, she was startled to find him at her side, curtly inviting her to dance.

Without waiting for an answer, he deftly swung her into a space on the crowded floor.

Not sure this was a sensible idea, she looked for Jason to rescue her, only he had disappeared into the traffic jam fronting the bar, leaving her defenceless.

Neither would Linda be intervening. She was already on the dance floor with the deeply tanned older man who'd earlier joined her and Greg. "Martin Wallace he is. Someone big in advertising, or maybe television," had been the word passed along the grapevine.

There was no avoiding it so Fenella gave in gracefully and followed where Greg led her, pretending that he was dancing with her because he desired her company.

Pretending, for the length of the dance, that the luxury of being in his arms was hers by right.

Silently, two pairs of eyes conscientiously averted from each other, Greg and Fenella circled the perimeter of the dancefloor.

Until they drew level with the door leading to the veranda. Tonight it stood wide open to let the cool sea breeze waft in.

A strategic twirl, and Greg thrust Fenella through the door and steered her down to the empty, darkened corner, out of earshot of the few couples taking advantage of the fresh air.

"I thought we'd reached an understanding," he accused her, "but where Jason's concerned you're absolutely determined to ignore my advice, aren't you Fenella?"

Greg's opening broadside caught Fenella off guard, her pleasant imaginings having led her in an altogether different direction. Temper beginning a slow burn, she gathered her wits, scattered by his bitter, unyielding stance.

"Your advice, Greg? Now what advice would that be?"

Assuming a nonchalance she didn't feel, Fenella edged away, turning her back on his threatening bulk to lean over the veranda rail, apparently more interested in the garden below than her companion.

"You know what I'm talking about," Greg sneered. "I advised you once before to leave Jason alone. You've deliberately ignored me, haven't you; flaunting your pitiful little triumph in my face. First this morning on the beach and again tonight."

Tightly leashed anger vibrated through the softly hissed accusation. Dreading another slanging match, yet determined not to back down, Fenella shivered.

In accepting Jason's friendship, she had done nothing wrong. Nothing to be ashamed of. Nothing to be reviled for. Indignation got the better of her.

"Advised me!" she spat back at him. "You didn't *advise* me about anything, Greg Kendall. All you did was warn me off, as if Jason is an infant who can't fend for himself. How insulting is that? You're darn right I ignored you. You've got no right to dictate to either of us. *As* I told you before."

Her heart hammering against her ribs, she struggled to contain the hot tears threatening to break free in an anguished torrent.

The pain of loving a man who didn't want her and hadn't the slightest respect for her as a woman was doing her head in. She swung round, desperate to escape. "I don't have to stand here listening to this rubbish. I'm going back inside."

She attempted to push past him, but he used his large frame to unfair advantage, blocking her passage.

"You'll stay and listen whether you like it or not, Fenella Wilkins. You may not be what I first thought you were, but I was right about one thing. Jason's too young for the likes of you. He'll only end up hurt trying to play in your league."

"Too young! I admit he is younger than me, but actually Greg, I don't imagine Jason's any more of an innocent than any other twenty-something male." More than a touch of sarcasm infected Fenella's tone.

"Don't be obtuse Fenella," Greg raged. "Jason may be adult in years, but he's nowhere near you in experience, is he? Let him go Fenella."

Experience? Fenella was astounded at Greg's argument. *What experience?* As far as she knew he didn't even know she'd been married and divorced.

Ignoring what she couldn't explain at the moment, she returned to her attack on Greg's unjust stand.

"Why?" she fired back. "Give me one good reason why I should, Greg. Just one! Jason and I are friends. That's it. Friends. Nothing more. So why are you getting all steamed up?"

"Alright, I'll spell it out for you. You've just said it yourself. There's nothing serious on your side. You're only fooling around, amusing yourself with him. Unfortunately, Jason's in love with you, as you're quite well aware, aren't you?" He made a derogatory statement of it rather than a question.

Before a flabbergasted Fenella could formulate her defence, he reiterated his demand. "Let Jason go Fenella, before he gets hurt."

"You're out of your tiny mind, Greg Kendall," Fenella informed him through clenched teeth, annoyed with herself for being reduced to issuing childish insults.

This time when Fenella attempted to leave, Greg contemptuously stepped aside, thrusting his fists into his pockets as if to avoid strangling her.

Fenella felt the blistering heat of his anger scorching her back as she strode away from him, head high, studiously casual, battening down her own fury. This time she wouldn't allow the infuriating man to provoke her into making a public exhibition of herself! Once had been more than enough.

Some of the rubbish he'd spouted though, gave her food for thought. Ducking into the restroom for a few moments of much needed privacy, she re-evaluated the situation.

If Jason really was in love with her as Greg asserted he was, it would be unkind of her to permit him to believe his feelings could be reciprocated. However, upon reflection she was certain Greg had gotten the wrong end of the stick. Admittedly, Jason was pretty free with his hugs and kisses, but she was positive his affection was brotherly, not lover-like.

I'll tackle Jason later and find out for sure though, she decided. Exiting the restroom, once again comfortable with her conscience, Fenella came slap up against Linda Beck.

"You think you're smart don't you Ms Fenella Wilkins; playing Greg and Jason off against each other." A feral snarl contorted Linda's perfect features into an ugly mask.

A shiver of foreboding shook Fenella's assurance.

"You can have Jason for all I care, but Greg's mine, and don't you forget it; or you'll be sorry! It'll take more than tricking him into five minutes alone in the dark to take him away from me. Greg would never be seriously interested in an ordinary little nobody of a country school teacher pretending to be a great artist. He likes his women sophisticated and beautiful. You don't measure up on either count, do you?"

She preened herself in front of Fenella, who had great difficulty refraining from slapping her across her carefully made-up face. Slapping her hard. Especially when Linda concluded triumphantly, "You're a joke, Fenella Wilkins!"

How dare Linda Beck threaten me?

Fenella fumed silently, lips pressed firmly together, not deigning to answer. Hand tingling in frustration, she shoved rudely past.

Damn Linda and Greg both! She'd show them they couldn't intimidate Fenella Wilkins.

Storming back to the dance floor Fenella proceeded to do just that.

For the remainder of the of the evening she stayed close to Jason. Very close. She gazed up at him in lover-like adoration and danced cheek-to-cheek, snuggling into his arms as if she belonged there.

"Act as though you're besotted with me,' she'd hissed casting a dark glance to where Greg, one arm laid possessively across his fiancée's shoulders, sat chatting to Martin Wallace, the holidaying television executive who was a friend of Linda's.

Eyeing Fenella warily until, highly amused, he realised her request had nothing to do with affection for himself and everything to do with annoying poor old Greg, Jason devilishly wrapped long arms around her, playing up to her for all he was worth.

Just what had his fool of a brother done to rile Fenella this time? He'd noted their unobtrusive exit together and Fenella's return, alone, a few minutes later, and wondered about it.

"Is this besotted enough, do you reckon?" he whispered, pretending to nibble on her earlobe. Fenella's burst of laughter was instantly mutated into a seductive chuckle.

"That'll do very nicely thank you," she whispered back. *Let Mr Busybody Kendall stick that in his pipe and smoke it,* she thought with unwonted savagery.

While Jason walked her home under a star-spangled sky, a great yellow moon rising majestically out of the ocean, Fenella sighed. It was a night custom made for romance, and although Jason, with his robust, boyish charm was very attractive, it wasn't his arm she longed to feel around her shoulders but that of his idiot, bad-tempered, someone else's property, older brother.

Her mind drifted, reviewing her latest set-to with Greg, replaying his bitter, hurtful words. Uncomfortably, she also recalled how she had let lacerated emotions goad her into using Jason in callous disregard of any possible grief she might end up causing him.

Guilty conscience eating away at her, she realised that Jason, as well as the iniquitous male at whom they were aimed, might easily have misinterpreted her actions. Stopping abruptly, she studied Jason's face under a street light.

"Jason, you aren't falling in love with me by any mischance, are you?"

"Not in the slightest, Fen darling," he replied immediately. "I appreciate your friendship, but my heart is quite safe." A second or two later he asked mischievously, "Is that good or bad?"

Fenella laughed, relieved that her reading of Jason had been accurate, unlike his brother's.

"Very good as far as I'm concerned."

She laughed, then explained what she meant by that very personal question.

"You're a terrific guy Jason, and I thoroughly adore you, only I'm not the teeniest bit in love with you. I'm so glad you're not in love with me either."

Jason's explosive laugh was so spontaneous, so genuine, that any lingering misgivings fled and Fenella joined her laughter to his, telling him of Greg's accusations, much to Jason's amazement.

Privately, he thought his brother's behaviour smacked of a dog-in-the-manger jealousy. It would be interesting to see what happened if he ever rid himself of Linda. He didn't think Fenella was sufficiently objective to appreciate this idea though, so he kept it to himself.

"As I said earlier," he said, picking up the conversational thread, "Greg persists in thinking of me as a kid. He always watched out for me when we were younger. Guess he's still trying to, even if he is misguided. One day he might realise I'm all grown up and can fend quite adequately for myself."

Jason mused silently on the matter for a few metres then spoke again in fond, exasperated tones.

"If I get half a chance I might point out to him which of us it was who rushed headlong into marriage like an idealistic fool, only to end up divorced a couple of years later. Old Greg's got no common sense where women are concerned. No sense of self-preservation. Even though he's never lacked feminine company, it's usually been the wrong sort for lasting happiness. Now Linda's got her hooks into him. She set a nice little trap and blind as a mole, he walked right into it."

They walked silently on, each ruminating on their own thoughts.

"Actually, Fen," Jason, sounding unusually diffident, broke the silence first. "I couldn't fall in love with you anyway because I'm already in love with someone else. Her name's Rosie. Rosemary Parrish," he amended. "She works in my office block and I've known her for ages. Just lately we've got to know each other a whole lot better. I'm pretty sure she's The One."

Fenella turned this new information over in her mind, aware from Jason's reticent tone that there was more to it than he'd told so far. Treading delicately, she ventured a hesitant question.

"Have you told your family about her yet?"

Drawing in a deep breath, Jason halted, then walked a few steps away from her. Shoving his hands in his pockets he stood looking out to sea, shoulders hunched.

Finally, he answered her.

"Not yet. You see, Dad's a wee bit biased. To tell the truth he's a dyed-in-the-wool racist. Still lives in the days of Menzies and the White Australia Policy and all that. Rosie's mother is from Malaysia," he elucidated.

"She came to Australia as a RAAF bride. Met her husband in Penang, like a lot of others. She's a lovely woman Fen. Like my Rosie. I'm worried that the old man might cut up rough at first, and I won't have them hurt. Which is why I'm not saying anything until I'm one hundred percent sure of my feelings. And Rosie's."

He turned back to face Fenella, an expression of sheepish uncertainty flickering across his face.

"'It hasn't bothered you has it? The way I fool about when I'm with you, I mean. I just can't resist getting up Greg's nose. Especially since he's being such an ass over you."

Calmly, Fenella reassured him truthfully that she wasn't at all bothered by his nonsense. He linked arms with her and they sauntered on.

"I'd like to meet your Rosie some time Jason," she said thoughtfully. "I have to be in Sydney in a few weeks for a Friday appointment. I'm planning to stay on for the weekend, so perhaps we could all have dinner together?" Jason agreed wholeheartedly with her suggestion.

"You and Rosie are going to like each other," he murmured. A little later he added, "It's wonderful to have a friend I can talk to about Rosie. I had hoped to get Greg on my side, but since Linda got her claws into him, he's changed. Now there's no knowing any more how he'll take things."

12

The peace and quiet of the following week came as a welcome respite after the weekend's dramas. It was a busy week for Fenella, and a particularly exciting one for her class of five-year olds.

On Friday, for the very first time, they were to host the school assembly to which their families had all been especially invited. Each child would have a particular task to perform; the more confident among them sharing the emcee duties, using the microphone to make the announcements. Aimee Kendall was one of these; indeed, the first to speak since Fenella was trusting her to welcome their guests. Well-rehearsed, the children were nervously agog, ready for their big event.

Making her last-minute dispositions on stage and settling her charges, Fenella scanned the gathering of proud parents filing into their seats, catching a glimpse of Mr and Mrs Kendall, Aimee's grandparents, entering the school auditorium.

"Kelly," she called softly to one of the older children assigned as ushers, "show Mr and Mrs Kendall to a seat up front please."

She indicated the older couple who appeared bewildered in the midst of all the busy confusion.

"Seats with a clear view of the stage, if there are any left," she added, catching sight of the video camera in Mr Kendall's hand. They waved their thanks to Fenella and followed Kelly. Attracted by the sound of her own surname, Aimee spotted her grandparents.

"Grandma! Grandpa!" she called, her piping soprano ringing out clear as a bell above the quiet murmurings and shufflings. Jumping up excitedly, she waved to them from the stage.

"Hello there Aimee love," her grandfather boomed back, while his wife shushed him, blowing a kiss to her granddaughter at the same time.

"Ms Wilkins, did you see? My Grandma and Grandpa are here. I didn't know they were coming, did you? I can't see Daddy though. He better hurry or he'll miss me."

Anxiously she scanned the auditorium, worry puckering her forehead, lower lip trembling ominously.

Restoring the child to her chair and diverting the incipient tears, Fenella also wondered where Greg Kendall was. Steeled for a possible meeting, she had not once doubted that he would be here to share his daughter's proud moment.

In Fenella's experience, the parents of kindergarten children rarely missed their little ones' special events unless prevented by work or illness.

Surely that didn't apply in the Kendall's situation since Greg Kendall ordered his own schedule.

After delaying as long as possible there was no option except to go ahead. She couldn't wait any longer.

"But it's okay Sweetheart. Your Grandpa's got his video camera," she soothed Aimee.

"Cheer up and give him a big smile. If your Daddy's too late he can still see you on the video."

There were all the usual easily forgiven mishaps when stage fright caused small troupers to drop things and forget their lines, however the audience was sympathetic and finally it was safely over. Guiding her class off the stage, Fenella heaved a huge sigh of relief.

Among the proudly doting parents who followed them back to their classroom were Aimee's grandparents.

"Well done Aimee darling," they praised. "We're so proud of our baby girl. Ask Ms Wilkins if we can come in to see some of your work, will you dear."

Ms Wilkins, duly consulted was only too happy to grant permission. It was time for the morning break anyway and many of the parents had elected to join their children, several also studying the children's work displayed around the room.

"We're very impressed Fenella," Mrs Kendall confided. "Peter and I haven't been inside a classroom since Jason was young. Things have changed a lot, haven't they?"

Fenella agreed, then, more seriously, Mrs Kendall asked, "Do you know what's happened to Aimee's father? We were rather disturbed to see neither him nor Linda here today. He didn't send a message, did he? Only he loves Aimee so much, I'm afraid something awful must have happened to keep him away."

"I'm sorry, Mrs Kendall, I've had no message. Aimee was disappointed too. I sent the usual notes home, so they knew about the assembly. After all, he told you, didn't he? I do hope nothing is seriously wrong."

Earlier she had felt nothing except annoyance with Greg for so carelessly hurting his daughter's feelings. Now though, concern for his well-being creased her brow.

"Actually dear," the older woman hesitated, "Greg didn't tell us. Aimee told us over the phone and we couldn't resist surprising her."

"Linda threw my invitation in the bin."

Unobserved at her grandmother's side, Aimee had been listening. Now, fearful and uncertain, she dropped this bombshell into the conversation.

"Daddy was in Sydney and Linda threw my invitation in the bin," she repeated. Their attention encouraged the child to elaborate on her bald statement. "I told her it was really, really important, but she said I was being cheeky and sent me to my room. She said Daddy was much too busy to waste time on such nonsense."

On a roll, Aimee got all her stored-up grievances off her chest at once.

"Linda's always throwing away the things I take home to show Daddy. She says I shouldn't bother him with all that rubbish, but Daddy likes to see it. So now I hide everything until she goes away, and I show him then."

The floodgates were well and truly open, though now Aimee was whimpering and knuckling back tears.

"Linda will be mad at me for telling," she sobbed into her grandmother's embrace.

"No, she won't!" Mr Kendall, voiced his indignation.

"Don't you worry about a thing young Aimee. I'll have a talk with Linda. And while I'm at it," he added pugnaciously, "I'll have a talk with your daddy as well. Seems he might need a few things set straight for him."

His thunderous countenance, so like his son's when Greg was in a temper, convinced Fenella that sparks were likely to fly during that conversation!

She almost felt sorry for Greg. Almost, until she glanced at Aimee wiping tears from her eyes, and hardened her heart. Defiantly, she hoped he, and Linda, got what they deserved.

"Cheer up Aimee dear," comforted Mrs Kendall. "You stop worrying now and leave it all to us. Grandpa and I will sort everything out for you, you'll see."

Linda Beck wasn't going to be happy at being 'sorted out'.

*****

"Regret to tell you Fen, I missed the big row," Jason informed Fenella the next morning. They were on the beach, out of earshot of Aimee, who was throwing a ball for Zilla, while Jason filled her in on the latest drama in the Kendall household. "Dad was still hopping mad though. He took me for a walk on the beach and poured it all out after I arrived last night. Seems Mum felt there might be unpleasant repercussions for Aimee and tried to persuade him to be a bit diplomatic in handling it. Fat chance," he sniggered.

"Dad and diplomacy are oil and water. First, he tore a strip of poor old Greg who hadn't a clue what he was going on about. Called him a lousy excuse for a father. Poor Greg. He asked Linda to 'please explain'. Apparently, she made up some flimsy excuse trying to blame poor little Aimee for losing the note. Dad saw red and next thing he'd lost his cool and was repeating what Aimee had said, about Linda chucking it away, etc. Told her in no uncertain terms that if she expected to be Aimee's mother then she'd better smarten up her act and start acting like a mother. Wish I'd been there to hear that."

He broke off and ran his hand through his hair in the manner typical of all the Kendall men, a wry grin twisting his lips.

"I've been on the receiving end when Dad's got the bit between his teeth; and it's not pleasant." Jason shuddered at past memories.

"The Old Man's quite formidable when he gets going; specially when he knows he's in the right. Mum was trying to calm everyone down and Greg got more and more uptight as it finally dawned what Dad was so irate about. Then he tore into Linda too. Seeing they were all against her, Linda turned on the waterworks and begged Greg's forgiveness. Claimed she hadn't understood that parents are supposed to join in with these sorts of things; that her parents never had. Could even be true I guess." Jason shrugged, reluctant to grant even that tiny concession.

"Glossed over the rest of it rather slickly," he continued.

"Anyway, Greg relented. Ended with the two of them going off to their room for a serious discussion. Must have been some discussion," Jason's lip curled scornfully.

"Today Linda's being all lovey-dovey, putting on a contrite act and Greg's come over ultra-protective of her. Says it's merely a storm in a teacup and ought to be forgotten."

Envisioning the scene Jason had described so graphically, Fenella once again felt the disturbing tremor of apprehension that had assailed her the day before. Today it made her seriously uneasy. Linda had a spiteful streak a mile wide as she'd learnt to her cost. Her shortcomings publicly exposed, even if she managed a successful cover-up, Fenella felt afraid that someone would be made to pay.

As long as it's not Aimee, she thought, protective instincts to the fore. Should her worst fears be realised, she was unsure how effective her limited guardianship would be.

That she herself might be made Linda's scapegoat worried her not one iota. She wasn't a defenceless child. In her present mood, she might even enjoy taking the other woman on.

Fenella's intense, tigerish expression informed Jason to his delight he wasn't alone in his dislike of his future sister-in-law. Their confidences came to an end as Aimee ran up, Zilla yapping at her heels. Before parting they finalised their plans for Fenella's upcoming weekend in Sydney when Jason intended to introduce her to Rosemary Parrish. A meeting she looked forward to.

✶✶✶✶✶

How could two brothers so alike be so very different, Fenella wondered sadly, watching Jason stroll down the beach, hand in hand with his niece.

Why should she like this one so much, yet fail to respond to his vibrant masculinity that could in no way be viewed as less than his brother's? And why, why, did the older brother, whom she wasn't at all sure she even liked, affect her so powerfully that merely to think of him had her burning for his touch? Yearning for his love. Fenella bewailed her fate.

It's just not fair. But then, as we've been told, life isn't meant to be fair, she paraphrased. Laughing bitterly at her foolishness, she whistled Zilla to heel and wandered home, feet dragging.

13

After Aimee's weekend exuberance in the company of her much-loved grandparents and her favourite uncle, her subdued demeanour on Monday morning was not all that surprising. Adopting a bracing matter-of-factness, Fenella mopped up a tear or two, eliciting no response other than a woeful sniffle.

"I wish Grandma lived here all the time," was the closest to an explanation for her tears that the little girl produced. Quite possibly missing her grandparents was all there was to it, so Fenella had to be satisfied.

That afternoon, shortly after the children had departed, Aimee dragging her feet more than usual, Fenella answered a knock on the classroom door, surprised to find a sober visaged Greg Kendall hand in hand with a now beaming Aimee.

"Hello Fenella. Aimee wants to show me her classroom, if it's okay with you." Fenella waved them in. His interest came better late than never, she supposed.

"It's very much okay. Parents are always welcome. I'll leave you in Aimee's capable hands."

Returning to the work on her desk, she left the two of them alone studying the colourful displays. Scrutinising Greg's shadowed face from across the width of the room, she couldn't help observing that he appeared weighed down; almost as depressed as Aimee had been that morning.

Sensing her gaze upon him, Greg turned, as if there was something he needed to say. Something weighty. She selected a folder from the shelf beside her desk and met him half-way.

"Being a writer yourself, Greg, you might be interested in these stories Aimee's been writing." Fenella proffered the folder with a professional smile, spoiling the effect by winking at the child by his side. "I rather think your daughter may have inherited your gift with words."

Greg scanned the enclosed pages keenly, then sat on the corner of the nearest midget-sized desk and invited Aimee to read some of them to him. A request she eagerly complied with.

The story folder finally restored to its rightful position, Greg rose tiredly to his feet, running a hand through his hair in the gesture that had endeared itself, and him, to Fenella. With difficulty, she resisted the temptation to reach out and smooth his disordered locks. In his present mood she rediscovered why she loved him so impossibly.

"Fenella." Determination to discharge an unpleasant task was writ large on Greg's unsmiling countenance. "As well as looking over Aimee's work; with which I am more than happy by the way; I came to have a word with you. I assume Jason told you about Friday's misunderstanding."

His lips twisted distastefully and Fenella merely nodded, not sure what answer, if any, would be appropriate.

Misunderstanding was a masterly understatement if ever she'd heard one.

"Well...," he hesitated. Straightening decisively, he came to the point. "There won't be any more misunderstandings of that sort. Linda, Aimee and I have talked it over and arrived at a system for handling notes and suchlike. Linda and I are both out of touch with modern school procedures. We didn't realise that these days parents are encouraged to get involved in what the kids are doing. You'll be seeing more of both of us in future." Greg clamped his mouth shut as if swallowing a particularly nasty medicine.

If he thought he could get away with it as easily as that, Fenella had news for him.

"That's precisely why we hold parent-teacher evenings," she informed him tartly.

"It's a pity Linda, and yourself," she added drily, "didn't see fit to accept our invitation at the beginning of the year. We teachers spent over two hours explaining routines and procedures, discussing the syllabus and answering questions. The two of you would undoubtedly have found it a most beneficial evening. Certainly, it would have saved your family a lot of unnecessary fuss."

She glared severely at the arrogant male she addressed, pleased to note a repentant flush staining the tanned cheeks. Or was it annoyance at her impertinence?

Fenella didn't wait to see. Turning aside, she spoke more moderately over her shoulder.

"If you've got a minute, my notes are still in the computer; I'll print you a copy to study at your leisure. Come and see me again if you have any questions. Here, you might as well have these, too."

While the printer chattered away, she rifled through a box of assorted papers and came up with copies of that term's weekly newsletters. "This lot ought to bring you up to date with what's been happening."

Considerately mollified, Greg accepted the bundle of notes she presently thrust towards him, offering what appeared to be genuine thanks. Ushering his daughter out the door, he halted at the last moment.

"I'm sorry we got off on the wrong foot, Fenella," he uttered impulsively.

"I seem to have been wrong about a lot of things where you're concerned. Hopefully we can be on better terms in future." He raised a questioning brow, appearing to be relieved when Fenella nodded; her surprise and pleasure easy to read on her expressive features.

"Maybe I was wrong about your being bad for Jason, too," he muttered, voice muffled as he hurried off, Aimee skipping along beside him.

Tempted to run after him and pour out the truth, she recalled that he didn't yet know of Jason's burgeoning love for Rosemary Parrish and it wasn't her place to inform him.

Besides, as long as Greg Kendall thought there was something between herself and Jason, he wouldn't suspect the true state of her emotions.

With a bit of luck she might succeed in subjugating her love for him, thereby ensuring her safety from detection by the time Jason could no longer be relied on as a shield. She must, she thought desperately, since it tenaciously refused to be willed out of existence as she had first hoped.

"Damn love; and damn all men," Fenella muttered, resentful she couldn't control her deepest feelings.

✱✱✱✱✱

Her happiness over her father's school visit subsiding, Aimee stoically accepted her less than perfect situation, although Fenella noted that often her face assumed an unhappy droop.

Such misery was never meant to be the natural state for any child.

Angry and frustrated by her inability to wave a magic wand and set the world to rights, Fenella's fertile brain churned out impossible miracles one after the other, none of which had the slightest hope of coming to pass.

This remained the situation when she left for her appointment in Sydney. Saving Aimee was beyond her capabilities, so, shelving the whole sorry situation she resolved to enjoy herself in the Big Smoke. Apart from the dinner with Jason and his Rosie, she was meeting with a gallery owner to whom she had previously sent samples of her work in the hope that he would agree to be her agent.

Lack of fortune in love had spurred her into reviving ambitions shattered by Paul Fremont's cruel repudiation of her worth as an artist as well as a woman.

Jealous when the student protege he married looked set to become more successful than himself, he had deliberately broken her confidence along with her heart. Even her bread and butter career as art teacher in a private secondary school had been rendered untenable when she fell into a deep depression following her divorce.

Floundering in despair and disillusion, Fenella had resigned and crept into hiding on her parents' farm. Lacking sufficient motivation to drag herself back from the depths, there she stayed; a victim to depression until her pregnant sister-in-law urgently pleaded for help at the day care centre of which she was both owner and director.

Needing an extra assistant during her late pregnancy and maternity leave, Margaret refused to listen to excuses. A great believer in the curative power of hard work, she'd adamantly hauled Fenella out of her emotional quagmire.

Once familiar with the routines, Fenella discovered in herself a hitherto unsuspected affinity for working with small children. With everything to learn, coupled with a natural delight in shape and colour, the children's enthusiastic responses to her art 'lessons' had prompted an interest in early childhood education. Suitable post-graduate courses had expanded her teaching qualifications, then, a final stroke of luck, she was appointed to the staff of Topaz Sands Central School.

Sun, surf, an interesting new job and the undemanding small-town lifestyle completed her healing. A whole woman once again, her artistic gifts taking off in a new direction, she carved a niche for herself as a children's book illustrator. Taking her courage in her hands, she now ambitiously sought a more upscale market for her other, more serious, work.

✳✳✳✳✳

"Hey Fen! Over here!"

A beaming smile on her face, Fenella waved back and threaded her way between the tables to where Jason stood waving both hands above his head to attract her attention. "Sorry I'm late." She reached up to plant a sisterly kiss on his cheek then slipped into the chair he pulled out for her across from a truly beautiful girl whose waist length gleaming dark hair was tied back in a high ponytail.

"Fen, meet Rosie. Rosemary Parrish. Fenella Wilkins. What can I get you, Fen? I'm just off to the bar."

"I'm so happy to meet you at last, Rosemary. Jason has told me so much about you I almost feel I know you already. My shout, Jason, and it's bubbly all round. I'm celebrating."

"Good news Fenella? Jason said you were nervous and very mysterious about your appointment. He was worried because you had to take time off work. I think he was imagining some terrible illness."

Fenella winced at Rosemary's faintly admonitory tone.

"Worried? Oh Jase, you should have said. It was nothing bad, I just didn't want to say anything in case it all came to nothing. But it hasn't!"

She waved over a waiter and ordered the champagne. Turning back, she grinned, all jubilation.

"I had a meeting today with John Remington from the *Remington & Browne Fine Arts Gallery* in the City. I'd met John years ago when I won a student art competition he sponsored".

She took a sip of her drink.

"Back in January I wrote to him and he remembered me and asked me to visit with some of my work. He liked what I brought and agreed to be my agent. He said if there's enough interest he might even give me an exhibition of my own later in the year."

"Wow, Fen. That's great."

"More than great, Jason. Remington & Browne is one of the best. Congratulations Fenella. Well worth the champers. Jason told me you painted, but you must be really, really good for them to take you on."

Fenella blushed. Today's meeting meant even more to her than recognition of her talent. Success might be just the panacea needed to ease the anguish of unrequited love. Success, and the hard work necessary to achieve it.

"You'll both be giving me a swelled head shortly," she laughed. "Enough about me. Tell me what you've been up to."

The conversation ranged far and wide and by the time the other two dropped Fenella off outside her hotel, she knew she could add Rosie Parrish to her list of friends. She had no doubts either that those two were made for each other, even though their love was not without its problems. They'd launched into what was obviously a well-rehearsed argument when she'd asked about their future plans.

"We have no plans," Rosie had declared, lips tightening to a thin line. "I was brought up to respect family, Fenella, and I refuse to come between Jason and his family."

"And I refuse to give you up, Rosie darling," Jason had shot back with a matching mulish tilt to his chin.

"We're going to get married just as soon as I can persuade this stubborn woman to say yes."

"I will say yes only when your parents welcome me as a daughter."

"What do your parents say, Rosie?" Fenella asked, hoping to defuse the suddenly tense atmosphere.

"They like Jason, but they agree with me that we should have his parents' approval."

"Then it seems to me, Jason, that it's up to you. Talk to your parents. Tell them how you feel. Until you do, you're only guessing at their reaction."

"I agree, Fenella. I have told him so many times but he is afraid."

"Only because I couldn't bear it if they came between us. I love you Rosie, and my future is with you, not my parents, although I would hate it if they threw me out."

"Well they haven't thrown Greg out, and you say they don't like Linda at all. I say give them a chance, Jason." Just at that moment the waiter came with their desserts, and they all tacitly agreed to change the subject when they were alone again. Fenella prayed that love for their son would be strong enough to overcome prejudice and allow the elder Kendalls to open their hearts to his chosen bride.

Thumping her pillow into more comfortable contours, she reflected on how much simpler life had been before she became involved with the Kendalls.

And how much duller, was her last rational thought before sleep claimed her.

14

"Where's Aimee? I've been waiting at the gate for ten minutes and I've got better things to do than hang about here."

At this strident, petulant outburst Fenella turned abruptly to where a thoroughly irritated Linda Beck stood framed in the classroom doorway.

"But Aimee's not here," Fenella gestured round the empty classroom, gathering her scattered wits.

"Then, where is she? It's just like her to make a nuisance of herself," Linda snapped. Thoroughly alarmed, Fenella answered slowly, her mind racing as she began considering possibilities.

"Aimee isn't here, Linda," she repeated. "In fact, she hasn't been at school at all today."

"Not at school! She certainly was at school!" Linda's voice rose to a sharper pitch. "If this is your idea of getting even, Fenella Wilkins, I'll see that you pay for it." Her beautiful face assumed an ugly, threatening cast.

Repelled, Fenella took an involuntary backward step. Pulling herself together, she firmly took charge of the situation.

"When did you last see Aimee, Linda?" she asked quietly, watching fear replace anger as Linda's thoughts began to run along the same path as her own. Bowing to Fenella's authority, she answered apprehensively.

"Not since breakfast. Greg took her in the car. He was on his way to Sydney and said he'd drop her off." Wringing her hands, Linda burst out with desperate accusations again. "She must be here. You're hiding her to upset me."

"No." Fenella's denial was implacable. "No. You know I would *never* use a child like that. Any child." Linda, instinctively recognising this to be true, deflated before Fenella's eyes.

"Then, ... where is she? What on earth has happened to her? What will Greg say?" She wrung her hands helplessly once again. Fenella felt like wringing her own by now as well, only someone had to take the initiative.

Aimee had been missing all day. God only knew what evil had befallen her.

"Could Greg have taken her with him?" This, her last faint hope for a happy resolution, was dashed by Linda's incredulous reply.

"Greg? Whatever would he do that for? He was taking her to *school*. If she was with *him*, he would have rung me."

"Then I think we'd better take this to Mrs Crammond."

Fenella led the way to the principal's office where she repeated the story succinctly. Mrs Crammond put several brief questions to the two of them then reached for the phone.

"Time to call the police in, I think."

Her concise report given to the officer in charge, she listened carefully, nodding her head from time to time as she jotted notes. Putting the phone down, she sent her secretary to make a cup of tea for Linda who had crumpled alarming and was now sobbing helplessly, and crisply directed Fenella to locate Aimee's special friends.

"One of them may have seen her when she was dropped off this morning," she said. A thorough search of the school premises was also set in motion, so that by the time the police arrived it had been ascertained that the little girl was not hiding in either the grounds or buildings.

The teacher on early morning playground duty didn't know Aimee, but, an avid car buff, was sure he'd seen Greg Kendall's distinctive electric blue BMW among the stream of vehicles dropping children off in front of the school that morning.

"He didn't park and come in, just stopped in the drop-off bay and let a kid out. I think it was a little girl, but you know how it is. They all look alike in shorts and polo shirts and those wide-brimmed hats. One thing I am sure of though; the kid came in through the gate. I would definitely have noticed any child in uniform going *out* at that time."

On the heels of that report Fenella confirmed that Aimee had indeed arrived at school. Her phone canvassing of Aimee's friends had resulted in several reported sightings of the child that morning.

"Susie seems to know the most," she informed the sergeant.

"Her mother's bringing her in now to talk to you, but the gist of her information appears to be that about the time the five to nine bell rang, Aimee told Susie she felt sick and was going to the sickbay. Susie went to line up, then we had a visit from the school nurse and she forgot all about Aimee."

From there on matters were entirely in the hands of the police who notified Greg. Desperately worried, he set off for home immediately. By the time he arrived after dark, the police sergeant was looking grim. A house by house search of the town had netted no sign of the child and the SES were organising a full-scale search to begin at first light.

Although Aimee's photo was on the morning news accompanying a general police alert, it was not until the middle of the morning that she was found, when she limped up to the kitchen door of a farmhouse almost fifteen kilometres from home.

Hungry and thirsty, feet blistered from walking, the tearstained scrap of misery had seen a safety house symbol on the mailbox and gone in search of help.

There had been no foul play; "And thank God for that," said Sergeant McLain. Aimee, unhappy at being left yet again with Linda while her father was tied up in Sydney with the filming of his book, had felt sick with dread.

On a sudden whim she had left the school unobtrusively while everyone was at morning assembly and begun walking to her grandparents' home near Gloucester.

Except that it turned out to be much further than five-year-old legs could accomplish.

Afraid, she had hidden in the bush every time she heard a car coming, finally crawling into a tumbledown shed to shelter for the night. In the morning, too exhausted to go any further, she admitted defeat and knocked on the farmhouse door.

Fenella, who had spent a good deal of the night with one of the search parties, had more of the story from an indignant Mrs Kendall several days later. Alarmed that her granddaughter had been desperate enough to run away from home, she had come to stay, to reassure herself that Aimee really was safe and well.

"I would love to have her live with us, only Greg won't hear of it. He says he and Linda and Aimee are a family and will just have to work harder at making a success of it." She spent a few moments lost in melancholy thought.

"Of course, he's right, I suppose. As I see it, it's Linda who's the problem. She's too hard on the child. Aimee's always being punished for something it seems, and absolutely dreads her father's trips to Sydney. So much so, that this time she ran away."

Fenella passed tissues to the older woman who was fumbling for a misplaced handkerchief.

"Thank you dear." She dried her eyes and resumed her confidences.

"Linda's all defensive tears, claiming Aimee is exaggerating the situation. Whether she is or not, and honestly Fenella I'm afraid she isn't, Linda's had a good scare. I believe things will be better now. I hope so, anyway." She sighed deeply and rose to take her departure. "Greg told me he's going to arrange for the two of them to go to parenting classes together as soon as possible."

"That sounds like a positive move, Mrs Kendall," Fenella observed with encouraging optimism while remaining personally unconvinced it would prove to be sufficient. Some things, love for a child being one of them, couldn't be taught.

"Yes," Mrs Kendall uttered doubtfully, mirroring Fenella's unspoken thoughts.

"At least it's a step in the right direction. Fenella, you're a good friend of Jason's and I know you have Aimee's best interests at heart. That's why I came to see you. I'm leaving this afternoon. If anything bothers you that you don't feel you can discuss with my son, don't hesitate to call me, will you?" she begged. "I won't suggest you talk to Linda. Since she holds you in such unreasonable dislike I doubt she'd listen if you did."

Fenella doubted it too; though, anxious as Mrs Kendall was, the idea of going to her behind Greg's back made her uncomfortable.

That would definitely only be a last resort.

"I'll watch out for Aimee as well as I can," she temporised, seeing her guest out.

She would too, she vowed, recalling how she had thought some time back that Aimee was scared of Linda. Seemingly she had been right about that. How she wished she'd been wrong.

✳✳✳✳✳

Over the next few weeks Greg made a conscientious effort to minimise his outside commitments.

Now Linda was the one frequently absent from home.

One evening Fenella, and everyone else in Topaz Sands saw her in a television advertisement for an outdoor clothing company.

Grudgingly, Fenella was forced to admit that Linda came across well, even if considerably more glamorous than the average camper. The fortunate upshot of the new routine was, that with her father spending more time at home and Linda less, Aimee was a happier child during the last days of the term.

"Daddy says if I help Linda learn to be a good mummy she won't get so cross with me," Aimee confided to Fenella soon after her return to school following her attempt to run away. "He made us all sit down and work out proper rules for everything, so we all know what to do."

"Are the new rules helping?" Fenella felt justified in asking that much.

"I suppose ..." As Aimee's voice trailed off Fenella cast a sharp eye over the earnest little face upturned to hers. "Linda doesn't rowse at me so much now, but I still wish she wasn't going to be my new mummy. Mrs Peterson can help Daddy look after me, then I won't need a new mummy."

Ingenuously, she offered what seemed to her child's mind an eminently satisfactory solution to her father's parental difficulties. Fenella had to turn away to hide her painful grimace.

She could think of an even better solution; one she was sure would be acceptable to the little girl. Only it would be totally irresponsible of her to undermine an already delicate balance by voicing it. Soberly she made the diplomatic response her conscience dictated.

"From what I hear, Mrs Peterson is already being a big help, isn't she?"

Aimee nodded happily. "She's really nice Ms Wilkins, just like an extra Grandma. She tells me stories about when her children were little."

"That's lovely Sweetheart, but I'm glad you're being good about helping Linda. Your Daddy loves you both." It stuck in her craw to say it, but it was the truth, wasn't it?

"It will make him happy if you can get along nicely together." Fenella chose her words carefully as she continued. "You know Aimee, there are lots of people you can talk to if you ever feel really upset again. There's your Daddy; or if he's away you've got me or Mrs Peterson. Your Grandma and Grandpa can help too. Even your Uncle Jason. Don't ever think you have to run away because you're unhappy and think no-one will listen to you. That gave everyone a dreadful scare. Bad things can happen to little kids who are all on their own."

"I know about all that now Ms Wilkins. That nice policeman 'splained it to me and so did Daddy. I promised I won't ever, ever, *ever* run away again."

Susie called her then and Aimee dashed off to join her friend in the playground.

"… just so you know," Fenella concluded.

Upon consideration she had decided to give Greg an edited version of her conversation with Aimee when they next met; an opportunity that occurred quite soon, now that he paid frequent visits to the classroom.

He also met other parents during these afternoon visits, resulting in the happy outcome for Aimee of now being able to visit her friends' homes for after school play, and have them visit her in return. An infinitely preferable arrangement in Fenella's opinion than the child's former isolation with none but adult company out of school hours.

"Thanks for your support Fenella," Greg replied.

"When Aimee came to live with me, I didn't appreciate how difficult a job parenting is." His candour disarmed Fenella. "Neither did Linda. We both love Aimee and want what's best for her. It seems a pity we've made such a botch of it when our intentions have been so good."

"It was a difficult situation, especially with Aimee grieving for her mother. Usually parents learn as their babies grow; you had to begin in the middle. It's not surprising there were setbacks."

A sympathetic smile accompanied Fenella's words. She wished she could offer more; knew she mustn't.

"I guess so." Greg smiled back, a warmer smile than she'd had from him since they'd first got to know each other.

"Being away so often with the filming of my book hasn't helped either. That's almost finished, thank God. Next week is hopefully the last of it; then we can settle into a more normal routine."

A bitter-sweet ache in the region of her heart, Fenella watched Greg's commanding figure disappear down the path.

It was an ache she was becoming all too accustomed to.

With the comforting promise that her Daddy wouldn't have to go away again for a long time, Aimee coped with his absence during the last week of term more cheerfully than usual.

"Even she seems to have mellowed a bit," was Fenella's observation on noticing Linda in animated conversation with a group of women at the school gate. Her television ad had led to Linda's being recognised locally as 'someone famous'; recognition which was balm to her ego, lacerated as it had been by the Kendall family's disapproval.

She hadn't mellowed towards Fenella though. The looks she'd directed towards her when Aimee dragged her in to inspect the Easter display were sour enough to curdle milk. The small problem of another child's lost lunch box gave Fenella a welcome excuse to avoid having to go through the motions of making polite conversation, in spite of their mutual antipathy.

15

Since everything in Aimee's world was running smoothly, Fenella was taken by surprise when she went to her car on Friday afternoon.

Normally she walked to work, enjoying the stroll along the creekside path. Today, anticipating a quick getaway to collect Zilla then off on her holiday, she had driven her car. Her parents expected her at their home near Kempsey in time for dinner, and Saturday night they were celebrating their fortieth wedding anniversary with a big family reunion.

Fenella was eagerly looking forward to that; and to the two weeks of freedom ahead of her.

Two weeks free from Greg Kendall's disturbing proximity.

To her surprise Aimee Kendall, the only child still in sight, was sitting on the bench beside the school gate.

"Ms Wilkins!" she called, relief clearly evident in her voice. "Linda's late. Do you think she'll come soon?"

So much for her quick getaway. Fenella shrugged, casting a regretful glance at her watch. A delay, hopefully a short one, appeared inevitable.

"Let's go in and phone her, shall we." It was nearly half past three. Surely Linda could have got herself here by now, or phoned to explain herself if she couldn't.

The phone rang out unanswered.

"She must be on the way Sweetheart. We'd better go back outside to meet her." Catching Aimee's uncertain expression, Fenella hurriedly reassured her. "It's okay. I'll wait with you till Linda gets here."

"Thank you, Fenella," beamed the relieved little girl.

The two of them sat chatting idly with an increasingly annoyed Fenella taking surreptitious peeps at her watch. After a further fifteen minutes passed fruitlessly, her patience ran out.

More than enough time had elapsed for even the slowest person to traverse the short distance between the Kendall's house and the school. Unbelievable as it was, it appeared that Linda wasn't coming. Fenella escorted the now visibly distressed child back inside the school.

Beginning with the house on the esplanade she rang every number in Aimee's contact file. There was no answer on any of them, not even Greg's mobile, on which she repeated the same terse message she'd left on all the others.

She raided the staffroom for biscuits and lemonade for Aimee and a much needed, sustaining mug of coffee for herself, thinking hard all the while.

Yet another call, to a gossipy neighbour elicited the information that Mrs Peterson wasn't answering her phone because she had gone to visit her daughter for the school holidays.

"So, I can't leave Aimee with her." Mentally, Fenella crossed off another option on what was a woefully short list. Annoyance was vying with concern for supremacy, and they were running a dead heat.

"Damn the Kendalls," she muttered under her breath.

Returning to Aimee she pinned a bright, cheerful smile in place and cleared away their snacks. Making up her mind, she bundled the child into her car and drove to the Kendall's house, uncertain what she might find.

As she feared, it was locked up and silent. No cars could be seen through the dusty garage window, certainly not Linda's sporty red job. A terse note for Greg, whom she learnt from Aimee was due home late that afternoon, was quickly written and taped to the security door. Then Fenella took Aimee to her own home.

Might as well be comfortable while I wait, she thought grimly, hoping Greg wouldn't be too much longer or she'd never make it to Kempsey in time for dinner

Jerked out of a fitful doze by the shrilling of the telephone, Fenella snatched it up before it could wake Aimee. It had taken her the dickens of a time to soothe the child's fears sufficiently to allow her to sleep.

With a groggily muttered "Wilkins," into the mouthpiece, she squinted at the clock. *Two seventeen am,* she noted furiously. *It was about time!*

"Fenella, Greg here," she heard, waiting stonily silent to see what lame excuse he came up with. It had better be good, she thought, seething righteously.

"Fenella," Greg repeated tiredly, "I've just arrived back and found your note. Thanks for looking after Aimee. I'll be right round to pick her up."

So! Fenella fumed silently. *Just thanks for looking after her. No explanation. No anything.*

It was too much for any red-blooded woman to take, particularly one with as short a fuse as Fenella. And especially at two seventeen am when she had been forced to change her own holiday plans.

"Oh no you won't Greg Kendall," she hissed. "The poor little mite was so upset it took me hours to get her to sleep. Pick her up in the morning. You know, you don't deserve to have a child; going off and leaving her in the care of someone capable of simply taking off and abandoning the kid to her fate."

She was in full spate now, fairly ripping into him. "It's no wonder she ran away, only it wasn't fear of punishment that drove her to it; it was knowing herself to be unloved and unwanted that did it."

It was a pity she couldn't see Greg flinch as if he'd been struck; his skin blanching to a sickly pallor beneath his tan.

Fenella wasn't finished yet, though. Not nearly finished. She'd been bottling her emotions up for too long.

"I'm sick and tired of getting caught up in the middle of your domestic crises," she stormed on, "and the next time it happens I'll do what I should have done today. I'll call the police and hand her over as an abandoned child. With your record, the welfare people are bound to place her with someone else." Running out of breath, she gulped in a fresh lungful of air and continued her tirade.

"Someone who'll love her and take proper care of her. Someone she really wants to be with." Running out of steam, Fenella was dismayed to discover tears streaming down her face.

"Damn you, Greg Kendall," she sniffled; her anger quickly burnt out having received no opposing argument to keep the fires stoked. "We've both been worried sick. Where the hell have you been?"

"It's a long story Fenella. Can it wait till morning?" She could hear exhaustion, and something weighing far heavier, dragging at his voice, slurring his words. Grudgingly she assented.

"Thanks," he whispered gratefully. "I know how much I owe you Fenella. I really do, you know. If you meant what you said about leaving Aimee with you till morning, I'll do that. I'll give you the whole story then, I promise."

Greg hung up quietly and Fenella's forlorn "Okay" was addressed to an empty dial tone. At least one of her desperate prayers had been answered. Her mind churning chaotically, she struggled to recapture sleep.

The man was still alive; and back in Topaz Sands where he belonged.

Although he'd be lucky if she didn't kill him herself, one of these days.

The promised explanation left almost as many questions as it provided answers for.

Groggy and heavy eyed from receiving less than her full quota of sleep, Fenella had to forgo her morning run due to the presence of the child, still soundly asleep in her spare bedroom. Automatically she headed for the kitchen when she crawled out of bed before seven o'clock. This morning she would have to rely on the stimulus attained via the coffee pot.

Taking her mug to the porch overlooking the water, she discovered Greg Kendall sitting there patiently; Zilla, the traitor, ensconced at his feet, enjoying a tummy rub.

Handing him her mug, she wordlessly fetched another for herself, inordinately pleased that she was wearing her favourite maroon and ivory satin pyjamas. The ones delicately patterned with a scattering of butterflies across the top. Her wild curls were still an uncombed tangle that defiantly she refused to tame.

Returning to sit in the cane armchair opposite, Fenella studied Greg, not bothering to disguise her stare. Less than his usual debonair self, he was pale and drawn.

Dark puffy circles underlined blue eyes that had lost their sparkle, and a livid bruise adorned his right temple. Narrowing her own eyes suspiciously, Fenella was sure she discerned the outline of heavy bandaging beneath his thin shirt.

"Fenella...," Greg began, only to be interrupted simultaneously.

"Give me a minute first Greg," Fenella begged, "then I'll listen to whatever you have to tell me." She dragged in a bracing lungful of air and met his curious, defensive gaze full on.

"Last night, for hours and hours I was worried sick and furiously angry at the same time. Aimee got all worked up remembering the day her mother didn't come home, either. By the time she finally settled I was exhausted. I was thoroughly annoyed for myself, also; disappointed at not getting away on my holiday, as planned." She looked away, but honesty demanded she say her piece eye to eye. "I'm afraid you copped the lot, Greg. I said a lot of things I shouldn't have, and I apologise. I know you really love Aimee, as much as any parent ever could. Also, that you've done your best in a difficult situation. Coping quite well, too, most of the time. You didn't deserve to be dumped on so unreasonably. I'm sorry."

Hands gripping her coffee mug against her chest, Fenella sat hunched in upon herself, head bowed, bracing herself for the blistering response she expected. When it didn't eventuate, she cautiously raised her head, braving that piercing cerulean stare she was certain would now be in evidence. Amazingly, she caught what couldn't possibly be admiration flickering across Greg Kendall's face.

Not for her, surely.

"You never fail to surprise me Fenella Wilkins," Greg stated, combing restless fingers through his hair.

"I readily understand how you felt last night, and you have no need to apologise. None at all, Fenella," he reiterated.

"You've earned the right to speak your mind. I don't have all the answers to yesterday's events yet, but I'll give you those I do. Before I start though, how come Aimee's with you, not Mrs Peterson? I found a note from Linda saying she'd asked Mrs Peterson to collect Aimee after school."

With Greg now watching her in a strange, calculating manner she didn't quite trust, Fenella considered the implications of that last statement.

It didn't fit the facts as she knew them. Mrs Peterson was too responsible a person to have forgotten such a commitment.

"When?" she asked finally. "Did Linda say at what time she spoke to Mrs Peterson?"

"Does that matter?" Impatiently Greg dismissed her question as irrelevant, then answered it anyway.

"According to her note, it must have been after one o'clock because she said the phone call for her to go to Sydney was at lunchtime."

His lips tightened ominously, however Fenella felt confident his spurt of annoyance couldn't be directed at her. Not this time. Straightening to military erectness in her seat, she explained.

"It matters," she answered, striving to keep her cool, "because Linda couldn't possibly have spoken to Mrs Peterson so late in the day. Mrs Peterson left for her daughter's in Newcastle at half past nine yesterday morning."

Disbelief written large on Greg's countenance, he opened his mouth to refute her statement, then closed it again; incipient anger darkening an already grim expression.

Let's see Linda wriggle out of that one, she thought.

An unaccustomed maliciousness seized Fenella. It was high time Greg's eyes were opened to Linda's shortcomings, even if it failed to endear the messenger to him. At the same time, she suffered acute pain at inflicting the blow. Suppressing the pain, she ploughed on.

"So, you see, Linda shot through to Sydney leaving poor little Aimee sitting at the school gate with no-one to pick her up."

She made sure he got the message loud and clear.

Eyeing the indications of injury with palpable curiosity, she changed the subject when he refused to comment on her accusations. Shrugging carelessly, Greg shook himself out of his dark reverie.

"What happened to me? I had a final meeting that ran overtime. Result – I got caught up in the holiday evening traffic jam exiting Sydney. Then I got trapped in the middle of a multi-car prang on the expressway just south of Gosford."

Fenella nodded, paling at his explanation. On the late news she'd heard a report of an accident involving a semi-trailer and several cars, resulting in two deaths and a number of minor injuries.

Her worst fears aroused, she had prayed desperately that Greg was merely delayed by the accident and the heavier than usual holiday traffic; that he had not become a road accident statistic himself.

Reminding herself that Greg was alive, sitting safely across from her, Fenella unwound her tightly entwined fingers, swallowing hard to quell her rising nausea.

"Go on," she urged.

"I'm okay Fenella. Really" he assured her, observing her sudden loss of colour with interest. He clasped her two icy hands between his, chafing them gently back to their normal warmth. Resisting her initial impulse to snatch them back, Fenella permitted herself this one tiny luxury.

More than her hands were warmed by Greg's kind gesture. Seeing a natural pink seep back into her cheeks, Greg continued his story.

"I escaped the worst of the pile-up. Ended up with no more than a nasty bump on the head and a couple of cracked ribs. The car won't be drivable for a while, so when the hospital released me I called Jason to come and get me. Had to wait an hour or so for him to arrive. Hence the ungodly hour we hit home. I'd been trying since before I left Sydney to call Linda and couldn't get through. Didn't have my mobile since I managed to drive off without it the other day." He shook his head at his carelessness.

"I thought Linda would be the one sitting worrying herself sick." He compressed his lips, angry again at how wrong he'd been about that. "Anyway, I persuaded Jason to bring me straight home. Now you know as much as I do Fenella." He spread large, well-manicured hands expansively.

In the end Greg and Aimee, overjoyed but teary at finding her father sitting on the end of her bed when she woke, stayed for breakfast. The last plate wiped clean and put away, Fenella shooed them out the door.

"Make yourselves scarce," she told them, "I'm late for my holiday and getting later every minute."

Breathless, and utterly speechless, she waved a trembling hand after them.

Greg had followed Aimee's example and kissed her goodbye. Except that while Aimee's kiss landed on her cheek, Greg's was full on her surprised lips.

"Thank goodness it was over so fast I didn't have time to give myself away," she muttered to Zilla. Stars in her eyes, she traced the imprint of Greg Kendall's firm, warm lips on her own.

Dropping her bag on a chair a few minutes later, she returned to the spare bedroom.

Unwrapping her sea god from his swaddling she caressed his beautiful, masculine face, a goofy smile on her lips. Walking into her own room she took down the innocuous seascape above her bed, giving that prized position back to her pagan god.

16

Yet again it was Jason, not his brother, who satisfied Fenella's curiosity. Spending a few days of her holiday with friends in Sydney, she phoned, inviting him and Rosie to lunch.

"Jason, how's Aimee?"

The question tumbled from her lips, cutting short the flurry of greetings when he and Rosie joined Fenella at the restaurant. Even before he answered, Jason's rumble of laughter and beaming smile reassured her.

"Wonderful Fen. Absolutely wonderful. Awful though it was at the time, Aimee's getting stranded was the best thing that could have happened. Sure opened Greg's eyes to a thing or two. I fancy something you said must have hit home as well. Anyway," his eyes twinkled at her impatience, "Greg was pretty sore and fragile so I stayed the weekend to give him a hand. La Linda finally turned up, all sweet innocence. Only this time Greg wasn't buying it. He'd had two days to stew over it and was out for blood. I did the gentlemanly thing and got the kid out of earshot so he could have his uninhibited say in privacy."

A mock bow invited applause at this point.

"Later Greg joined us on the beach and took us to the Mermaid for dinner. Told us he and Linda had decided not to marry after all. By the time we got back she'd packed up and left. As you can imagine, Aimee was ecstatic. Her joy was the last nail in Linda's coffin, I guess. Greg took it hard, realising how miserable the kid had been."

Mouth clamped grimly shut, Jason lost himself in a dark reverie. Snapping out of it moments later, he flashed his irrepressible grin at the two women.

"You'd have been proud of me ladies. For once in my life, I kept my mouth shut. No need to rub salt. After Aimee went to bed Greg opened up a bit. You remember that Martin Wallace, Fen? That friend of Linda's who was at the Mermaid that night?"

She nodded.

"Seems he's had a lot to do with getting her into television advertising; introducing her to the right people and all that. She's pretty keen to keep in good with him."

His expression left Fenella in no doubt of his feelings regarding Martin Wallace. Or maybe it was Linda he was thinking of.

"When he rang, inviting her to a party where she'd be guaranteed introductions to a number of useful people, she fell over herself getting there. Left a message on Mrs Peterson's answering machine when she couldn't raise her, and considered that that was Aimee taken care of with Greg due back before dark," he snorted.

"Some sense of responsibility, huh! I sort of gathered the gloss had been wearing thin on the relationship for a while. Linda was getting fed up with playing mother and didn't put up much of an argument when Greg told her he'd had enough."

Greg Kendall's domestic problems adequately covered, the three of them moved on to other topics of mutual interest until Rosemary and Jason returned to their respective offices.

Alone, Fenella allowed herself to dwell on Jason's news. Overwhelming relief rendered her light headed.

Linda's gone! Linda's gone! The words marched through her mind in time to the joyful tapping of her heels on the pavement. On the train to her friend's house, the refrain became a miraculous, *Greg Kendall is free! Greg Kendall is free!* echoing the clickety-clack of the wheels. Much later, alone in Laura's guest room, her euphoria ebbed, leaving a cold, empty space in the region of her heart.

Yes, she lectured herself, *Greg Kendall is free, but that doesn't mean he'll want me. When did he ever show the slightest interest in me?*

Gloomily she reminded herself that quite the contrary was true. Although, in the circumstances, what indication of interest a decent man could have given, she didn't know. On the edge of sleep, she recalled his kiss the morning he'd collected Aimee; the last time she'd seen him. Afraid to build hopes on such flimsy foundations, she repressed them ruthlessly sure that the kiss was just his way of saying thanks.

✻✻✻✻✻

The next morning saw Fenella on the road to Wollemi National Park.

Arriving at Dunn's Swamp, she wasted no time pitching her tent and launching the aluminium dinghy she'd borrowed from her father.

Seven days of uninterrupted painting among the spectacular pagoda shaped rock formations that were the park's most distinctive feature, were what she'd promised herself. It made an interesting change to populate her pictures with bushwalkers, wombats and the ubiquitous purple swamp hens instead of surfers, sunbathers and seagulls.

Totally immersed in painting by day and campfire activities of an evening, she successfully banished Greg Kendall's image from her mind during waking hours, only to have him intrude into her dreams.

More than once Fenella woke, aroused and aching with unfulfilled desire, crushingly disappointed to discover that the passionate lover of the night was no more than a figment of her over-active imagination manifesting itself in dreams.

Fenella returned from her holiday buoyed up by a comfortable sense of achievement when she studied the sketch books and canvasses she'd filled. She refused to analyse the deeper cause of the bubbling anticipation that persisted in permeating her whole being.

Soon enough, she'd discover whether the dreams she'd failed to squelch had the slightest chance of being realised. She greeted the sea god with a beaming smile, confident she'd come face to face with his alter ego sometime soon.

It was with a sanguine glow of optimism that she recognised Greg Kendall's voice when she answered the phone that Sunday morning.

Earlier, she had already been welcomed by a cheerful wave and a shouted 'Good morning Fenella,' from Aimee in her usual perch on the deck of the blue house.

A greeting which warmed her heart, instilling in her as it did, a certainty of the rightness of her world.

"I'm glad you're back." Greg's tone was pleasantly friendly, his words utterly prosaic. Nevertheless, Fenella's pulse raced and it became difficult to breathe past the lump in her throat.

It wouldn't do to sound as breathless as a star-struck adolescent, she thought, fighting to control her reactions. Managing a commendable equanimity, she answered equally prosaically, voice quite steady.

"Hello Greg. I'm glad to be back. How may I help you?"

"By joining us for lunch."

Fenella's imagination produced a picture of an intimate meal for two, hastily discarded when the 'us' registered.

"Mum and Dad brought Aimee home and stayed for the weekend. They'd both like to see you to thank you personally for being there for Aimee."

Not Greg who wanted to see her, but his parents. Her hearted plummeted, only to rebound at his next words.

"We'd all like you to come, Fenella." His voice caressed her nerve ends down the phone. "I do a mean steak on the barbecue, you know."

Fenella needed no further coaxing.

"What a temptation. I'll be there," she laughed. "Make mine well done with lots of onions."

In case he thought her too eager, she added, "I look forward to seeing your parents again. They're good people."

Briskly concluding the call, she raced off to sort through her wardrobe for something fit to wear. It wasn't a date, but it was going to be the first amicable social occasion she'd spent in Greg Kendall's company, so it required more thought than she usually gave to her attire.

Unruly curls tamed into an orderly French braid, a near-new sundress and the light application of make-up to bolster her confidence and she declared herself ready. Snatching up a matching jacket in case the afternoon sea breeze grew chilly she was halted at the gate by a plaintive bark.

Poor Zilla. She'd spent the last week in a boarding kennel since dogs were not permitted in national parks, and was still feeling unsettled by the separation.

"Come on then," Fenella relented, rewarded by the small dog's obvious delight. She only hoped Greg wouldn't object.

She needn't have worried, she realised a short time later, watching a smiling Greg Kendall crouch in front of Zilla, offering his hand for a doggy shake. At that moment a squeal of joy announced Aimee's arrival on the scene, flinging herself into her friend's arms.

"Fenella! Fenella! Grandma, Fenella's here at last. Zilla's here too. Come on Zilla, come and shake paws with Grandma and Grandpa."

By the time the hubbub generated by Aimee and Zilla died down, Fenella's attack of nerves was over.

Greg hadn't fallen on her with delight.

Not that she'd expected that for one second, as in her more realistic moments she was all too well aware that her love for him was entirely one-sided, but he had welcomed her quietly and sincerely to his home.

While treating her as an honoured guest, he maintained a pleasant, impersonal air which Fenella returned philosophically. Less than her heart yearned after, it was still more than she'd dare hope for.

No-one mentioned Linda, until later that afternoon. Following the elder Kendalls departure, Greg and Aimee were walking Fenella home along the beach, Aimee chasing seagulls with Zilla.

"I don't know what you've heard Fenella," Greg enunciated crisply, eyes fixed midway between sea and sky, avoiding hers, "but Linda and I have parted. Amicably. As it turned out, she wasn't really the villain of the piece at all, just woefully inexperienced in taking care of children."

Fenella winced inwardly, feeling his words to be a condemnation of her antipathy towards his erstwhile fiancée.

"However, she prefers living in Sydney. Also, she decided she wasn't cut out for a maternal role. I felt sorry for her. She really did love both of us but couldn't adjust to our lifestyle. Unfortunately, I'm not prepared at this time to uproot Aimee all over again and return to Sydney just to please Linda."

His expression darkened to sadness, tearing at Fenella's sensibilities. "I guess neither of us loved the other enough."

Fenella's fingers curled into claws, itching to scratch the other woman's eyes out, although it was a toss-up whether her reason was Greg's broken dreams, or jealousy over his avowed love for Linda. She had forgotten that not-so-minor fact in her jubilation at his freedom. As long as Linda held onto a piece of Greg's heart, he'd never be truly free.

Without another word, or so much as a sideways glance, Greg jogged off to join Aimee, leaving Fenella to follow at her own pace. She supposed she should commend him for his loyalty. And so she would, if she could get past her jealous longing to be its subject.

A longing which it became abundantly clear in the following weeks, was futile.

Greg accorded Fenella nothing beyond a casual friendship. Peculiarly enough, Fenella found herself relaxed and almost contented during this time necessary for Greg to lick his wounds. There was no ecstasy; and thankfully, no agony either.

For the first time in their relationship they were learning to know each other as friends in a normal, everyday manner.

As long as the hiatus wasn't unduly prolonged, since she was developing distinctly possessive feelings for him which went way beyond friendship.

17

How long that state of affairs might have lasted, there was no way of knowing.

Mothers' Day, followed by a wonderfully warm phone call from Susan Kendall, Aimee's grandmother, to tell Fenella how thrilled she was with Aimee's portrait, came and went. While Greg had meetings with his agent and publisher, Aimee had a few days off school to visit her Granny Stone.

Now it was almost June; the Queen's Birthday long weekend the next event on Fenella's professional calendar. The first ripple heralding a change of tide in her life came in a phone call from Jason.

"I've made my decision Fen," he announced.

"Rosemary and I are getting married in November. You're invited, by the way. We're both absolutely sure of our feelings, so I talked matters over with Rosie and her parents to work out the best way to deal with the Old Man if he cuts up rough.

"His prejudices are *his* problem, not ours. It's up to *him* to come to terms with them."

His expression assumed a pugnacious aspect.

"We all agree we can't let him dictate our lives. That would be giving in to emotional blackmail, and that's just not on! Even my soft-hearted Rosie can see that."

Nodding to herself, Fenella wasn't given time to voice her whole-hearted agreement as Jason rattled on.

"So here's the plan, Fen. I'm off to Gloucester to tell the parents. If the Old Man doesn't chuck me out on my ear and order me never to darken his door again, I'll take Rosemary up with me for the long weekend. Let them get to know her. Dad will have had a whole week to get used to the idea; and if I can get Mum and Greg onside, he'll be outnumbered. Wish me luck Fen."

"I'll be praying hard Jason," she assured him. "But you never know, he may be more amenable than you think. Give him a chance. He might surprise you."

Fenella smiled faintly at her optimism. Peter Kendall was every inch as stubborn and hot-headed as his sons.

"And I just saw a squadron of pigs fly past!" Jason's snort of derision echoed down the line, mirroring her own opinion. "As you say Fen, I'll give him a chance. It'd be really great if he does accept Rosie without too much fuss."

Was this another Kendall crisis brewing?

However did I survive without the constant excitement they generate, Fenella wondered drily as, all alone, she sipped coffee on the porch, watching a lovers' moon rising from the sea.

If Peter Kendall knew what a lovely young woman Rosie was, surely he would be happy for Jason. Was there anything she could do to help?

Frowning in concentration, she applied herself to the problem. The situation was too delicate for an outsider to simply go barging in. An idea burgeoning in her mind, she let it simmer while she took Zilla for her evening walk.

"Yes," she told Zilla. "That can't do any harm. It may even help." She would wait till Jason had broken the glad tidings, then a day or so later, phone Susan Kendall, ostensibly to congratulate her on her good luck in acquiring a jewel of a daughter-in-law.

Any mother would want to support her son, and maybe Susan would find another woman's good opinion encouraging.

And wives influence their husbands in so many subtle ways, she mused, recalling with amusement some of her own mother's marital coups.

As it happened, Fenella didn't have to wait that long for her chat with Susan Kendall. The older woman called *her* as soon as Jason left on Sunday night.

"Oh Fenella, we've just had the most dreadfully upsetting weekend," a distracted Susan poured out as soon as Fenella picked up the phone.

"It seems Jason's gone and got engaged to some Eurasian girl. Peter got on his high horse, saying some truly frightful things I won't sully your ears with, about foreigners in general and Asians in particular."

Running out of breath, Susan gasped audibly, rushing on to get the worst of her story off her chest as fast as she possibly could.

"So then Jason got really angry too, and told his father a few home truths about his attitude. That didn't go down very well either. Fenella, it was just dreadful! I had to call time out and send Peter out to his shed and Jason off for a long walk. By the time he returned, he was in a mood to be a bit more conciliatory and Peter had cooled down enough to listen, even if he wasn't ready to make any concessions. At least they're talking to each other again. Jason's bringing his girlfriend to meet us next weekend. Now, that's why I'm calling you, Fenella."

Susan had slowed to a normal conversational tempo and Fenella began mentally rehearsing what she intended to say.

"I wouldn't be troubling you with our family problems at all Fenella," Susan was saying nervously, "except that Jason told me you've met Rosemary several times. Fenella, would you mind very much telling me what you know of this girl?"

Now, it was Fenella's turn.

"Susan, you've absolutely no need to worry about Rosemary Parrish," she began, in the warm, comforting, supportive tone she used when counselling her students

Over the next ten minutes of talking and answering questions she went a long way towards allaying the worst of the other woman's fears.

Now for the clincher, she thought, mentally crossing fingers and toes.

"You know Susan, I was really impressed with the way you and Peter were prepared to accept Linda, even though you didn't like her; simply to prevent an estrangement with Greg."

She paused to let the comparison she was making sink in. "I'm sure you'll be equally capable of opening your hearts and minds to Rosemary; and this time I predict a far happier outcome. Jason's worth it, isn't he?"

She held her breath, afraid she may have been too boldly outspoken.

A whooshing sigh of relief whistled down the phone line. In a firm, assertive tone Susan answered her.

"You're so right Fenella. My son *is* worth whatever effort we might need to make. And you can be sure I'll tell that to Peter. After this little chat, Fenella, I feel so much better. I don't like airing our dirty linen outside the family, but I was quite upset."

Fenella's lips twitched at the masterly understatement.

"I turned to you because you're the only person I know who's actually met the girl. Besides, you're almost as good as family, Fen. For a while there, we all thought it was you Jason was falling in love with, you know."

Shared laughter at that absurdity brought the call to a cheerful conclusion.

"Thank goodness I've got safely over that hurdle," Fenella murmured.

✱✱✱✱✱

"Remind me I owe you a whopping great kiss," was Jason's reaction.

After he'd given Fenella his colourful version of events, she'd cheered him out of his depression with her report of the conversation with his mother.

"If anyone can bring the Old Man round, Mum can. She's worked a small miracle or two in the past, so here's hoping."

"Well, well. Look who's here," she interrupted. "A duo of Kendalls just walked through my gate. Bye Jason. Give my love to Rosemary."

She hung up with Jason's hoot of laughter and his admonition not to let Greg blame her for any of *this* lot echoing in her ears.

While issuing a cheerful greeting to the visitors, she cast a wary, sidelong glance at Greg to assess his mood. The sight of his tight-lipped frown sent her heart plunging into the depths. Refusing to be daunted by his scowl, she deliberately broadened her smile, infusing her next words with a gay lilt.

"Have you two come to share the good news with me? You're way too late if you have. I've just been on the phone with Jason."

She noted Greg's eyes take on an even steelier glint at the mention of his brother's name; and pushed her luck a little harder.

"It's terrific news, isn't it? I'm so happy for him, aren't you Greg?"

"I suppose so," he grunted, visibly lacking in enthusiasm, "although Dad's rampaging around predicting doom and disaster."

"So I've heard. He hasn't met Rosemary yet. When he does, I predict he'll soon change his tune."

"That's right. You've met the girl haven't you Fenella?" She ignored his low growl accusing her of she knew not what.

"I have," she assented, relieved to note that Aimee, uninterested in adult conversation had run into the back garden, chasing after Zilla.

"I've met Rosemary several times and like her enormously. You know something else Greg? She and Jason are so obviously head over heels in love that anyone seeing them together can't help feeling happy for them."

"You're certainly a faithful friend, Fenella. I hope that damned young fool appreciates just how loyal you are." Indignation overtook Greg's civility. "After the abominable way he's treated you, you'd have every right to be mad as hell at him."

Fenella's surprise showed. Greg had done an abrupt U-turn from his earlier stance! What was going on here? Running his hand through his hair, Greg threw some light on the situation.

"Ages ago I realised I'd got entirely the wrong idea about you. I'd even begun to think the two of you might be right for each other."

He glared down at Fenella from his superior height as if his misconception had somehow been her fault.

Which maybe it was, she thought, guilt making her squirm when she recalled how she had used Jason as a shield to hide her love behind.

"I don't give a damn right now how Jason feels about this Rosemary, but I am angry with him. On your behalf Fenella. I hope you appreciate the irony of that, after all the times you were the butt of my temper."

She did.

Fenella was hard put not to laugh. Somehow, she didn't think Greg would appreciate being laughed at right now. Lips quirking, she decided it was time to straighten out the misunderstanding before it grew any more complicated.

Waving Greg to sit, she plunked herself down in the other chair and set herself to the task.

"Greg, it's extremely gallant of you to be so protective of me, and yes; I do appreciate it. Only I'm not clear what you're accusing Jason of. You don't still think we're sweet on each other, do you?" His expressive face told her that, yes, he did. Exasperated, she explained. "We both told you, several times, that all we shared was friendship. That's the truth, Greg! Has always been the truth."

He still looked sceptical, so she essayed another approach.

"Jason told me about his Rosie soon after we met. He had to talk about her to someone and wasn't ready to introduce her to the family. I filled the bill."

Deciding on yet more honesty in this clearing of the air, she continued.

"He told me he couldn't resist teasing you about me after you cut up rough," she told him in a desperate attempt to convince that stubborn, self-opinionated male sitting so stiffly in her best armchair.

Had he been nurturing this silly misconception all these months? She feared he had.

Unbelievable, she thought, then caught her breath as a whole new world of possibility opened up before her.

If Greg had truly believed she and Jason were an item, how would he react now that both of them; she and Greg - not Jason - were free of their old loves?

Now there was an idea to conjure with! A warm blush suffused her cheeks, and Fenella lowered her eyes from Greg's discerning gaze.

Damn Jason! Greg thought, not believing for a moment that Fenella was telling the truth.

Not when she blushed so guiltily. That was a sure sign she was fiddling with the truth.

Oh, he now believed that *Jason* felt only friendship. But Fenella? Nothing would convince him her heart hadn't been involved. His own heart ached for her, sitting there so courageously, trying to cover up for his worthless brother.

"Okay Fenella," he agreed mendaciously, allowing her to save face. "You've convinced me."

He still intended to give that unrepentant young rogue a piece of his mind when next he saw him.

Meanwhile, he'd keep a judicious eye on Fenella. See to it she didn't have time to mope. In retrospect he felt guilty over his past aggression. *I'll make up for it now*, he decided. Stubbornly setting his chin at a determined angle he took the first step in his campaign of atonement.

"This business of the engagement aside, Fenella, I came for another reason as well," he said impulsively, turning his back on the strict truth.

"Aimee and I would like you to have dinner with us tomorrow. No excuses allowed," he commanded when she didn't answer immediately.

Blushing again, Fenella found her voice and croaked out a tepid assent. The joy exploding through her veins was anything but tepid, however.

18

The mouth-watering aroma of onions sizzling on the barbecue filled the salt-laden air, a light breeze wafting it to a gathering flock of gulls. Keeping a wary eye on the gulls, Greg surreptitiously tossed tiny chunks of meat to an ecstatic Zilla when he thought Fenella wasn't watching.

Sipping a perfectly chilled Barossa chardonnay, Fenella listened to Aimee prattling on. Bursting with excitement now she'd been informed of her favourite Uncle's impending marriage, she couldn't wait to tell Fenella all about it.

"And you know what else Fenella? Uncle Jason says my new Auntie Rosemary wants me to be a flower girl at the wedding. I'm going to wear a special dress and have flowers in my hair like a fairy princess."

Starry eyed, the little girl became rapt in dreams of wedding finery until Zilla dropped a ball at her feet, nudging her to pick it up.

"Can Zilla and I play on the beach, Daddy?" she begged.

"Okay Poppet, as long as you stay in sight. You have until I finish cooking dinner."

Alone with Greg, Fenella took advantage of the opportunity she'd been waiting for.

"I take it you'll be off to Gloucester to meet Rosemary, then Greg?"

He nodded tersely. He'd heard more than enough about Jason, his Rosie and the wedding. He specially didn't want to subject Fenella to any more of it.

"Jason asked me to give him a bit of moral support. Not sure I'll go that far, but I'm prepared to meet Rosemary with an open mind."

At the risk of souring their amicable new relationship, Fenella pressed gamely on.

"I'm glad, Greg. You've said in the past you considered Jason to be just a kid, still wet behind the ears. You're wrong about that."

She ignored Greg's repressive glare, determined to finish what she'd started.

"Oh, I know he carries on with a lot of nonsense; joking around and teasing and all that, but it's nothing more than a front. Underneath, he takes life pretty seriously. Jason's really quite a mature young man, Greg. One who's more than ready for marriage. You'll be pleasantly surprised if you look beneath the surface. And I hope you will support him. Please, Greg. Don't let your father upset them. He'll listen to you."

Although unable to withstand Fenella's ardent championing of his brother, Greg felt a severe pang of jealousy.

No woman had ever taken up the cudgels so vigorously on his behalf.

Glancing down to the beach, he tried to shake off the uncomfortable sensation. He was peeved with his brother. That's all it was. It was small-minded of him, but he convinced himself it was because Jason was the centre of everyone else's attention. His emotions had to be quite unrelated to Fenella since he didn't feel anything special for her. He couldn't.

That sort of emotion just wasn't in him any longer.

Nevertheless, he avoided those intense brown eyes, pretending the steaks needed his attention. Using a carefully neutral voice, he gave her an answer he thought she'd be satisfied with.

"All right Fenella! Since I was wrong about you, I'm willing to concede I may have been wrong about Jason, too. If he wants to talk, I'll listen. I'll even arrive early and have a go at reasoning with Dad as well. It's high time he abandoned that ugly bigotry of his and embraced our modern multicultural society."

A bark of a laugh lightened the atmosphere. Turning to Fenella he shared the joke. "He loves Asian food. Next step is convincing him to love Asians. Some of them, at least."

Their conversation turned to general topics over the meal. Succumbing to Aimee's blandishments and reading her two bedtime stories, Fenella then made her excuses, wary of outstaying her welcome.

"It's a weekday, Greg, and I've got marking to finish for tomorrow," she explained. When Greg let her go without protest, she was glad she hadn't lingered.

"I can't leave Aimee, or I'd see you home," was all he'd said. "Walk down the beach so I can watch out for you."

As Greg stood on the deck watching Fenella saunter down the moonlit beach, sandals swinging loosely from her hand and Zilla scampering round her bare feet, he was fighting a sudden impulse to run after her and crush her in his arms. *Lust*, he told himself. *Just normal, healthy lust.*

Her perfume lingered on the deck chair cushions and the remembered taste of their first, catastrophic kiss filled his mouth, arousing a desire for more.

She wouldn't welcome his kisses anyway, he sighed. Her championship of his cause plainly shows she's still in love with Jason.

Although he was not in love with Fenella, Greg finally admitted what, until now, he had strenuously rejected. Fenella Wilkins was an attractive, desirable woman. Now he was alone, he missed the pleasures of feminine companionship.

If Fenella should ever turn to him for consolation, he'd be more than willing to oblige her.

*****

True to his word, Greg left early on the visit to his parents. On Thursday afternoon he popped his head round the classroom door.

"Can't stay to chat Fenella. Just letting you know Aimee won't be in tomorrow. We're beating the weekend traffic and leaving right now. See you next week."

A quick wave of his hand and he was gone before Fenella could respond. Wandering over to the window she caught a flash of sunlight glinting off electric blue paintwork as the Kendalls disappeared down the street. Feeling like Cinderella watching the stepsisters leaving for the ball, Fenella fell prey to self-pity.

Now I wait it out till someone thinks to tell me whether Peter Kendall comes on like a fire-breathing dragon or purrs like a kitten.

Idly she considered the odds. Her bet was that he would play it cool. He might be irascible and overbearing at times, but no-one could ever call him stupid. He would have cooled down enough to mind his manners, and be a gracious host. Shouldn't take long before he learnt to love Rosie for herself.

Casting her gloom aside, she reminded herself that she had plans of her own for the break.

The Kendalls and their dramas were consigned to the back of her mind while she settled down to getting her paper-work up to date.

She was right not to worry, Fenella discovered.

On Tuesday afternoon Greg suggested she pop in for a drink after he'd put Aimee to bed, and he'd bring her up to date on the family saga.

She would have been even more eager to go if she'd known Greg, driven against his better judgement to seek her company, had clutched at the first handy excuse that came to his mind.

"Dad still wasn't too happy," he confided, "but he'd got over his initial belligerence, accepting Rosemary as an innocent party. He turned on the charm for her. Took Jason off for a round of golf. Told me he didn't want me tagging along, so I don't know what was said, except they were both in better spirits when they got back."

"And...?" Glowing with pleasure at this confirmation of the happy outcome she'd predicted, Fenella begged to hear more. Greg threw up his hands, conceding defeat.

"Alright Fenella," he chuckled, "you were right. Rosemary Parrish is everything you claimed her to be. I'll even concede that you're probably right about Jason, too. He wasn't larking about the way he usually does, and I was pleasantly surprised at the change in him."

Their conversation turned to other topics until Fenella decided it was time to be on her way.

Rising to see her out, Greg, both hands clasping her shoulders, turned her gently towards him. An unaccustomed sultry gleam darkened the blue of his eyes as he captured her wide-eyed gaze.

"What would the Kendall family have done, Fenella, if we'd never met you?"

The murmured caress of Greg's warm baritone as he half whispered these words set Fenella's pulse racing. Eyes locked on his, she stood, mesmerised.

Casting caution to the winds, Greg gave in to the desire which had been building within him all evening. In slow motion he lowered his lips towards hers, allowing her all the time in the world to take evasive action.

If she chose to.

It lit a triumphant flame within him when she didn't.

Light as the brush of a feather, Greg's lips teased Fenella's, confidently increasing their pressure when they met no resistance. Hands slid from her shoulders, stroking her back and drawing her firmly into his embrace.

Fenella gasped, heat flooding her body as hard masculine angles meshed sweetly with feminine curves. Greg's tongue slipped smoothly between her parted lips, inciting the flames dancing across her nerve ends into blazing ferocity.

Almost of their own volition, her hands crept around his neck, fingers tangling in locks overdue for a visit to the barber. Pressing herself urgently against his exciting hardness, Fenella surrendered to long suppressed desire, revelling in the joy of mutual discovery while her world trembled on its axis.

Chests heaving as they gulped in much needed oxygen, they drew reluctantly apart.

Face suffused with the flush of undisguised desire, Greg threaded the fingers of one hand through Fenella's rampant curls, bending his face towards hers again, clearly intending to follow that earth-shaking kiss with more of the same.

Seized by inexplicable panic, Fenella stepped back, out of the dangerously exciting temptation of his arms.

"G… goodnight Greg," she whispered huskily, knowing there was no way he would believe her fiery response had been a simple farewell embrace.

Stumbling a little, she backed further off, then fled to the door.

"You may have a good night Fenella," Greg barked, reluctantly allowing her unimpeded departure, "but after this, I know I won't!"

Stealing an uncertain glance over her shoulder, Fenella slipped out and away so fast Greg had to open the door again for Zilla, barking her distress at being left behind.

✶✶✶✶✶

"Oh Zilla, I don't know what came over me."

Safely ensconced in her favourite armchair, Fenella muttered into the ears of the pet clasped to her bosom for comfort.

"There I was in Greg Kendall's arms being kissed as I've been yearning to have him kiss me, when all at once it was too much. It all happened so suddenly. There we were, one minute discussing the council elections, then out of the blue he was kissing me. He must think I'm a real idiot to run off like a scared virgin when I'm anything but."

Misery reduced her trembling voice to silence as Fenella contemplated her confused emotions.

Straightening from her defensive huddle a short while later, she carried Zilla to her basket in the kitchen.

A cheeky grin lifting her mobile features out of their despondent droop, she addressed the little dog again.

"One thing's for sure, Zil. Next time I won't be taken by surprise. I'll be ready for him; and it'll be a different story then, I reckon."

If there was a next time.

She met newly doubtful eyes in the bathroom mirror, the hand wielding a ruthless brush through her unruly mop dropping to her side.

No. She tilted her chin determinedly.

That was no way to be thinking! Greg Kendall was man enough to understand her attack of nerves for the minor setback it was. There *would* be a next time!

Fenella clung to that positive thought as she dropped into a dreamless sleep watched over by her sea god. Buoyant expectancy put an extra bounce in her step the next morning.

19

"It's a really rotten day," wailed a woebegone Aimee, plunging over the doorstep into Fenella's lounge room. "Daddy says it's too windy for our picnic."

The wintry blast that snatched the door out of her father's hand, slamming it on his heels was a sure confirmation of this edict, if one had been necessary.

This was Fenella's first social meeting with Greg since their fateful kiss. Though neither had spoken of it, on more than one occasion during the last few days, Greg's kindling gaze issued a warning that he hadn't forgotten. Therefore, Fenella wasn't altogether surprised when, ostensibly visiting the classroom to read Aimee's stories, he set up today's date for a picnic.

More familiar than the Kendalls with the chilly winter winds that often blew for days on end along the coast, Fenella had armed herself with an alternative suggestion.

No way did she intend to miss out on his company.

"What do you mean, Sweetheart?" she asked facetiously. "This is beautiful weather."

She made a show of looking out the window. "Yes. Absolutely perfect." Both Kendalls eyed her dubiously. How could anyone consider such a wild day perfect? Chuckling, Fenella took pity on them. "Remember our new song, Aimee?" she prompted, relishing the delight dawning on the child's face.

"The kite song!" she squealed. "Are we going to go kite flying?" Then she slumped into a chair, tears threatening. "I haven't got a kite Fenella," she wailed.

"Not yet you haven't," was her friend's intriguing reply.

"What have you been up to now, Fenella?" A grin a mile wide lifting the corners of his sensuous mouth, Greg leaned indolently against the window frame enjoying their by-play.

"Come and see," Fenella invited. "I won't see you on your birthday Aimee, since it's during the holidays, so I'm giving you your birthday present now." She led the way into her studio where she handed the child a gaily wrapped package. "I chose a small one she should be able to handle with a bit of help from her dad," she explained to Greg while Aimee carefully undid the tape and removed the paper from a brightly coloured fabric shape.

"Look Daddy. Fenella's given me a bird kite."

Aimee held it up to his admiring gaze, studying it intently to see how it could be made to fly.

"See, Daddy. If you tie the string on just here," she pointed, "then my bird kite will fly. Won't it Fenella?"

"It sure will. And today the wind is just right to make it fly really high. Zip up your jacket Sweetheart, and put that beanie back on, then let's go fly this kite."

Suiting her actions to her words, Fenella reached for her own parka and woollen hat on the rack by the door. In a remarkably short time the three of them were making their way up to the broad grassy plateau that topped the jutting southern headland of Topaz Beach. The precious kite, now attached to its reel of string, fluttered eagerly against its owner's chest.

For the next hour they raced about madly battling the wind while the kite dipped and soared, taking on a life of its own. Finally, cheeks pink from exposure to the chilly blast, Fenella deemed it time to seek shelter.

"Okay you two," she shouted, "reel it in and let's head home. I've got a fresh pot of soup and homemade bread waiting to warm us up. There'll be plenty more good days to fly that kite, young Aimee," she stated firmly, quashing the incipient protest trembling on the pouting lips, "but if we don't go inside and warm ourselves up, you'll get a chill. Then there'll be no more kite flying at all."

Subsiding with a shiver, Aimee reluctantly agreed.

"It is cold, isn't it," she uttered forlornly.

"Sure is Aimee love. Come on Fenella, lead us to that soup you mentioned. I hope it's good and thick, with lots of chunky bits I can get my teeth into."

The simple meal was as big a success as the kite flying expedition had been.

"This is good bread Fenella, better than any I've been able to find. Where do you get it?" Greg demanded to know. Trust a man and his stomach, Fenella thought, laughing.

"Let me show you. Here, Aimee. You can help with this." Fenella hauled a bread maker and a bag of flour out of the pantry. Letting Aimee do the measuring of ingredients, she set the machine to work.

"There you are Aimee. Now you can tell everyone you're a baker. You can take that loaf home with you when it's cooked." By the time the novelty of listening to her bread mix chugging and sloshing through the mixing cycle wore off, Fenella had her small kitchen spic and span.

"What'll it be, you two? Ludo, or snakes and ladders?" she asked, rummaging in the hall cupboard.

In the end both games were played. Greg Kendall, self-proclaimed Master of Sneaky Tricks, entered into the spirit of things with unalloyed enthusiasm, always appearing suitably contrite when he was caught out, as he invariably was.

Until the next time.

"You're cheating Daddy!" Aimee's shrill squeal echoed round the room yet again.

"You put that back where it was. Right now." She rolled the dice, triumphantly counting off her move. "One, two, three, four. I win! I win! See Daddy. I win, don't I Fenella?"

"You sure do, Kiddo." Greg rolled his daughter on her back, extracting his revenge with a ruthless tickling until she begged for mercy.

"Stop it, Daddy! Fenella, make Daddy stop tickling," Aimee pleaded through her giggles.

Retrieving the last of the game pieces scattered by the rough housing, Fenella yielded to irresistible impulse.

Attacking Greg's unprotected back, she got in a few good tickles of her own, revelling in the glorious freedom the game allowed her to touch his body.

"Help me out here Aimee," she gasped, as Greg rounded to meet his attacker. "We women have to stick together, you know." The ensuing melee ended in Fenella's ignominious defeat. Lips a teasing pout, she wriggled provocatively under the weight of Greg's body pinning hers to the carpet.

"I surrender, Greg. I surrender," she giggled huskily. The pout broadened into a wicked grin as she discerned an unmistakable reaction in the blatantly male body atop hers.

A tiny moan escaped her lips and her half-closed eyes began to glaze over as Greg ground his hips into hers, further arousing them both.

Heart beating wildly, Fenella watched Greg lower his mouth towards hers. A pink tongue tip moistened lips tingling in anticipation of the kiss that was surely coming her way.

"I've got you now, Daddy," shouted the small demon who launched a new attack, unaware that the adults were now playing a new game entirely.

"Okay Love, I surrender too," the man growled softly, his last words directed not towards his daughter, but towards the woman beneath him whose delectable curves and enticing lips were leading his thoughts in directions only his child's presence prohibited him from pursuing.

Unable to resist, he helped himself to those lips, making a thorough job of sampling their sweetness.

"Spoils of victory, Fenella," he claimed, the devilish glint in his eyes telling of the delights he would have claimed if not so adequately chaperoned.

"Me too Daddy." Aimee tugged at his arm. "I won too," she reminded him, puckering her sweet child's mouth to receive the kiss she deemed her due.

"You too Love," Greg agreed. He rolled easily onto his side, releasing Fenella from her blissful imprisonment to reach for his daughter.

Steaming mugs of hot chocolate topped with marshmallows, a Disney movie for Aimee, and a chessboard for the two adults filled in what was left of the lazy Sunday afternoon.

When he saw Fenella setting out the chess pieces, Greg slid insinuating arms around her, dragging her back against his manly bulk till she was aflame, the hard shape of his body indelibly imprinted on her back.

Large, sure hands stroked across her midriff beneath her sweater.

"More games, Fenella?" he breathed into her ear, exposed by hair tied back neatly again.

"You must be a glutton for punishment. You won't win, you know."

He interrupted his challenge to drift a string of tiny kisses along the tender length of her neck. Turning her head slightly, Fenella instinctively offered more smooth, bare flesh for his delectation.

At the same time his questing hands strayed upward; and her body arched in silent supplication.

Accepting the tacit invitation, Greg cupped her breasts, thumbs lightly teasing the sensitive nubs erect, thrusting against the filmy lace and satin confining them.

"The odds are stacked in my favour," he murmured seductively. With a tantalising lack of haste, he trailed his hands back to her waist and eased himself away from her warmth, reluctantly mindful of Aimee's presence nearby.

Frustrated desires and eager anticipation roiled within Fenella's breast; and 'The Lion King' played on in the next room, reminding them both that this was neither the time nor place for *this* game.

Pulling herself together, Fenella smiled archly at her tormentor.

"Maybe I can win, maybe I can't. That's something only time will tell, isn't it?"

Not quite sure which game she meant, the comment being applicable to both, Fenella seated herself demurely behind the chessboard.

It was a leisurely game, both considering their moves carefully, each taunting the other mercilessly when they achieved small victories. Each offering tempting distractions when their gambits failed.

Barbed insinuations and double entendres provided an intoxicating stimulus; specially for Fenella who had been without a special male companion for so long. And such a man who'd finally found her! Lost in contemplation of the direction their relationship may be going in the near future, Fenella forgot the game on the board.

"It's checkmate Fenella." Greg's foot nudged her out of her daydream. "Nothing can save you now. You're mine. Accept defeat."

Those words were even truer than he thought. If only he meant them in the same way she did.

"Alright, I give up." She sighed in mock despair. "It seems you know all the moves, Greg Kendall."

"Maybe not all," he drawled, lowering his lids to eye her lasciviously through blue slits, "but I know a good few, and can make the rest up as I go along."

Was he talking chess, or a more exciting game? Then he left Fenella in no doubt.

"I'll be claiming my prize, Fenella." Greg lowered his voice suggestively. "Later." Fenella savoured the delicious tingling in all her nerve ends, anticipating the nature of his prize.

She may have lost the chess game, but she knew she was on the verge of winning big in this other special, high-stakes game. Goose bumps erupted beneath her sweater.

'Later' had better not be too long; waiting had never been so hard.

*****

"Girls, how's this for an idea." Greg's voice fell into the flat void at the end of the afternoon when Fenella was thinking her guests were about to pack up and decamp, leaving her alone and lonely after the most enjoyable day she'd had in ages.

"What idea Daddy?"

"Well Poppet, after all the fun we've had today it seems pretty tame for us to go our separate ways. So why don't we take Fenella home with us Aimee? You'd like that, wouldn't you?"

His sidelong glance included Fenella in his question. Encouraged by her dawning smile, he continued.

"I can get some fish and chips from Charlie's and we can have a picnic dinner at our place. How does that suit you?"

"Suits me just fine." Fenella's ready assent was nearly drowned out.

"My bread Daddy. We can have my bread too, can't we?" Aimee ran to fetch the loaf, cooling on a rack in the kitchen.

"Very definitely we'll have your bread, Aimee love. I can't wait to taste the very first loaf of bread my clever little miss has baked. Grab your coats girls," he ordered, "and let's go."

✱✱✱✱✱

"Greg! Ooh yes. Again, please," Fenella begged, voice a breathless whisper.

Obligingly Greg did.

Then he began kissing her all over again. His tongue laving the sensitive hollow at the base of her throat elicited a satisfied moan; or maybe it was his questing hands plundering the treasures disclosed by the shirt buttons they had just popped open, which were responsible?

Fenella didn't know; and lost in long dreamt of carnal delights, was past caring.

Her own hands, their task with other shirt buttons long since completed, played erotic games in the light thatch of blond chest hair, buried in which flat, brown, masculine nipples grew taut under the attentions she lavished upon them.

Greg's lips climbed the slim column of her throat, finally reclaiming moist, red lips; swollen and tender from the surfeit of kisses he'd already bestowed on them. Her body writhing beneath his on the sofa silently urged him on to more intimate explorations.

Mutual explorations, in which she was not afraid to lead the way when he dawdled, engrossed with discoveries already made.

Steadily lower Fenella's hands trailed, following the narrow line of body hair arrowing enticingly below the waistband of his jeans. Both their sweaters had long since been discarded, two colourful pools of knitted fabric on the carpet, and now two shirts fluttered down to join them.

Returning to the lounge room from tucking a heavy-eyed Aimee into bed, Greg had pulled Fenella into his arms, tumbling her onto the sofa to be kissed senseless. Now he raised his lips fractionally from the mounded breast they'd been ravishing, to speak, voice husky with unsated desires.

"It's later, Fenella," Greg whispered expectantly, intent eyes observing her reaction.

Dizzy with passion, Fenella opened dazed brown eyes wide, momentarily missing his allusion.

Oh, that later.

Her lips widened into a lazy, taunting smile as the import of Greg's statement penetrated her passion induced haze.

"Later, Greg?" she purred provocatively. "Is that supposed to mean something significant?"

The mischievous twinkle in Fenella's eyes belied the bland innocence of the question.

"Most definitely, you saucy wench." Greg nipped her lightly, punishing her for teasing. "It's time I collected my winnings. In full." He nipped her again, kissing the spot better immediately.

"Are you going to pay up tonight or let your debts accrue?"

Oh, the darling man!

After all the flirtatious innuendos bandied back and forth between them throughout the afternoon, and her abandoned pleasure in their kisses just now, he was still allowing her the option of backing out if she felt unsure.

A wave of tenderness overtook Fenella. Any lingering doubts she may have had were utterly dispelled by this show of consideration.

Sable lashes fluttering, she peered coyly up at him.

"I could never do that, Greg," she protested demurely. "I was brought up to pay my debts promptly."

With a muffled exclamation of triumph, Greg rose to his feet. Steel muscled arms scooping her high against the warm flesh of his bare torso, he strode purposefully towards the master bedroom.

"Aimee?" whispered Fenella, belatedly recalling that she and Greg were not alone.

"Sleeps like a log," she was assured with a tigerish grin, the bedroom door closing behind them with a portentous click.

Fenella was cast lightly into the centre of the king-sized bed needed to accommodate a man of Greg Kendall's height and breadth in comfort.

Stripping off the remainder of his own clothes, Greg made short work of divesting Fenella of what she still retained of hers. A deeply indrawn breath paid an appreciative tribute to the flaring curves of hip and breast laid bare to the blue orbs roving intimately over them.

Fenella's own eyes employed on an equally enthralling sightseeing tour, she reached out a hand in mute supplication. Pearl tipped fingers stroked male flesh that had hitherto been taboo to her touch.

"Come a little closer Darling," she murmured. "I want to begin paying those onerous debts of mine."

No second invitation necessary, Greg lowered himself onto the sheets alongside her. Merging creative talent with piratical instincts, he gave as generously as he took. What followed was the most gloriously satisfying experience of Fenella's twenty-seven years.

And still she craved more.

Long past midnight, after another, more leisurely, loving, Fenella defied Greg's vigorous protests. Leaving his bed with a regretful glance at the tangle of male limbs and sheets, she gathered her clothes, dressing as she went.

Greg, in hastily donned jeans, caught up with her at the front door. "I do wish you'd stay, Fenella," he grumbled.

Evaluating the inflexible tilt of her chin, he sighed. "Let me find my shoes and I'll drive you since you're set on abandoning me," he offered. "Aimee will be fine for five minutes."

20

Monday and Tuesday nights were a repeat of Sunday's. Arriving at Greg's house after Aimee's bedtime and insisting on leaving before morning, Fenella followed her instincts for self-preservation which urged her to become neither a slave to Greg's wishes nor to flaunt their affair too openly.

Fortunately for her, the citizens of Topaz Sands preferred to spend cold winter nights indoors, drawn curtains shielding the peccadilloes of their neighbours from view. It was her glowing countenance announcing her new-found joy, which drew curious glances from a number of interested persons; although thus far none had ventured to ask intrusive questions.

Not yet secure in her love, Fenella was making the most of what she guessed would be a short breathing space to build solid footings for her run-away emotions. Greg Kendall fulfilled her wildest desires and, except that no words of love had yet passed his lips, was proving himself a gratifyingly demanding lover.

Was she anything as special to Greg as he was to her?

Or was he merely satisfying his needs with the most readily available woman, namely herself? Fenella craved the certainty of knowing her love was reciprocated.

Either way, until she knew, she felt best advised to play it cool herself.

Wednesday night was different.

Oppressed by thoughts of their impending separation, Fenella succumbed to temptation and spent the whole night exactly where she most wanted to be. Thursday's dawn was casting a pink glow above the horizon before she dragged herself from the comforting haven of Greg's cradling arms. The heralds of a new day informed her it was time to be going. Dressing quietly, she tiptoed back to the side of the bed to gaze once more upon Greg Kendall's beloved face before leaving. Sleepy blue eyes cracked open and he muttered drowsily.

"Be right with you Fen. Give me a moment to get some clothes on." In his befuddled state he thought it was time to drive her home.

"Shush. Go back to sleep Darling." Fenella pushed him gently down into the pillows, taking the opportunity to steal a lingering farewell kiss. When she saw him later in the day there would be too many interested spectators for such liberties.

"It's breaking day. I'll jog home along the beach" she whispered, reluctant fingers drawing away from his warmth.

"More exercise Fen?" Wide awake now, Greg relentlessly drew her down until she lay sprawled athwart his body in the tangled bedclothes.

"I would have thought you got all the exercise you needed last night, but if you insist on more, I'll do my best to satisfy you." He poked sly fun at her, enjoying the blush that spread across her cheeks.

After their escapades of the previous three nights the woman could still blush! Amazing.

"It'll be more fun than jogging, I promise." Greg began nuzzling below Fenella's ear, hands tugging at fastenings she had only just closed.

Chuckling, Fenella planted one hard, swift, final kiss on his ready lips then levered herself upright once more, batting away the large hands that sought to tip her back onto the bed.

"Unhand me, you lecherous beast," she giggled. "Seriously, Greg. It's morning. I really must go; but how I'm going to miss you until you get back."

"Not half as much as I'll be missing you, woman." He swung his legs sideways, unembarrassed by his nudity, reaching for the bathrobe flung across a chair. "If you must go, at least let me see you to the door."

The robe secured, they walked, arms circling each other's waists, through the dark, silent house, stopping for one more deeply arousing embrace before Fenella opened the door. Stepping through it she looked back, filling her sight with a last view of the large, tousled, unsmiling man she loved to distraction; mentally adding it to the other freshly acquired memories that would be all she had to sustain her till after the weekend.

"Bye Greg," she called softly. The door closed as she slipped out the gate and she imagined him crawling back into the still warm bed for another hour's sleep. Therefore, she was gratifyingly surprised, when, on reaching the sand she looked back to see him watching from the deck. A tall, brooding figure, hands thrust into the pockets of his long, navy robe. Lifting her hand in a silent wave, she tore herself away, jogging south along the beach at a fast clip.

She had been none too soon making her escape. A bewhiskered Matt Sykes, plaid collar high around beanie covered ears, fishing rod and tackle box in hand, greeted her as he trudged towards the rocky point to cast a hopeful line.

"Mornin' Fen," he called gruffly. "Where's the furball today?"

"Matt! Good morning." Fenella slowed her pace to return his greeting.

"Zilla's in bed. Too cold for her this morning," she answered, guiltily aware she had been neglecting her faithful companion. *I'll make it up to her, starting tonight,* she vowed.

Having Greg Kendall for a lover was totally wonderful but he had thrown her whole routine out of kilter. Her thoughts drifted forlornly to all the extra time she would have on her hands over the next few days.

Friday night was to be the gala premiere of the film of Greg's book, 'Lethal Fancies'. Fenella looked forward to seeing it, but it wouldn't be this weekend. She was to be godmother at a christening in Coffs Harbour on Saturday morning; too far from Sydney to attend both events.

"I do wish you could be there Fen," Greg had grumbled, although he understood that she couldn't let her friends down at the last minute.

Fenella's prediction regarding their lack of privacy that afternoon was well founded.

When Greg, all packed up for a quick getaway, collected Aimee, he found Fenella surrounded by chattering women and children.

They had to content themselves with a public exchange of eloquent glances and carefully casual words.

"See you Greg. All the best for tomorrow night. Bye Aimee. Have fun with your Granny Stone, Sweetheart."

"Thanks Fenella. See you next week."

"Bye-bye Ms Wilkins."

✳✳✳✳✳

Eagerly tuning in to the breakfast show on her motel room television, Fenella waited to see if there would be any coverage of the premiere. Yes! There it was on the Morning Show agenda, although it would be too late in the program for her to catch today. She'd set the recorder on her home set before she left and planned to watch it on her return.

On the way home the next morning, she bought the Sunday papers. *Maybe I should start a scrapbook,* she thought. In her imagination she saw a bulky collection of clippings recording her man's successes over the years.

Aren't I the optimistic one, she jeered at herself. *My man indeed!*

Maybe he was for now, but who was to know for how much longer? He might prove to be one of those who men who enjoy the pursuit more than the capture. She didn't really believe that, however a chill of foreboding crept up her spine at the reminder to herself of how little she knew 'her man'.

✱✱✱✱✱

Zilla a comforting warm bundle on her lap, a mug of coffee in one hand, Fenella rewound the videotape then fast forwarded to the segment she wanted. Fully alert, she absorbed the comments made by actors, producer and director. She was beginning to fidget impatiently when the camera zoomed in on the face she'd been hoping to see.

Leaning forward intently, she missed not one syllable of the brief interview with the author of 'Lethal Fancies'. Sighing when the ad break came and the program moved to a new topic, Fenella turned off the television and sank back in her chair.

Greg hadn't said much. Didn't the man realise she'd be here sharing his triumph, however vicariously? He could have been a bit more expansive. Possibly he had been, she shrugged, knowing the show's producers would have cut the recorded interviews quite ruthlessly to fit the time slot allowed. Brightening, she decided she was lucky they'd kept the tiny snippet they had.

Suddenly restless, Fenella jumped to her feet.

Wrapping Zilla up warmly in her snug dog coat, she coaxed her out, braving the gusting wind for a long, bracing walk over the headland to the next bay.

Windblown and chilled to the bone, but mercifully free of the crochets that had bedevilled her all day, she settled Zilla on her rug in front of the heater and went to prepare something easy for dinner.

It wasn't for some time that she became aware of the message light flashing on her answering machine.

"Fenella. Greg here. There's been a change of plan. Won't be back till late Tuesday. Maybe Wednesday. The parents are taking Aimee and will get her to school. Call you when I get home."

A sharp click ended the terse message. *Oh no! Another two or three days before she saw him!*

There had been a lot of background noise, music and talking and women's laughter. Where was he calling from? Fenella replayed the message, checking the time it was sent. Twelve thirty-seven am Saturday morning. He must have called from the post-screening celebration party.

"Well, not much I can do about it," she told Zilla. Nevertheless, the harsh, practical tone and absence of any endearment, or even regret at the delay, extinguished her upbeat mood. Trailing into the kitchen to retrieve her dinner from the microwave oven, she noticed the unread Sunday papers tossed onto the corner table in her haste to see the taped television report.

Seated on the lounge room carpet amid a sea of scattered newsprint, she finally found what she was looking for. First on the film review pages, where the critics had been quite kind, and then on the social pages where the premiere had garnered a whole two-page spread of photos.

Fenella gloated over the glamorously dressed men and women. Sydney's social set had turned out in force for one of their own.

Her smile froze into a grimace, her eyes skidding to a disbelieving halt, fixed on one particular photo near the bottom of the page.

Greg Kendall hadn't photographed particularly well, unlike the very photogenic, very beautiful blonde clinging possessively to his arm, gazing adoringly into his downturned, and seemingly equally adoring face. An all too familiar blonde. It didn't take the caption to tell Fenella she was looking at a photo of Greg Kendall lovingly entwined with Linda Beck, but she read it anyway. '...author of 'Lethal Fancies', Gregory R Kendall and his lovely fiancée, well-known model Linda Beck.'

An icy sweat breaking out all over as she was suddenly attacked by nausea, Fenella felt her dinner rising alarmingly. *His fiancée*, the paper said. *But she wasn't, was she? That was over and done with, months ago. It must be a mistake.* Studying the photo again, Fenella now noticed what she'd first missed. That great, ostentatious diamond ring flashing exultantly on Linda's left hand. Yes, Fenella checked, definitely the left hand.

Was this what Greg meant by 'change of plans'? Was this why he'd uttered no endearments. Why there was no tenderness in his voice?

Because he and Linda Beck had made up their differences and taken up right where they left off – in love and engaged to be married?

"Nooo!" wailed Fenella. "I don't believe it! I won't!" she whimpered. "Not unless he tells me himself."

Sick to her stomach and shivering from shock, Fenella stepped over the newspapers strewn untidily about the floor, reaching for the phone.

Greg will surely have seen this, she told herself. He'll tell me what a ridiculous furphy it is, and we'll laugh ourselves silly over it.

The call to his mobile rang out unanswered.

Fenella left a subdued word of congratulation for the good reviews on the message bank and hung up. Greg knew she'd be home tonight. He'd ring her back for sure.

Except that Greg Kendall did not ring.

Fenella received no comforting reassurances. As hope gradually ebbed, bitterness filled the void. Bitterness and an acid, gnawing sense of loss.

By Monday evening anger was edging out the shock-induced numbness that had allowed her to function automatically during the day. A pretended impending cold excused her unusual lack of vitality.

Driven by the need to do something, anything, Fenella snatched the offending paper from where it lay, mute witness to her pain. Cutting out that loathsome photo, complete with its incriminating caption, Fenella scrawled a note, folded the two neatly together and tucked them into an envelope. Gregory R Kendall, she inscribed with a flourish.

She raced down the sands and up the beach steps, the shortest route between their two houses. Without giving herself time to reconsider, she poked the letter through the slot in Greg's mailbox.

There, that should give him the message. She brushed her hands fastidiously.

Deflated, now that she was deprived of the urgency of affirmative action, Fenella wandered listlessly home, where, in a fit of healthy temper, she once again relegated the sea god to the spare bedroom, out of her sight.

And its model out of her mind? No, she was afraid she couldn't yet manage that feat.

The next morning, she phoned in sick, citing a migraine as the cause, an excuse that unfortunately had the virtue of being true. By Wednesday she'd pulled herself together, determined not to fall into a decline. Employing work, her previously successful panacea for spiritual ills, as her crutch, Fenella was back at school.

Exhausted, emotionally battered, damning all men and one in particular, she was still functioning; if not at full efficiency.

No man was ever again going to lay Fenella Wilkins low. Head high, a militant expression defying fate, she faced the world bravely.

21

"Damn the woman! Wouldn't you think she'd have the sense to know it's just a stupid mistake?"

Greg threw Fenella's note with its accusing clipping violently onto the table, biting back an even pithier expletive in deference to his mother's presence.

He'd arrived home shortly before ten pm on Wednesday night, weary and wanting nothing more than a little peace and quiet and a good night's sleep.

It had surprised him to discover how much he missed the susurration of the waves, rolling and hissing up the beach below his bedroom window. The muted roar of Sydney's traffic hadn't lulled him to sleep as effectively on this visit as it usually did.

Or had it been the absence from his bed of one particular passionate, brown-eyed houri who occupied more than her share of his thoughts lately?

His arrival had been warmly hailed by his parents, and replete with coffee and hot buttered toast, he had picked up the bundle of mail.

Flicking through the accumulation for anything urgent, Greg had instantly recognised Fenella's distinctive script on the hand delivered envelope, and seized on it eagerly.

Disgust and disappointment had given rise to his furious outburst.

"Problems Son?" inquired his father mildly, glancing up briefly from the latest Lee Child novel in which he was engrossed.

Susan, more alert than her husband, dived on the newspaper clipping fluttering to the carpet to lie half under the sofa.

"Oh dear," she gasped. She and Peter not being readers of the 'Sun-Herald', she was seeing it for the first time.

"Oh dear, indeed, Mum," Greg ground out impatiently. "I've had that revolting photo, and its idiotic caption, thrown up at me everywhere I've gone for the past three days. Now here's more of the same, from Fenella, of all people."

Why single out Fenella in particular?

Susan's maternal antennae quivered, at full alert. However, a more urgent issue demanded her attention.

"This *is* the mistake you're referring to, Gregory dear?" She asked, laying the picture down with a distasteful grimace.

Dread aroused by suddenly reawakened fears, she prayed that a mistake was all it was, although the photo hinted strongly at a continued intimacy between her beloved first-born and the ex-fiancée she'd been so pleased to see the last of. Her diffident tone pleaded for reassurance.

"Of course, Mum. Either a misprint or some journalist too lazy to verify her facts. The cause is immaterial anyway." He smiled tightly. "I felt entirely justified in calling the editor and giving him a blast; which I trust he passed on to the true culprit."

Perking up, his mother chose at this time, not to ask the obvious question, namely 'What was that woman doing, draped all over you so possessively?'

"Did you really? Call the editor, I mean?"

"Yes Mother, I most assuredly did," Greg replied. "And now I'm going to do the same with Fenella Wilkins."

Alarmed at her son's grim expression as he reached for the phone, Susan was tempted to offer advice, thinking better of it at the last moment. Greg was a grown man. One moreover, who wasn't given to welcoming unsolicited interference in his affairs.

Unashamedly she settled down to listen in to his end of the conversation. If Greg wanted privacy, Susan reasoned, he could go into another room. Besides, she was consumed with curiosity regarding his relationship with Fenella. Some idle words of Jason's had led her to nurture quiet hopes in that direction and so she considered she had a vested interest.

Fenella didn't answer immediately. Susan heard the phone ring seven times before it was picked up.

"Fenella, it's Greg," she heard her son say, wincing at his aggressive tone. "What the hell did you mean with that snide little note?" Just moments later he slammed it down on its rest, seriously endangering its delicate technology.

"She hung up on me!" Greg stormed, a thunderous scowl mantling his clean-cut features.

"Well, she's gone too far this time," he ranted. "She needn't think I'll let her get away with hanging up on me. Or with this rubbish either." He snatched up the note and clipping, stuffing them roughly into his pocket. Striding for the door, he called over his shoulder as he shrugged into his jacket.

"Don't wait up for me. She's a stubborn woman. This could take a while!"

"What's all the shouting about?" Peter Kendall, emerging grumpily from his book, demanded as the door snapped shut behind Greg.

"Don't ask Dear. Just pray he doesn't ruin everything," his wife soothed. Irritated, Peter stared at Susan.

"Ruin what?" Then, pugnaciously defending his son, he asked, "Why would you assume he's likely to ruin anything?" His wife answered tartly, casting a speaking look at her husband.

"He's your son, Peter darling." A fulminating glare was the only answer to this impertinence, so, more conciliatory, she changed the subject.

"Put your book away Dear, and let's go to bed."

*****

A thunderous knocking on the front door brought Zilla dashing from her basket to bark her indignation at the rude visitor creating such a ruckus so late at night.

Fenella, shrugging in resignation, took her time answering the summons, as she had a short time ago answering the phone. Then, caller ID had informed her of the identity of her caller.

Now, after hanging up on Greg, she was pretty certain he was here in person to take issue with his treatment.

The intemperate thumping of the knocker carried the 'Greg Kendall in a snit' signature note.

She had hoped he wouldn't pursue the matter further. He had her note, and if that wasn't explicit enough, hanging up on him should have told him precisely what she thought of his behaviour.

"It's typical of the man," she fumed, whistling Zilla to heel, "he simply must have the last word."

Flinging the door wide, Fenella planted herself, arms akimbo, all bristling defiance, barring entry.

"You're wasting your time blocking the door, Fenella." Greg, blue eyes flashing a warning of primal danger, met glare with glare. "I'm coming in," he stated adamantly.

When Fenella refused to budge, he grabbed her round the waist and hoisted her across his shoulder. Kicking the door shut behind him, Greg marched into the lounge room.

Zilla, brave little champion that she was, did her best to defend her mistress. Snapping and growling, she latched onto Greg's trouser leg with a bulldog grip; refusing to let go when he tried to shake her loose. Greg turned a glowering countenance on his small attacker.

"Down!" he thundered. Zilla, recognising the voice of authority, subsided onto her belly, ready to resume battle with Fenella's attacker should it be necessary.

Not so her mistress.

Kicking and pummelling, Fenella struggled for her freedom.

"You too! Sit there and don't move!" Greg roared, dumping her unceremoniously among the cushions on the divan.

As if! Giving voice to her tempestuous fury, Fenella bounced back to her feet.

"How dare you come bursting into my home, attacking me and kicking my dog," she screamed.

"I did not kick your dog," he bellowed back.

When Fenella opened her mouth to argue the point, Greg recognised this unjust accusation for the diversionary tactic it was. There were more important issues between them than pointless, time-wasting bickering over whether or not he kicked the damned dog; which that infuriating woman knew full well he hadn't.

"I did not kick your dog!" he yelled again, forestalling her.

Fenella closed her mouth.

Greg continued to glare at her. Unyielding determination in every inch of his towering form, he sought to dominate her by will alone.

It occurred to Greg that he was beginning to enjoy himself. Maintaining his angry stance in spite of it, he was determined to teach Fenella Wilkins a lesson!

Unquestionably the wronged party, he'd had time to reflect on the walk between his home and Fenella's. Uncomfortably Greg acknowledged to himself that being confronted unawares by that bit of journalistic malfeasance had probably upset Fenella a bit.

Probably!

No doubt about it, it had. He would make it up to her, but really, she should have had more faith in him! Enough at least to not go jumping to all the wrong conclusions. Righteous anger continued to simmer, blazing high at Fenella's belligerent reception.

"Sit down!" Greg barked, surprised when Fenella obeyed. Instantly. Pleased at the unexpected success of this tactic, he ventured again. "Quiet!" he commanded, even though Fenella, busily regrouping her defences had made no attempt at further argument. Some slight easing in her opponent's attitude had made itself felt, so, faced with the inevitable, Fenella, not the least bit afraid of his anger and bluster, resigned herself to listening to the infuriating man's excuses.

In some far recess of her heart, hope cautiously raised its head.

Greg cared; or he wouldn't be here yelling and shouting at her in the middle of the night.

"This better be good," she warned, unwilling to give in too tamely.

Lips clamped together, fists decorously folded in her lap, she composed herself to listen. Eyes relentlessly tracking his movements, she watched Greg pull a chair close and sit, facing her.

Alert for danger signals, Greg pulled Fenella's inflammatory note from his pocket, the photo fluttering to the floor. Tersely he read aloud.

Congratulations on the success of 'Lethal Fancies'.

Congratulations also on the resumption of your

engagement. I assume that was an unpremeditated

development? The change of plans you mentioned.

"What do you think I am woman!" he roared. Again, he read aloud the relevant passage from her note.

"How could you imagine me capable of callously treating you so badly, Fenella Wilkins?" he demanded, grimly forcing her into a defensive position. "After what we discovered together, how could you belittle our feelings for each other? I ought to put you over my knee and give you the spanking you so richly deserve," he concluded.

Fenella sat unmoved. She needed more than bombast before she forgave him.

Greg adopted a less aggressive stance.

"All you had to do Fenella, was ask. If you had simply asked, you could have saved yourself a lot of unnecessary upset." Silently he pleaded with her to believe in him.

"Agreed," Fenella bit out. "I called your mobile. When nobody answered, I left a message. You didn't get back to me."

Greg ran his fingers through his hair and muttered under his breath.

"What did you say? Speak up Greg."

Fenella pretended she hadn't heard. She had him now, and intended to make the most of her victory. Casting a black look at her, Greg complied.

"I forgot the blasted mobile. Why didn't you ring the flat?"

"Because the number's unlisted and you didn't give it to me!"

Greg stared, realising she was right. He hadn't. It hadn't occurred to him to do so. He ran his hand through his hair again, frustrated that an argument with so much damaging potential had arisen from such a simple cause.

Melting at the sight of the familiar, honest gesture, Fenella, practically convinced, played her advantage a little further.

"Okay Greg. You say all I had to do was ask. I'm asking." She drew in a deep breath and asked the question which had haunted her for the last few days.

"What was that picture, and its caption, all about, Greg? What does it mean to *us*?"

"Nothing." Relieved Fenella was now behaving reasonably, Greg answered her second question first. "It means nothing to us, because some journalist's careless mistake is all it was. As for the photo, Linda was there with friends. Other friends," he explained, forestalling the next question.

"She came over to congratulate me just as the photographer popped up in front of me. Shove a camera in front of her and Linda poses automatically. I was a bit put out with her over it, if you must know. Especially when everyone started ragging me over the blasted photo." His expression darkened again, recalling the unwelcome teasing.

Fenella nodded slightly. Greg's words had an unmistakable ring of truth, but she needed to be totally sure.

"So, you and Linda Beck are not re-engaged, then?" Where did she stand now? Had she blown it with Greg, or would he give her a second chance?

"We definitely are not!" Observing the strained expression on Fenella's face he moderated his tone, now almost pleading for her understanding.

"I'm sorry Fenella, I should have called, regardless. Only I hate phones, and I was flat out with meetings and publicity appearances, etc. When I didn't hear from you, I assumed either you hadn't seen it, or else you'd recognised it for the load of rubbish it was. I should have made time for you."

Had she forgiven him? He hoped so. Fenella Wilkins had come to occupy rather an important place in his life, although quite what that place was, he didn't know.

Fenella breathed again.

Greg hadn't used the 'l' word, but the situation looked promising again. His next words reinforced that conviction.

"I'd like to make time for you now, Fenella."

When this hopeful sally wasn't rebuffed, Greg moved to sit beside her on the divan.

He took her hands in his, smoothing the fingers from their tightly clenched fists, heaving a sigh of relief when they relented.

It would be alright, he thought, exultantly, amending his certainty to a more cautious maybe.

To Greg's dismay, fat, silent tears began rolling down Fenella's cheeks.

He was murmuring assuaging inanities and wiping ineffectively at the deluge with unsteady fingers when Fenella cast herself upon his chest, arms gripping tightly around his back.

Soothing hands stroking, and tender lips brushing comforting caresses over any available patch of bare skin, Greg weathered the storm. When Fenella's snifflings into the front of his shirt finally ceased, he took his handkerchief and gently turning her face up, blotted it dry.

Dropping an affectionate kiss onto still trembling lips, Greg whispered against them.

"It's over now Darling. It was all a mistake and it's over now. Don't cry anymore."

Feeling an easing in the arms binding her to him like a lifeline, he kissed Fenella again, and yet again; more insistently, until she was kissing him back as if her life depended on it.

All relieved, masterful male, Greg picked her up, far more tenderly than he had upon his arrival, and carried his now willing burden into the welcoming haven that was Fenella's bedroom. They made love and slept; to wake and love each other again.

*****

Greg was still sleeping soundly when Fenella slipped from his enfolding arms, being careful not to wake him. Showering and dressing in a rush, she only just made it to work on time.

A good hour later, Greg woke; disoriented to find himself in a strange bed, until he recalled the events of the previous night. Yawning, and stretching luxuriously, smug satisfaction spread a broad grin across his face.

The crackle of crushed paper sent him searching through the bedclothes, coming up with a square, pink post-it page bearing the lipsticked imprint of a pair of generous feminine lips. Fenella's lips.

Greg chuckled, his own lips tingling with the memory of those same full lips pressed hungrily against them. Most women he knew would have woken him up and turfed him out before leaving for work. He yawned prodigiously again.

Fenella's got one hell of a temper, alright, Greg mused fondly, *but when she gives, it's unstinting.*

He swung his feet to the floor where they were met by a fierce growling.

"Ah, the valiant protector." Greg spoke aloud, addressing the bristling terrier.

"Here Zilla." He snapped his fingers encouragingly and held his hand out for her inspection.

"Come on old girl. Your mistress has forgiven me, so how about you and I make it up too?"

Recognising the voice as that of a past friend who had apparently been reinstated, the little dog crept over to the bed. Tentatively touching a moist nose to the outstretched hand, she gave it a delicate sniff, then touched her tongue briefly to Greg's wrist, looking up as if to say, "Sorry about last night, but you know how it is. A dog's got to do her duty."

Greg understood, and made much of Zilla to the small animal's delight.

Borrowing Fenella's bathroom, Greg was surprised all over again to discover a towel and toiletries, including a disposable razor and a toothbrush still in their cellophane wrappers, stacked neatly next to the hand basin.

Men's toiletries, he noted coldly.

Who did Fenella keep those for? He slammed the can of deodorant back down on the benchtop, his mind roiling with images of *his* woman entertaining herself with other lovers; until he recalled she had a father and a brother, either of whom could have left these things here.

Virtuously, he decided to give her the benefit of the doubt. Besides, he was pretty sure that any previous lovers Fenella had had were well in the past, hence none of his business.

A niggling doubt lingered, disturbing his complacency. He knew he wasn't the first man in her life. There was even an ex-husband, he recalled. Yet the image of Fenella in the arms of any man other than himself remained an uncomfortable one.

22

Susan Kendall had been on the lookout for her son all morning, though when he finally returned, discretion ruled and she held her tongue.

"There you are Greg," she called when he walked through his front door, "I was about to pour the coffee. There are fresh muffins, too. Straight from Charlie's oven."

Lost for an explanation for his prolonged absence that wouldn't embarrass his mother, Greg stalled for time, burying his nose in his coffee mug.

"I've been on the beach," he finally offered, placating his conscience with the fact that it was quite true, though no-where near wholly, true. He had taken the beach route home from Fenella's.

"That's nice dear," his mother accepted blandly, biding her time. Not so Peter Kendall. He fixed his son with a piercing stare and came to the point immediately.

"I take it that business last night with Fenella Wilkins has been cleared up satisfactorily?" he demanded, dispensing with frivolous pleasantries.

"Entirely." His son answered as succinctly as possible, his defiant air giving notice that no-one need expect further details.

Pointedly leaving the conversation to his parents, Greg centred his attention on the plate of muffins, wolfing down three in quick succession.

"Stay a moment Mum," Greg asked as Susan began gathering empty plates and mugs. "I've got a huge favour to ask of you both." He stopped a moment to gather his thoughts.

"Go on then," urged his father. "Now that you've deigned to resurface, stop wasting our time. We need to get going."

"Yes, well," Greg hesitated. "That's part of what I want to talk to you about. Time. I've got way behind on the current book, what with one thing and another over the last few months, and my publisher's yapping at my heels. He's set me a deadline I'll be hard pressed to meet, what with the school holidays starting this weekend."

He paused hopefully, but his parents both sat in silence forcing him to make his pitch unaided.

"I was hoping you two might offer to take Aimee for me," he begged. "It's an imposition, I know," he added quickly, catching his father's incipient scowl, "but if I could have two straight weeks with no interruptions, I could catch up."

"Oh, yes Dear," Susan jumped in. "We love having Aimee to visit. Don't we Peter?" She wasn't going to permit her husband to voice any objections.

Peter merely grunted his acquiescence, although already mentally planning what he and his precious granddaughter would be getting up to, while exhibiting a dour expression designed to keep that son of his on his toes.

"There's no point in leaving today, then, is there Peter? If we stay till the end of the week, we can take Aimee with us and save Greg a trip. We can go to her sports carnival on Friday afternoon, too," she added, warming to the change in plans.

"No need to go on and on, woman," Peter grumbled. "I'm not arguing."

He patted her affectionately on the shoulder as he got up to phone his excuses to the captain of his bowls team. He would miss this week's game, chasing around after the family like this.

"Then how about lunch in Forster? On me," Greg offered. His problems solved, he could afford to be magnanimous. The day was too far advanced to get any serious work done anyway. And tonight, there would be Fenella.

✷✷✷✷✷

Lunch over, the three Kendalls were browsing through the shops when Susan led the way into the dim recesses of an antiques shop to see if she could find replacement pieces for her grandmother's tea-set; a treasured inheritance which she had almost restored to full strength.

Tucked away at the back of a display case, Greg spotted an Art Deco brooch. A dragonfly set with diamonds and a glowing yellow topaz that reminded him of Fenella's preference for yellow – the sunshine colour that brightens the gloomiest day, as he had heard her describe it to Aimee.

She would love this. Impulsively, he bought it, anticipating her pleasure when he gave it to her tonight.

Dropping his parents off at the house on their return from Forster, Greg drove straight to the school to collect his daughter. Propelling her back inside on the pretext of wanting to see the work she'd done during the week, he waited till Fenella was alone, wanting to speak privately with her.

Buoyed up by her reunion with Greg, Fenella had sailed through her day, looking forward to the time she could be with him again. Ushering the last of her other visitors out of the classroom, she finally turned to where Greg and Aimee waited patiently, a beaming smile lighting up her whole face.

"At last!" she exclaimed. "I was hoping to see you Greg. We have so much to talk about." She threw him a sparkling, significant look across the top of Aimee's bent head.

"Only not here," he murmured back, his warm perusal of her bringing a proud blush to Fenella's cheeks. Reaching out a gentle finger, Greg caressed the pink glow.

"I'll come to you tonight, will I Fen?" he asked, voice deepening in anticipation. She nodded happily, too choked up with emotion to speak.

*****

"Talk first Fen, then we can concentrate on ourselves." Regretfully putting Fenella slightly away from him, Greg's husky whisper brought her back from the heights his hello kiss had taken her to. She had greeted him rapturously on his arrival, and he had responded in kind.

Now, before the situation got out of hand and they ran out of time, there were a couple of issues Greg wanted settled. There were one or two issues Fenella was longing to bring to his attention, too, so she obediently complied.

Pouring them each a drink, she snuggled up against her lover's side, his arm holding her reassuringly close, waiting for him to proceed.

Telling her first of the outcome of his meeting with his publisher, Greg kissed her lightly.

"You see Fen," he murmured, lips close to the delicate skin below her jaw, "we're going to have to be a bit disciplined about this. Much as I would prefer, I simply can't spend all my time making love to you. I'm going to have to set aside regular hours for writing."

"That's one of the things I wanted to discuss too," Fenella replied seriously, readjusting her position to one that allowed fewer distractions. Gazing earnestly into Greg's face, she elucidated.

"You need to write; and I need to paint, to prepare for my exhibition, Greg. Also, after the holidays, I'll have school work to fit in somewhere as well."

She grinned impudently, eyes dancing.

"You can have the holidays all to yourself to write. I'm off to New Zealand for a week's skiing with friends. It's been booked for ages. Then I was intending to spend a few days in Sydney with my friend, Laura. That one's negotiable though," she volunteered.

Unhappy that the next two weeks were not going to be spent quite as enjoyably as he'd been envisaging, still, Greg agreed that Fenella should go ahead with her holiday.

On her return, he told her, they would tailor their times together to fit flexibly around their busy schedules, thereby winning an extra encomium of approval from Fenella.

Greg accorded her work equal status with his own! A courtesy she'd never known from Paul Fremont.

Emptying his glass, Greg put it aside. Taking Fenella's from her unresisting fingers, he disposed of it too. Wickedly suggestive blue eyes caressed her intimately.

"Now, Fenella darling, let's get down to some serious loving." With that, Greg suited his actions to his words.

✳✳✳✳✳

Susan Kendall had not been deceived by her son's non-committal, "Be back later," as he slipped out the front door following Aimee's goodnight story. She'd noted his impatient glances at the clock while he helped her clear away the dinner dishes.

Kissing her granddaughter goodnight, her patience was rewarded. A sleepy Aimee murmured an explanation.

"Daddy's going to see Fenella." Pretty rosebud mouth adopting a sulky pout, she added, "I wanted to go too, but Daddy said they have lots to talk about, and it's too late and I need my sleep."

It was long after Susan and Peter went to bed that the front door opened quietly, closing again with a muffled click.

Footsteps tiptoed heavily down the hallway to the master bedroom.

"One twenty am," Susan noted drowsily. "Must have been some talk Greg was having with Fenella."

Acting on her own initiative the next morning, she ordered Greg to his computer straight after breakfast.

"You get busy with that writing of yours," she commanded. "Peter and I will walk Aimee to school. I think I'll invite Fenella Wilkins to dinner tonight," she added, a carefully contrived afterthought that brought Greg's head up.

Waiting with bated breath, Susan was happily relieved when he blandly accepted her suggestion.

"Good idea Mum. You do that," was all he said; but it was all the encouragement Susan needed.

"It's such an age since we had a nice long chat, Fenella," Susan said, putting her plan into action. "Do you think you could find the time to have dinner with us tonight? You see, it's our last night here, this visit. Tomorrow morning we'll be heading home with young Aimee for the holidays." She eyed the younger woman hopefully, slyly tossing in an extra incentive. "I checked with Greg. He agrees it's a good idea."

"I'd love to Susan," Fenella agreed cheerfully. "You can tell me all about the wedding plans."

*****

"Is Zilla going too?" Aimee asked. The dinner table conversation had arrived at Fenella's plans to go skiing in New Zealand. "I don't think she'd like all that snow."

"She certainly wouldn't," Fenella laughed. "She hates being left in the boarding kennel, too, only I'm afraid I have no option.

"Why don't you let us take her?" Peter offered unexpectedly.

"Our baby would like that, wouldn't you Aimee, love? Besides, my doctor has been badgering me to walk every day. If it works out with Zilla, I might get some sort of small dog of my own. You know, Fenella. Try before I buy."

His last words were drowned out by Aimee's gleeful shout.

"Ooh yes, Grandpa!" Responding to her father's signal to moderate her voice, Aimee continued persuasively. "Please, Fenella. Grandpa and I will take specially good care of her."

Fenella took very little persuading. Zilla would be happier with Aimee and her grandparents.

While Aimee splashed happily in the bathtub, and the men dealt with the dirty dishes, Susan and Fenella stood on the deck together watching the moon rise.

Diffidently, Susan broached the subject dearest to her heart, emboldened by the warm glances exchanged across the table between Fenella and her son. Also, surely the dragonfly brooch Fenella was wearing was the one she'd seen Greg looking at yesterday in the antiques shop.

In his own way, her husband had signalled tacitly that he considered Fenella part of the family. Now it was her turn.

"I'm so glad you and Greg have become friends," she said, plunging right in. "After that disastrous affair with Linda, Peter and I were quite worried about him and Aimee. You're so good for them both, Fenella."

Casting a sidelong glance at her companion, she noted her serious mien. "Greg is happier right now than he's been in years." Fear of being too pushy vied with the wish to assure Fenella of the Kendall family's approval of her.

Fenella made no pretence of misunderstanding.

"It's good of you to say that, Susan. I'll be honest with you. I love Greg, although I think you should know, he hasn't committed himself to anything beyond the moment," she replied flatly.

She felt horribly dejected at having to acknowledge that poor truth, when her love for Greg Kendall demanded so much more of him.

Fenella's fingers crept up to the brooch he had pinned to the lapel of her dressing gown last night.

Greg Kendall might not be ready to admit it, however, in her heart she was sure he loved her in return. Stroking the topaz dragonfly once again she allowed optimism to lighten her mood.

"Not yet, Dear." Susan patted her shoulder consolingly, reinforcing her surge of optimism. "Sometimes love takes time to grow. Especially when a man has been disillusioned in the past."

A call that coffee was ready brought this interesting tete-a-tete to an end.

23

Susan Kendall's sage words echoed comfortingly in Fenella's mind during the following weeks as her volatile emotions see-sawed alarmingly, from elation in Greg's company to frustration when alone. Greg's longed-for declaration of his love remained unforthcoming. Hardily acquired caution dictated that Fenella protect herself by concealing the full depth of her own feelings.

With this absence of complete honesty between them, though, Fenella gradually fell prey to a daunting accumulation of doubts. On becoming aware of the problem, she attempted an objective analysis.

It's my own fault, she concluded, *I should talk to Greg. Tell him how I feel and ask him to explain these things that are bothering me*. Good advice; except that she was afraid to. Afraid that the truth would disrupt their fragile relationship, making even so limited a union quite untenable. For her, if not for Greg.

I'll wait, she resolved, rationalising her decision by reminding herself it was actually not such a long time since they'd become friends. An even shorter time since becoming lovers.

All of Fenella's niggling suspicions stemmed from the same source – Greg's continuing relationship with Linda Beck. She was never quite able to determine precisely what their relationship was, only that a relationship still existed; and she was afraid to ask for enlightenment.

They were not engaged.

Greg said.

Neither did they plan to marry.

Greg said.

Although he'd never said he didn't love Linda anymore; only that he didn't love her enough.

Which was more than he'd ever granted Fenella.

That they still communicated, and even went out together during Greg's now less frequent trips to Sydney, she had discovered quite by accident. The three of them, Aimee, Greg and herself, had returned from an energetic Sunday morning ramble through the dunes to find the indicator light flashing on the answering machine.

Aimee had gone to wash her hands, while Fenella towelled Zilla dry in the laundry.

When Greg played back his message, Linda Beck's metallic tones had reached out to her from the lounge room.

"Greg darling. Wonderful news. Ring me. Soon. Let's have dinner again to celebrate next time you're down. Love you Darling. Linda."

There was plenty in that message to incite jealousy and suspicion in even the most complacent of lovers.

And complacent Fenella certainly wasn't. Trepidation filling her heart, she went to stand in the archway to the lounge room.

Hearing her approach, Greg turned to face her. Chin lifted arrogantly, he silently dared her to comment.

That had been the time to speak out, Fenella realised belatedly, only she had flunked it.

"You going to ring her back?" A feeble question, but all she could manage with her stomach churning rebelliously, her suddenly dry tongue cleaving to the roof of her mouth.

"Not right now." Greg glanced at the clock. "It's not a good time to catch her in."

Which confirmed that he knew way too much about his ex-fiancée's movements.

Greg had stared at Fenella defiantly until, shrugging her shoulders in pretended unconcern, she had pushed herself away from the supporting archway that had been all that kept her upright for several long moments.

She slunk back to the laundry and the patiently waiting Zilla. Busy feigning indifference, Fenella hadn't been a witness to Greg Kendall's slumping shoulders and bleak, tight-lipped expression.

Fenella never discovered whether or not Greg did phone Linda back; or whether or not they went to dinner. Again. And how many other times? Anguish tore at her heart.

That night, unable to bear the tension a moment longer, she'd walked out on Greg, returning home before Aimee's bedtime.

The following day's lesson preparation had been cited as the excuse, although these days she made sure her lessons were always prepared well in advance.

Greg had not protested, as, yearning for reassurance, Fenella had desperately hoped he would. His goodnight kiss had been too perfunctory to assuage her fears.

When they next met, however, Greg had treated her once again in the warm affectionate manner to which she had grown accustomed, begging her to come round that evening.

"You know I'd prefer to come to you, Fen, except I can't leave Aimee," he'd reminded her, his intimate inflexion melting her resistance. After all, what was a phone call, or even a dinner. There was probably an innocent explanation for both.

Without wasting time on pleasantries, they had fallen into Greg's king-sized bed with a minimum of preliminaries, making love with an almost desperate passion. Soon, their relationship appeared back to normal.

Foolishly, Fenella consigned her worries to the turbid depths of her subconscious. There they festered ominously, their poison gathering just below the surface, awaiting a catalyst to activate it.

For a time, during which Greg, consumed by his writing, had no time for trips to Sydney, Fenella buried her head in the sand, returning to the state of blissful, unruffled happiness she'd experienced following her holiday.

Greg too, seemed more than willing to avoid awkward confrontations, so they patched over the shortcomings of their relationship, ignoring the underlying pitfalls.

September arrived, warm enough for a bracing dip. People ventured forth, taking advantage of the balmy weather, the beach welcoming growing numbers of family picnics.

Children once again dug tunnels to China and wielded cricket bats on the sand.

The ranks of die-hard surfers who had doggedly pursued their sport throughout the cold, blustery days of winter were swelled by fair-weather devotees, Fenella Wilkins among them.

Wattle blossom spread a fragrant patchwork of gold across the landscape, and dive-bombing magpies defending their nests terrorised young and old alike.

Spring had arrived, lifting spirits. Hope burgeoned anew.

Humming a catchy tune, Fenella strode confidently up the beach steps. Greg had said five, and it was no later than four. However, she was planning a little surprise, so it suited her purpose when she caught a glimpse of his blue BMW disappearing around the corner.

She had her own key, given to her last week, in case of emergency when she'd minded Aimee during Greg's three-day round of publicity appearances.

Knowing how precious Aimee was to Greg, it had boosted Fenella's confidence no end to be entrusted with the child's care. Shaking back her hair, she ran exuberantly up the last half dozen steps. On such a glorious day even the darkest of spectres lost their power to haunt.

Closing the door behind her, Fenella went directly to the kitchen, setting her basket down on the counter.

Aimee had been invited to a birthday party this afternoon and was sure to be overtired, ready for an early night.

In her basket, Fenella had all the fixings for a romantic candle-lit dinner for two. Before Greg returned from collecting Aimee, she would set the scene in the dining room. Then she would shut the door on it and forbid entry.

About to begin her preparations, Fenella paused, sure she had heard a noise. Yes, there it was again. If Greg was home, who had driven off in his car? Or did she have that the wrong way round?

Cautiously, Fenella went to investigate.

Even her worst nightmares couldn't have prepared her for the scene she discovered in Greg Kendall's bedroom.

Normally immaculate hair in wild disarray, lipstick wiped from her sultry, red mouth - kissed off, whispered a chilling voice in Fenella's brain - Linda Beck was sprawled au naturel among the tumbled bedclothes.

As Fenella halted abruptly in the doorway, frozen by shock, Linda casually pulled the sheet up to cover her abundant charms, holding it across her chest with her left hand. Her fingers flexed, the movement causing light to refract in a rainbow flash from the unmistakable square cut diamond on her third finger.

A ring Fenella remembered all too well.

"You!" the apparition hissed.

"What are you doing in my bedroom, Fenella Wilkins?" Linda sneered.

A triumphant note entered her voice. "Because, make no mistake about it, this is still *my* bedroom. I told you once before that Greg Kendall is mine. That hasn't changed one iota, even though we've been forced to live apart because of the brat."

Observing Fenella's white, stricken expression, vicious satisfaction spread a mocking smile over Linda's face.

A few more knockout blows, then she'd better wind it up and get out. She didn't have much time before Greg would be back, and she had to restore the bedroom to its former pristine condition before then.

"You surely don't imagine that just because Greg finds you a convenient bed-warmer and child minder, that he's fallen in love with you, do you?" Linda jeered.

"Get real! Greg Kendall is all man, with a man's appetites. I don't like it, but since I know you're no danger to me, I can live with it."

I can't, Fenella screamed silently, vocal cords paralysed by shock; pain ripping through her chest.

"We had a lovely time last week, three whole days," Linda smiled cruelly.

"You know, this isn't the first time I've been to stay with friends near here. From nine to three, you and the brat are safely out of the way, so Greg and I play."

Linda was purring now, thoroughly enjoying this heaven-sent opportunity to get her own back on Ms Goody-goody Wilkins. When she'd seen her turning in at the gate, key in hand, she had been overcome by blind fury.

Reacting slowly, she'd almost missed her chance. Almost. Time was up, though, Linda realised, glancing at the bedside clock.

"Sorry Darling," she drawled. "The truth has come as a bit of a shock, hasn't it? I've got to get up now. Don't want the kid coming home and seeing me like this."

As Linda swung her legs over the edge of the bed, sheet still clutched modestly to her bosom, Fenella regained control of her legs.

Whipping round, she raced headlong for the door, snatching up her basket on the way. Linda Beck's mocking laughter spurred her precipitate retreat.

Mind whirling out of control, Fenella ran until exhausted, then collapsed onto the sand of the next bay from Topaz. Desperately, she strove to bring order to the chaos in her mind.

Greg Kendall had betrayed her. Used her. Just as Paul had.

Well, no more, Fenella vowed.

The evidence had been there all along, challenging her to give it credence; only, besotted, she had turned her back on it. Suspicion was one thing. A naked woman, all languid and tousled from his lovemaking, in Greg Kendall's bed in the middle of the afternoon, was entirely another.

That constituted proof.

And he'd told her not to come till after five.

Utterly wretched, the arguments in her brain going round and round in in a vicious circle, Fenella rose and turned homeward, feet dragging reluctantly.

The last rays of the dying sun faded, leaving her to pick her way home in the dark along the rough path over the headland.

✲✲✲✲✲

Greg Kendall hung up the phone, plagued by a premonition of disaster. A worried frown creased his forehead.

He glanced from Aimee, glued to 'Sleeping Beauty', to the clock.

It was dark outside, had been for at least half an hour. He should be getting Aimee off to bed, except that if anything had happened to Fenella, he might have to go out in a hurry.

"Where is she?" he muttered, pacing restlessly across the deck to study the beach, then realising it was too dark to see if Fenella was out there. Back inside again, he came to a halt beside the phone, and impatiently picked it up and dialled Fenella's number again.

Again, the answering machine picked up.

Greg left a third message, tersely demanding that Fenella call him, ASAP.

He had been expecting her to join Aimee and himself for dinner, and she should have been here at least two hours ago. Being late wasn't all that important. What really worried him, was that she hadn't left him a message; and wasn't answering her phone or returning his messages, either.

Aimee's movie coming to an end, Greg bundled her off to bed. Once again pacing the deck, he whirled at the shrill summons of his phone, plunging inside to snatch it up.

"Fenella! Is that you!" he barked.

"Hello Greg." It was Fenella's voice alright, but she sounded strained.

He'd left three messages on her answering machine, each more urgent than the last. Afraid that if she ignored him, he might come after her, Fenella had felt impelled to call him back.

Greg heard her draw breath sharply.

"I've been out walking and forgot the time. I had to come home in the dark. That's why you couldn't reach me," she explained, words tumbling over one another.

"Never mind all that, Fenella," Greg interrupted. "As long as you're okay." His voice softened. "I've been worried that maybe you'd had an accident, or something. How soon can you be here? I missed you this afternoon."

That patent untruth put steel into Fenella's backbone. The devil had to be faced sometime. Fighting off another bout of tears, she thought it might as well be now. Then it would be over and done with.

She straightened her shoulders, preparing herself for battle.

"I'm on my way," she stated firmly, and hung up.

✶✶✶✶✶

"I saw Linda today," Fenella stated baldly.

Her back to Greg, she stood staring out the window, arms tightly crossed, holding her sides while she watched his reflection in the glass.

Greg eyed her warily.

Fenella had turned her face away from his kiss, pushing his hands aside and taking up her present defensive position on entering the room a few moments ago.

His heart sank. He had hoped Linda's brief visit would escape notice. Shrugging, he realised he should have known better.

"She was picking up some things she missed when she left." he said, voice deliberately as bland as possible. Seeing how uptight Fenella was, the answer likely boded no good, so he was being careful not to provoke her further.

Fenella, facing his reflected image, had seen the shrug; signifying indifference, she thought.

That, and his bored intonation, brought her hackles up.

"She was here for a lot more than that, though, wasn't she!" Fenella snapped.

"She had plenty to say, too! Although she didn't need to say a word. A naked woman in your bed, all mussed up from lovemaking, is pretty self-evident, don't you think? Flashing that bloody great diamond of yours on her engagement finger, and all. She claimed that the two of you are still lovers. Still engaged and planning to marry sometime in the future. That you meet and make love whenever you're in Sydney, or she's up here visiting friends."

Fenella turned to face Greg, steeling herself to resist his flabbergasted expression.

"What, no comment?" she jeered.

"I've got plenty of comments, Fenella Wilkins," he roared.

"You've always been unreasonably jealous of poor Linda, but this time you've gone too far. Anyone who can go around making up such slanderous stories needs their head examined!"

Restraint thrown to the winds, Fenella entered the lists.

"Do you deny she was here?" Fenella yelled back.

"You know damn well she was here. You saw her. But not in my bed, you didn't; because she was never there. As you very well know."

Breathing heavily, he took a moment to control his raging temper, continuing more moderately.

"Linda hasn't been since we broke up. Broke up, Fenella. For good. She came here today to pick up some stuff she'd left behind when she moved out. And that's all."

Belligerently, Greg stood over Fenella, hands on hips. Fenella's head snapped back as if she'd been struck.

"I know what I saw, and it had nothing to do with left luggage," she retorted, unable to believe he was denying everything. Fenella couldn't see much point in arguing against such recalcitrance, but continued anyway.

"I know what I saw," she reiterated stubbornly.

"You're paranoid, Fenella!" Greg exploded furiously. "You need help."

"Maybe I do," she shouted angrily, holding on by a thread. "I made a big mistake getting involved with another two-faced bastard." She pushed past him, intent on escaping before she broke down.

At the door, she turned back, her hand on the knob.

"I don't want to see you again, Greg Kendall," she declared, her voice breaking as she uttered his name.

"I can't trust you."

Then she was gone.

"And I'm well rid of you, too, Fenella Wilkins," Greg shouted at the closing door.

But if that was true, why did he feel totally eviscerated?

24

"You're looking pretty glum, Old Boy. Anything you care to talk about?"

Jason was more worried than his light manner suggested. When he'd last seen his brother, Greg was on top of the world. Now, he was drawn and abstracted; lost in some dark, inner misery. Even his bright blue Kendall eyes were dulled and grey. He appeared to his brother's discerning eye to be a beaten man.

"Not really,' he muttered dully. "Not your problem."

Jason decided to push a little harder. Someone had to help the poor sod, and it looked as if he'd been elected.

"Mum said you have a good thing going with Fenella Wilkins. Hinted it could become a permanent arrangement any day."

"Then she was being grossly optimistic."

Greg walked away, plainly disinclined to discuss the matter further. But Jason could be tenacious when the occasion warranted. He kept pace with his brother, launching the next broadside a few seconds later.

"You blew it, didn't you?" he accused.

That would explain why Fen was avoiding all the Kendalls. He'd tried to phone her. Receiving no answer, he'd left a message to the effect that he and Rosie would be up on the weekend, and were looking forward to catching up with her. Fenella's answer had been a text message bearing the sketchy information that she'd be away, sorry to miss them. He'd thought at the time it sounded a bit suss.

Greg stubbornly ignored him, so Jason tried a different tack.

"Talk to me, Bro," he pleaded. "Maybe I can intercede with Fen. Help you straighten things out."

"It wouldn't do any good. She won't listen to reason," Greg snarled bitterly.

They had reached the end of the beach, and Jason urged his brother to sit with him on one of the scattered boulders lying half buried in the sand.

"Tell me," he persisted sympathetically.

In dribbles and spurts that built up to a raging torrent, Greg poured out the story of Fenella's lack of faith, her absurd accusations and wild delusions. Through it all, his own bewildered innocence proclaimed itself, convincing Jason that the unlikely tale he was hearing was the truth.

From one perspective, at least. He took his time, sorting through the confusion for cogent facts.

"Okay," he said, satisfied that he understood the problem. "Did you have a go at making up your quarrel with Fen?"

"Of course I did. First up, I phoned Linda to discover what had actually happened that day. Seems Fenella arrived unexpectedly for some reason or other and found Linda getting her things out of the cupboard in the back bedroom."

He turned to his brother to judge whether or not he was being believed. Satisfied, he went on.

"Not *my* bedroom, note, and certainly not naked in my bed as Fenella claimed. Linda said Fenella lost her temper and started abusing her, so she got out as fast as she could and left her to it." Frustrated all over again with the ridiculous story, he ran his fingers through hair already tousled by the stiff onshore breeze.

"I gave Fen time to cool down, then tried to talk some sense into her. Explained that we could sort the whole thing out if she was prepared to be reasonable. Told her there was no need for her to make up exaggerated fantasies. Told her I'd had the truth from Linda."

In his mind Greg replayed that conversation. Something about it, other than the obvious, made him feel uncomfortable, but he couldn't pinpoint what it was. His attempt at reconciliation had gone wrong, right from the first, with Fenella remaining obdurate.

"*I* told you the truth," she had declared. Receiving no answer, she added, "It's up to you which of us you choose to believe."

"Oh, come on, Fenella. How can you expect me to believe such a ridiculous cock-and-bull story? Admit it was all a fabrication so we can put it behind us," he had demanded.

"I thought we had something pretty good going for us," he had added persuasively when she said nothing.

Fenella had met his eyes steadfastly. Silently. Until he had begun to think she'd fallen into a trance. Finally, she looked away.

"Seems you've decided what to believe already," she said, quite calmly. Dismayed, he realised she had been waiting for him to say he believed *her*.

Only he didn't. How could he? It was a stupid pack of jealous lies aimed at destroying his friendship with Linda.

"I guess there's nothing more to say," Fenella had told him. Then turned and walked away.

"Fenella!" He had called after her, appalled to think that what they'd shared could be so easily dismissed.

Fenella had never looked back.

Remembering, Greg poured out his pain and confusion to his brother.

"I love her, Jase." Greg turned desperately unhappy eyes towards his brother.

"I didn't think I'd ever love anyone again. Didn't want to after the way I keep on messing up my relationships. But it crept up on me so that I didn't know I loved her till it was all over. I still can't believe she could do that to us. She won't even talk to me anymore."

Jason studied him curiously, considering his words carefully.

"I've always believed trust was an important aspect of love," he began obliquely.

"Same here," Greg muttered. "Only Fenella didn't trust me, did she? She even said so to my face."

"Nooo, apparently not," Jason agreed slowly, "but when it came down to it, you didn't trust her very far, either, did you?"

His words pulled Greg up short.

Jason pressed home his advantage. "Think about it, Greg. Fenella begged you to believe her. I know her story was outlandish, but ask yourself; what did she have to gain by it? Why would she make up such a story?"

"But, if Fenella wasn't lying ..." Greg wondered aloud.

"Then Linda was," Jason finished for him. "For sure one of them was lying, and I know which woman I'm more inclined to believe. Which one I trust."

Each with much to consider, they returned to the house in silence.

✶✶✶✶✶

The subject of Fenella Wilkins was shelved until after dinner that evening. When Greg rejoined Jason and Rosemary after seeing Aimee to bed, it was obvious the two of them had been discussing weighty matters.

"I've not told Rosie any of what you told me, except that you and Fen have had a falling out," Jason assured his brother.

"There's a story I want Rosie to tell you, one she's not at all eager to repeat. I've insisted, because I believe it's something you need to know."

He was earnestly compelling, so Greg nodded, turning expectantly to the apprehensive young woman clinging to Jason's hand.

"I'm listening," he prompted gently.

"I don't like telling you this," Rosemary's liquid brown eyes begged forgiveness in advance. "I'll be as brief as possible. You know where my parents live?"

Greg nodded. He had visited the Parish's home in Woollahra with Jason.

Rosemary spoke quickly, getting her unpleasant task over with.

"Martin Wallace is a neighbour of theirs. Mum knows Mrs Wallace quite well. Shortly after Christmas he started cheating on his wife with a younger woman. Mum put it down to a male mid-life crisis, but I just think he's a creep. Mrs Wallace told Mum he admitted to her that the affair started in February, while she was visiting their daughter in Melbourne."

She raised her eyes to glance across at Greg. Seeing he was listening attentively, she ploughed on.

"The affair is over now, and his wife's taken him back, not that he deserves it! Anyway, Mum saw him with this other woman, acting like a randy old goat, and her encouraging him all the way. That was in early March, while the affair was still going strong."

Rosemary's hands were twisting together in her lap, and she glanced nervously at Greg once again.

"She recognised the woman and pointed her out to me later in an ad on television. Mum didn't know who she was, but I did. It was Linda Beck." Rosemary kept her eyes discretely lowered.

"February and March, Greg," Jason hammered home the dates in case his brother had missed their significance. "Linda was cheating on you way back then. She was having an affair with Martin Wallace while she was still engaged to you."

Greg winced.

He'd worked that much out for himself.

Jason continued, making sure Greg couldn't sweep this information under the carpet as he had done in the past regarding Linda's inadequacies.

"It's my belief she latched onto you, thinking a successful novelist with a book being made into a film, would be a useful meal ticket; possibly a stepping stone to the acting career she used to talk about all the time. Then she used poor little Aimee to wangle a proposal out of you, pretending to be all love and concern for the motherless babe." Jason had the bit between his teeth and was pouring out his long-suppressed disgust and dislike for Linda Beck. Maybe now his brother was ready to listen to a few salient facts.

"Then you upped and turned your back on the Sydney scene. She didn't like it much up here, did she? No entertainment. Just you and the kid and the housekeeping. Another sucker turned up; Martin Wallace, who could do more for her career than you. Wallace used his influence to get her the inside running with that advertising company, didn't he? Now I hear she's landed a part in some soapie. Guess she dropped him when she found a more influential target."

"It's all old news now." Greg ran a weary hand through his hair. "I do realise why you wanted me to hear it, though." He mulled it over a while, the other two waiting silently.

"To throw your own question back at you, Jason," he said, "what would she have to gain if Fenella was telling the truth? That is what you're inferring with all this, aren't you?"

He waited, anticipating Jason's answer, pretty sure what it would be. His mind racing, a sick feeling invading his stomach, he was beginning to view various incidents from the past in an entirely new light.

Since his earlier talk with Jason he had already begun questioning some of his past judgements. This revelation of his ex-fiancée's duplicity accelerated the process.

"Revenge." Jason had no hesitation in arriving at a viable explanation.

"You know, woman scorned and all that. She had it in for Fen from day one. Which reminds me," he snapped his fingers. "You said something about Fen raving on about Linda's engagement ring."

"Yes. Fenella said Linda was wearing it on her left hand at the premiere, and also when ..."

Greg cast a shamefaced glance towards Rosemary and rephrased his words.

"When she saw her here at the house. I've tried to recall it, but I never take any notice of those sort of details."

"Me either. Not something we males are particularly interested in, is it? Rosie, can you recall it? Fenella only saw the photo in the paper, remember."

Rosemary stood, assuming the same posture Linda had adopted for the photographer, her left hand raised as Linda's had been.

"Yes! Look, it was her left hand on your chest, Greg, and she was definitely wearing a flashy ring on it. The girls in the office were talking about it."

"When I told her to keep it, I suggested she wear it as a dress ring," Greg commented thoughtfully.

"Bet she swaps it around for effect whenever it suits her." Jason got in that one last dig before the subject was dropped, leaving Greg with a great deal of food for thought.

25

Her lover did not believe her.

Did not trust her.

His loyalty and trust, and his love as well, still belonged to his ex-fiancée, Linda Beck.

Sustained by an unyielding determination not to bow under this fresh blow from an inimical fate, Fenella Wilkins had held her head high, and walked away from her faithless lover; unrelenting when he called after her. As the distance between herself and Greg Kendall lengthened, she fiercely blinked back tears.

Tears were a weakness she couldn't afford.

I made a mistake. I've corrected it. I go on, she told herself, repeating it over and over; a mantra powerful enough to dam the pain of a love that had failed, preventing its acid from eating into her soul and destroying her.

Last time she had been tested by fate, she had collapsed under the strain, but not this time, she vowed. She had learned to be strong.

To be a survivor.

Fenella had occasion to remind herself of these facts numerous times in the days and weeks that followed her rejection of Greg Kendall.

My decision. My choice, she lectured herself whenever her resolution wavered. Peculiarly enough, it was this affirmation that it was herself, Fenella Wilkins; and neither blind fate, nor any other person, who controlled her decisions, which became her greatest source of strength.

Work filled all her waking hours, a barrier between herself and her painful thoughts. When there were no more lessons to prepare or books to mark, her easel waited. As the term dwindled to a close, painting became her solace. Her refuge. And the raw emotion she refused to acknowledge anywhere else gave power to her paintings. John Remington was so pleased with them he had settled on a firm date for her promised exhibition.

Since this disaster had been self-inflicted, Fenella preferred not to burden anyone else with her troubles. Stoically, she struggled on alone, determined to win through by her own efforts.

When Jason phoned, she was tempted to confide in him, sure he would understand and be generous with his support.

Regretfully, Fenella knew she couldn't ask it of him.

To do so would be tantamount to asking him to choose between herself and his brother. Instead, she took the discretionary option of absenting herself for the duration of his visit.

During the week following, there were three messages left on her answering machine. All from Greg Kendall.

After the first – "Fenella, this is Greg. I need to talk with you. Call me to arrange a meeting." - which she missed accidentally, Fenella let the machine pick up, ascertaining her callers' identities before answering.

The second call came the next morning, early. "Fenella, Greg again. This is important. Please answer." *Important to whom?* She couldn't imagine anything new he might want to say, and she couldn't stand the thought of rehashing their last argument all over again.

Besides, she wasn't sure she was strong enough yet for a face-to-face with him.

The mere thought was a knife, twisting in her gut. Mercifully, since their break-up, Greg had not intruded on her peace at school; thus this meeting he wanted would be their first.

Fenella packed a bag and fled.

A few hours for consideration was sufficient to convince her of the foolishness of flight.

Sooner or later, they must meet. Topaz Sands was where they both lived and worked, and it was a small place. However, it was the spring break, so she needn't rush back for work.

Fenella took her time, relaxing in the protective bosom of her family, examining the events leading to the demise of her ill-starred affair.

If Greg's request had anything to do with this, then she'd be prepared. If not, she could only benefit from confronting her agony and coming to terms with it.

That achieved, there was no point in deferring the inevitable any longer.

Checking on her return, Fenella discovered the third of Greg's messages. "Fenella. Greg again. It's imperative we talk. You can't hide forever, Fenella. I'll be waiting."

Driving down the main street just now, Fenella had exchanged waves with Susan Kendall and Aimee. If Greg was home, he'd shortly know she was back. Courage high, she decided to forestall him.

Picking up the phone she slowly dialled Greg's number.

What a let-down! Fenella slumped into the phone chair, gathering her scattered wits after talking to Susan Kendall.

"I'm so glad you called, Fen dear. I know Greg's been trying to catch you. When he gets in, I'll tell him you called." Susan had continued chattering about inconsequential nothings for several minutes before hanging up.

Fenella fended off an invitation to afternoon tea with the excuse that she had only just walked through the door and was too busy. She shuddered at the thought of Greg walking in to find her drinking tea with his mother.

Until she knew what he wanted, she didn't feel up to socialising with any of his family.

Unable to settle, Fenella fidgeted restlessly from one make-work task to another, remaining within easy reach of the phone.

The afternoon storm which had swept in unexpectedly from the Tasman Sea, raging up the coast, exactly suited her mood.

Fenella stood at her window, watching the breakers clawing at the beach in their fury, until it was too dark to see more than a phosphorescent gleam surging back and forth.

Drawing the curtains and turning on the television for the news, she listened half-heartedly to reports of a number of small boats which had experienced difficulties during the storm. Even with the sophisticated monitoring devices used by the meteorological department, freak storms, such as today's, could still catch everyone unawares, the weatherman explained, pointing to his charts.

The seas were still running high, even though the wind had abated somewhat. Peeking through her curtains, Fenella saw the rain had stopped and stars were appearing through rifts in the cloud mass. It would probably be fine in the morning.

"Is Greg messing me about?" she asked Zilla, impatiently glancing towards the phone. "Wish I'd had the presence of mind to ask Susan when she expected him back."

She didn't know whether to have an early night or wait up to hear from him. When the phone rang, she pounced on it, relieved the waiting was at an end.

"Oh Fenella," whimpered not Greg, but a distraught Susan Kendall. "I don't know what to do. Can you come? I'm so frightened."

"Tell me what's wrong, Susan," Fenella begged, a foreboding chill sending shivers down her spine.

"It's Peter and Greg, Fenella. They went on an overnight fishing trip yesterday and haven't come back. They're hours overdue, and on the news, it said a boat was sunk in that storm."

Fenella could hear the other woman gulping back sobs.

"I don't know what to do," she reiterated, her voice rising in panic.

Fenella, an icy chill taking her breath away, felt near to panic herself, but someone had to stand firm.

"Sit tight, Susan. I'll be right there," Fenella promised. "We'll see this through together."

Fenella was backing her car out, this crisis being too urgent to waste time walking along the beach, when she slammed the brakes on and raced back inside.

There was no need to sit helplessly waiting for news to come to them, she thought, grabbing her address book. She knew quite a few people among the coastguard volunteers, who might be easier to get information from than the official sources.

Minutes later when she walked through the door of Greg's house, Susan flung herself into her arms, choking back tears.

"We might be worrying ourselves sick over nothing," she said, attempting to ease her friend's fears. "Maybe they put in somewhere sheltered to sit out the storm and will come walking in the door any minute."

"Do you really think so?" Susan's eyes strayed to the phone, silently pointing out the flaw in such hopeful reasoning.

If the men were safe, why didn't they call?

If there was no phone handy, they could radio the police or Maritime Rescue to relay a message. Another quick glance at Susan showed her the older woman was close to the edge.

"Let's phone the Maritime Rescue ourselves," she said, pulling her phone out of her pocket.

Susan sighed with relief.

"Are they fishing alone, or with someone else?" Fenella asked quickly. "I'll need to know the name of their boat when I ask for news," she said.

"They're with Matt Sykes, only I don't know the name of his boat."

"It's the *Osprey*. Everyone knows Matt," Fenella said, her matter-of-fact voice offering comfort. She reached out to clasp the other woman's hand while she spoke to the Maritime Rescue officer.

Susan was unable to follow the conversation, Fenella's responses being largely non-committal once she had given the relevant details. She ended by quoting their phone number and giving her thanks to the person she'd been speaking to.

Her brow wrinkled apprehensively, Susan sighed again when she saw Fenella's smile.

"It's not all bad. It was the *Osprey* that went down, just as you feared, but Matt was able to radio for help before it did."

She essayed a cheerful smile, but it didn't quite come off.

"He said the engine had packed it in and the boat was being driven onto the rocks. They were making for Broughton Island to sit out the storm when it happened. He said they intended to use the dinghy with its outboard motor to get ashore onto the island. Now that the storm's over, a boat has already been diverted to pick them up."

"If they made it. Oh, Fenella, what if the dinghy was swamped? Peter could be drowned. And Greg." Susan refused to be comforted.

Until their safety was confirmed, she would continue to fear for her menfolk.

"We should know soon," Fenella soothed. "They'll ring back as soon as they hear. They would have called earlier, except that they didn't know who was with Matt. Only that he wasn't alone. Let's have a cuppa while we wait, shall we Susan."

The two women had drunk the pot dry before the promised call eventuated. When it did, it was good news.

The best.

26

Hanging up the phone, Fenella smiled radiantly through the tears she was finally allowing to flow now the crisis was almost over.

"They've been picked up, all three of them safe and well, and they're being taken to Tea Gardens by the Water Police," Fenella announced joyfully.

"By the time you arrive to collect them, they should be there," she added, intending to offer to stay with the blissfully sleeping Aimee, whom Susan had tucked into bed, all unaware of the threatened tragedy, before calling Fenella.

Noting Susan's shaking hands, she changed her mind. Susan was in no condition to drive. She was a bit shaky herself. Not too shaky to fetch the men home, though.

"Bundle Aimee up warmly, and I'll drive you," she offered. "Throw in some blankets, and dry clothes, too. For Matt as well. We don't know what state they're in."

It was a long night, one that neither Fenella nor Susan would ever forget.

With Aimee awake now, drowsily fretful on the back seat, they sped south, arriving in Tea Gardens in time to see the Police Rescue boat cruising up the Myall River to the wharf.

Susan flew out of the car, flinging herself into her husband's arms as the men stepped ashore. Aimee followed, crying out to her father, who scooped her up in his arms, burying his face against her warmth. Silent tears streaked his face when he lifted his head, his mouth opening in surprise to see Fenella standing by his parents' car.

"Fenella!' Greg shouted, long legs closing the distance between them in a handful of strides.

Aimee squashed between them, he crushed her against his chest, his mouth descending to claim a kiss that left Fenella's senses whirling.

It was a while before they could leave, what with thanking their rescuers, and changing into dry clothes.

Throughout this time, Greg held his daughter on one shoulder, and kept Fenella pressed tightly against his other side, except for the few seconds it took him to change, after which he gathered them to him again.

Finally, they were able to begin their homeward journey, Aimee strapped into the fold down seat in the back, while Greg took the front passenger seat next to Fenella.

The older Kendalls, huddled close in each other's arms, shared the back seat with an exhausted Matt Sykes. Back in Topaz Sands, Fenella drove Matt to his front door first, then delivered the Kendalls home before transferring from their large four-wheel-drive and heading home to her own snug cottage.

Greg had ducked his head awkwardly through the driver's window to kiss her goodnight, balancing his daughter on his hip.

"I love you Fenella Wilkins," he had whispered, for her ears alone. "Expect me on your doorstep in the morning."

✶✶✶✶✶

Sunlight streaming through curtains inadvertently left open the night before, slanted tiger stripes across Fenella's face. Squinting against the glare, she rolled over to read the time.

"Seven thirty," she groaned, realising she had slept much later than usual. A toe-tingling stretch brought her fully awake. Memories of the turmoil of the night before came flooding into her mind. No wonder she'd slept late. It had been close to dawn before she made it to bed.

Reliving the events, she recalled the night's interesting ending, excitement sizzling along her nerve endings impelling her to rise and embrace the day.

And whatever it might bring.

Sitting up in bed, Fenella wrapped her arms around her shins, chin resting on her knees.

A dreamy, introspective smile lit her face while she contemplated the import of Greg Kendall's words and actions of the previous night.

An exercise that dimmed her exuberance a trifle.

Gathering Zilla into her arms she put her concern into words, directing them into her pet's sympathetic ears.

"He needn't think he can flimflam me with a couple of kisses and three little words. Even if they are the right three words at last, we've still got a lot of issues to sort out, and I don't know if we can." She frowned, contemplating those issues. "For now, all I can do is see where this takes us."

She put Zilla down and climbed out of bed, heading to the bathroom for a quick shower. "I know exactly where I want it to take us," she continued aloud, "Have done for ages. Here's hoping Greg wants the same. If only he does, surely we can sort out all the rest."

Too full of energy to wait patiently, Fenella fed Zilla, made her bed and began tidying up in her studio, unearthing her sea god who'd long ago been relegated to the back of a stack of unused canvases.

She'd been strangely shy of sharing him with his alter ego, and since she'd given Greg his marching orders, hadn't been able to cope with seeing his painted image every day, and had left it hidden away. Now it no longer mattered. Either way. This painting was still one of her best, and deserved its place of honour.

It was the work of moments to swap him back into his place above her bed.

Whether Greg ever shared her bed again or not, her sea god was too special to languish in hiding.

She stood back, comparing the two in her mind, her lips twitching into a rueful smile. Poseidon may be a god, she thought, but Greg Kendall is only a man; with all a man's faults. A man with feet of clay.

A run would have suited her restless mood, except that when Greg arrived she wanted to be sure of looking presentable for once; not sweaty and wind-blown. She laughed at herself.

Since when did Fenella Wilkins put herself out to impress a man?

Since Greg Kendall told me he loves me, she answered herself, peering dubiously into the mirror, studying the dark smudges under her eyes; products of too many sleepless nights recently.

Wearing her favourite denim shorts and yellow sleeveless knit top, she brushed her hair out loosely, holding it back with mother-of-pearl slides. A tinted moisturiser and copper lip gloss were sufficient make-up. She didn't want to overdo it.

Slipping her feet into flat leather sandals, she went to look again, even though she knew she was still alone. Zilla would let her know when Greg arrived.

Her smile faded, replaced by stern decision. This was her chance to set the record straight between herself and Greg.

And this time she wouldn't blow it by being a coward.

The coffee percolator had finished its work, so, pouring herself a cup, Fenella took it to the porch and settled in her favourite chair.

To wait.

Greg found her there a short while later. Bounding up the stairs he strode forward, arms outstretched. It was obviously his intention to greet Fenella with a kiss.

Adroitly side stepping, she dodged, Greg ending up with his hands round her mug of coffee instead. He grinned to himself as, without a word, she stepped inside to fetch another coffee.

Round one to Fenella, he conceded.

He supposed it had been too much to hope that his difficult darling would fall into his arms so easily. Biding his time, he made himself comfortable.

"A bit early, aren't you," she asked, choosing to conveniently forget her own impatience.

Putting the fresh coffee in front of him, she took back her own, seating herself opposite, where she could keep him under close observation while they talked.

"Couldn't sleep," he replied, flashing her one of his best smiles. "Too excited about being back on speaking terms with you, Fen."

Fenella compressed her lips, shooting a quelling look at him from beneath lowered lashes.

"Stop that right now, Fenella," Greg countered, his voice calm, but firm.

"Don't even try to pretend nothing's changed between us. Not after the way you kissed me back last night."

He waited for her to look him in the face, taking in her set expression. More gently, he stated once again, "I love you, Fenella Wilkins."

Fenella's expression eased slightly, although it remained non-committal.

"When did you reach that conclusion?" Feigning disinterest in both the question and its answer, she let her gaze wander out across the waves, as if they held greater interest for her than his answer.

"I probably fell in love with you months ago." Greg also feigned disinterest, serving some of her own medicine back to Fenella. He was beginning to enjoy this battle of wits.

"I'm a stubborn bugger though," he admitted, "so it wasn't until a short time ago I finally admitted it to myself."

Dropping the pretence, he snared Fenella's eyes with his own. "With all your shilly-shallying Fenella, there was a time yesterday when I thought I might never get the chance to tell you. You've no idea what it meant to me last night, to look up and see you standing there."

Greg's words and manner were imbued with a sincerity that overrode Fenella's carefully cultivated scepticism.

"Your mother thought you were dead," Fenella told him, a remnant of stark fear colouring her flat tone. "You and your father. For a moment there, when I heard the *Osprey* had sunk, I thought so too."

She took a deep breath and continued.

"Until I was told Matt planned to use the dinghy to make his way to safety."

Warmth edged out the cold dread that had gripped her, remembering that terrible moment. The crinkling at the corners of her eyes was the only sign of amusement, as she shared her relief with Greg.

"Matt keeps a pair of oars in his dinghy. I knew that you'd reach a safe haven, because if the outboard failed as well, he'd have you rowing. That great body of yours would be put to good use."

A warm chuckle greeted this sally.

"So you think I've got a great body, do you Fenella?" Greg purred seductively. "I can think of a few other, very pleasant uses we could put it to."

Fenella glared, and he chuckled again.

"I was referring to your size," she muttered, attempting to sound scathing, but only succeeding in sounding sulky.

"Oh, size," he murmured, leaning closer. "If size is important, I'm sure I can satisfy you." This time Greg's challenging grin was positively wicked.

Fenella thumped down her coffee mug, the contents sloshing onto the table. For a brief moment her annoyance showed, until she wrestled her emotions back under iron-fisted control.

Truth to tell, she would normally have enjoyed this exchange of double entendres, enthusiastically attempting to top Greg's quips.

Not this morning, though. Not with her whole life at stake.

"You said on the phone you wanted to talk," she reminded him, fixing her gaze on the middle distance.

"I'm listening."

Greg sat back, studiously composing his mobile features into a serious mode. It was to be business first.

Fenella was right, it was of the utmost importance they clear up all the misunderstandings that had driven them apart. After that...

"I've already told you the most important bit," he began. "I love you."

The words came more easily each time he said them.

"The trouble was, I'd sworn off love. Told myself I didn't believe in it."

He grimaced, then, squaring his shoulders, got the rest of his explanation out before he lost his courage.

"From past experience I felt a complete and utter failure when it came to a real emotional commitment, to love, so I deluded myself into thinking I was incapable of loving. You know something, Fen?" He swung round to face her again.

"I've discovered I have a real talent for self-deception. First, I brainwashed myself into believing Linda really was the sweet, kind, loyal helpmate she purported to be; then this rubbish about being immune to love. Stupid, huh?"

He checked for audience reaction. Fenella was raptly absorbing his every word. Encouraged, he went on with his confession.

"I was more relieved than anything when she finally gave me just cause to break that damned engagement; only she beat me to it. All pitiful regret that she wasn't equal to the task, even though she loved me, and Aimee, and always would. She made me feel guilty Fenella. I thought I owed her something, so I agreed to remain friends."

He recalled one of Fenella's sore points and hastened to address it next. "Our occasional meetings in Sydney were all instigated by her, you know. I agreed to them because I felt guilty for not loving her as I thought she deserved."

He glanced up, noting Fenella's expression now held a touch of frost. Sighing, Greg forced himself to persevere with this truly difficult task of baring his soul.

"There never was anything between Linda and myself after we broke up. However, at that time I was blind to her true nature. Still believed in the woman I thought she was. That was why I simply couldn't credit it when you told me what she'd done to you. To do so would have exposed as a lie so much I believed true. About myself as well as Linda. I wasn't with her, Fenella. Not that day or any other."

Greg's whole life was on the line now, as he put heart and soul into his plea.

"Please Fenella, you've got to believe me."

Fenella studied him impassively, gauging his sincerity. Deeming his words completely true, she relented enough to relieve his anxiety.

"I figured that out almost immediately," she said, ignoring his surprised gasp. "As soon as the shock wore off, I realised I'd been set up by an expert."

"Then why did you walk out on me?" Greg was astounded. If Fenella knew he was innocent, then why ...?

"I didn't know about the other times, in Sydney, did I? After what my ex-husband put me through, Greg, I was pre-disposed to suspect the worst."

Fenella choked back a sob. This was not the time to break down in tears.

"Linda told me I was no more to you than a convenient bed warmer and child minder. The facts as I knew them bore that out."

She frowned, remembering the pain this man had put her through. It was past time he learnt full extent of what he'd done to her.

"You never said, back then, that you loved me. You never took me out without Aimee in tow. Never suggested taking me to Sydney to meet your friends. When I thought about it, I felt miserably second rate. Unimportant to you except as the afore-mentioned bed warmer and child-minder."

A quiver shook her voice, forcing her to take a second or two to collect herself.

Greg's expression of utter horror bolstered her courage.

"It didn't matter so much at the time, but later, after she'd infected my mind with her poison, it rankled. On top of all that, you thought I was an hysterical ratbag." She sipped at her coffee, bolstering her resolution.

"I knew my story sounded incredible, but your choosing to believe Linda over me was the last straw. To have remained your lover after that would have meant total self-degradation. For the sake of my sanity and self-esteem, I had to make a clean break. It hurt like hell, Greg, because I've loved *you* from the very beginning."

A choked cry breaking from his lips, Greg reached for Fenella's hand.

Having her snatch it back was akin to a slap in the face. Never in his wildest imaginings, had Greg thought he had hurt Fenella so deeply.

So irreparably?

God, he hoped not.

"After you left me, Fenella," he forced through white, shock-stiffened lips, "it seemed my life spun out of control. I was utterly miserable. More so when I realised I had grown to love you. That's when I began to question my take on events. Finally discovering the truth regarding Linda's deceitfulness snapped everything into clear focus. I'm sorry Fenella. I never meant to hurt you, but I let my damnable temper get in the way of the truth."

Greg sat motionless, desperately craving words of forgiveness that never came.

Defeated, he heaved himself to his feet and trod heavily to the exit, too sick at heart to so much as glance sideways where he might be forced to read Fenella's rejection on her face.

Greg was leaving!

It wasn't supposed to end like this! Fenella's mind reeled. She couldn't just let Greg go. Not now, when they were so close to putting the past behind them and starting anew.

He was almost at the gate!

Clutching frantically at straws, she offered further encouragement, practically shouting at him in her urgency.

"Is that it then, Greg Kendall?" she shouted after him. "Was clearing your conscience all you came for?"

Greg halted at her first word, listening intently. He paused, one hand on the gate, turning slowly back to face her again.

Fenella moderated her tone to something approaching a cajoling purr.

"I hoped you might conceivably have had some other purpose in mind. One that included me, but all you've done is selfishly fulfil your own needs."

With bated breath, she watched him bound back up the three steps onto her porch.

"You really want your pound of flesh, don't you Fenella?" Deeply etched pain was erased like magic from his beloved face.

"Well I won't deny you. Yes, I had another purpose in mind alright. I came this morning, intending to ask you to marry me, because without you my life is incomplete. I'm incomplete."

He was breathing heavily by the time he ground to a halt. Fenella stared, open-mouthed.

"Nothing to say, Fenella? I thought you'd be gloating, seeing me abasing myself before you."

"Yes!" Fenella screeched. "There's plenty I could say, but one word's enough. YES! Yes! Yes! Yes!"

Fenella was standing now, nose to nose, toe to toe with Greg, pent up emotion spewing forth in a tidal wave.

Fists drumming against his chest, she collapsed against him, her one-word refrain repeated over and over through a flood of cleansing tears.

A shudder racking his frame, Greg gathered her into his arms, soothing her.

Kissing her

Fenella's arms crept around his neck as she sniffed back the last of her tears. Lifting herself on tiptoe, she gave him back kiss for desperate kiss, until the terrible fear seeped away, leaving only passion.

Long minutes later, Greg, cautiously jubilant, dragged his lips from Fenella's.

"What were you shouting 'yes' to, Fenella?" he asked, sober and sternly implacable.

Fenella stared blankly, till, wits working again, she had the most recent sequence of events sorted into order. Her lips quirked into a pseudo-innocent smile.

"What was your question, Greg, darling?" she inquired sweetly, her fingers tracking stealthily up and down his spine.

Greg threw back his head, a great shout of laughter half deafening Fenella.

"I do love you, Fenella Wilkins," he said, repeating the words Fenella would never tire of hearing. He dropped a quick kiss onto her upturned mouth.

"Now listen carefully, woman, while I ask you properly. And make sure you give me the right answer."

He paused for dramatic effect, earning himself a not so gentle thump from his impatient love.

"Fenella Anne Wilkins, will you marry me, to be my wife till death do us part?"

Fenella thought about teasing him further, changing her mind immediately.

"Yes," she answered solemnly. "Yes, I will marry you, Gregory Richard Kendall. To have and to hold forever."

"YES!" he shouted.

Whirling her round and round until, almost too dizzy to stand, he fell into his chair, Fenella in his lap, he proceeded to kiss her into willing submission.

Some considerable time later, he whispered slyly.

"Fenella, I feel awfully tired. Would you let me take a nap on your bed?"

"Oh, my poor darling," Fenella giggled. "You go right on in and lie down. I'll sit quietly out here and make sure you're not disturbed."

Greg assumed a pathetic hangdog expression that fell short of being wholly convincing.

"I'd rest more easily if you came and lay down beside me, Fenella darling," he pleaded hopefully.

This time Fenella simply took him by the hand and led him to her bed, pausing briefly to lock the front door behind them. It was a long time before either of them slept.

THE END

I hope you enjoyed reading *Loving Fenella.*

Please turn the page for a preview of Lena West's new Australian Historical Romance, *Unto Death.*

Here is Your Preview of
Unto Death

An Australian Historical Romance

LENA WEST

1

"Damn it all Stephen! Don't you turn your back on me! I'm your father, and the very least you owe me is the courtesy of listening while I try to instil a little common sense into your thick skull!" Thomas Fortescue's face, already beyond red, edged towards an alarming puce, the blood thundering through his veins.

"Stop shouting at me Dad! I'm no longer a child you can order around." Stephen, red-faced and equally furious, stomach roiling, took a deep breath, firming his grip on his own flaring temper. God only knew how much he loathed angry confrontations. Usually he found a way to avoid them, and wished it were possible now. Fighting with his father, whom he respected and loved deeply, would achieve nothing but grief; for them both. He strove for a more conciliatory tone when he continued.

"I'm a man now, Dad; and I have a man's right to live my life the way I choose. A man's right to make my own decisions; even if they don't meet with your august approval."

Gritting his teeth, he glared defiance, determined, somehow, to have his way in this, the most important argument of his life.

"Alright!" Stung by the unaccustomed lash of his son's anger, Thomas, hand pressed against tightly closed eyes, inhaled slowly, holding the breath till his unaccustomed excess of temper was safely reined in. He waited a moment longer, until the blood pounding within his head slowed and he once again felt himself capable of civil speech. "Alright, Stephen. I'm sorry I shouted at you. But even though you're grown, a man as you say," - although whether any youngster of twenty-one years had sufficient maturity to be classed a man, he'd take leave to doubt – "you're still my son. I care deeply about you, Stephen. I always will; and when I see you making a grave mistake I can't help trying to set you right."

"You only think I'm making a mistake because you're old. You've forgotten what it is to love." This was dangerous ground; the weak point in his argument. As Stephen very well knew, he was trespassing against all the rules of civilised society, and the uncomfortable position of knowing himself to be in the wrong had led him to lash out in retaliation.

"Stephen!" Thomas recoiled from the venom in his son's voice. Turning to hide his pain, he leant his forehead against the cool glass of the window.

He needed to set the boy straight, that was irrefutable, but he'd back down for now rather than destroy completely their formerly close relationship. Grimacing, he rubbed a callused palm over his chest where sudden pain warned him to go easy.

Taking another deep breath, he further calmed himself before once more facing his son; this time deliberately employing a soothing, semi-jocular tone.

"I will admit to being past my first youth, Stephen, but I'm yet a long way from my dotage. And son," he allowed the naked grief he still felt when thinking of his beloved wife's early death to show on his usually impassive face, "I loved your mother. With all my heart and soul. Our love for each other is the one thing I'll never forget. Never. My last promise to Georgiana was to take the very best care of you. Always. So please, can we sit down and talk this over like rational men?"

Thomas spent a long moment lost in thought, remembering the plans he and Georgie had made. His years in India with the army had been well spent. Through judicious business deals he'd successfully parlayed a comfortable inheritance into a sizeable fortune. Stephen, their first-born, was never meant to be an only child.

Their intention had been to establish a dynasty. Arriving in New South Wales in 1838, newly married and with a child on the way, he'd bought 'Eden Vale', one of the largest properties in this region, to become his family seat. With Georgie at his side they had built it into the highly profitable estate, producing grain, fruit, wool and prime beef, it now was. As well, he had his fingers in quite a few other profitable colonial pies. After Georgie's death, all his hopes for the future became centred on his only child, Stephen, and the grandchildren he anticipated. Now, in 1860, with Stephen of marriageable age, those hopes had seemed near to fruition.

Until the extremely undesirable liaison the boy had recently formed placed this dream for the future in jeopardy.

Thomas gave himself a shake. Now was not the time for introspection, he had a crisis on his hands; one in which he was terribly afraid he might fail. But oh, how he wished Georgie, with her wise counsel, was at his side today.

A quick glance informed him his son had lost the bitter, angry expression which had struck fear into his heart. He breathed a little easier. "Son, I was wrong to lose my temper and start shouting. I promise to listen to your arguments if you'll listen to mine. All decisions will then be up to you." A silent prayer that common sense would prevail accompanied his words.

Stephen relaxed as the tension in the room abated. That sounded fair enough. Maybe his father wasn't as hide-bound as he'd thought.

Stomach settling, he nodded agreement and flung himself into his accustomed armchair to the left of the library fireplace. Truth be told, he was ashamed of his childish outburst. How could he expect the Old Man to take him seriously if his behaviour mimicked the tantrums of a spoiled brat? Which he'd never been permitted to become. From his earliest years he'd been trained to the responsibilities of his position, his father even going so far as to make him work alongside the men, learning how to do every single task necessary to the successful running of 'Eden Vale'.

At the same time, Stephen was desperately serious in his love for Isabella Cummings, in spite of the seemingly insurmountable obstacles in their way. Never having fallen in love before, his first glimpse of Isabella's ripe, sultry beauty had struck at his heart; a thunderbolt aimed by a particularly mischievous god.

The heart-stopping intensity of his emotions in that moment had swept him off his feet; and, although he would be the last to admit it, swept away every vestige of common sense he possessed. His whole concept of right and wrong had been turned on end and cast to the wind. And due to the necessarily secretive nature of the affair, he'd been unable to confide in anyone. The guidance afforded by his father's sage counsel had been sorely missed.

Disposed, therefore, to meet his father half-way, he hoped Thomas could steer him towards an acceptable solution to his present dilemma. Provided the solution was one which would grant him his heart's desire.

He didn't really hold out a great deal of hope, though. His father's social mores were too rigid, too old-fashioned, to allow his father to accept a forbidden love such as the one he and Isabella shared.

Thomas, breathing in the cleansing, aromatic scent of eucalyptus, let his gaze linger briefly on the gleaming brass ewer of fresh, purplish gum tips which presently filled the hearth; a tribute to the paucity of flowers now there was no woman of the house to take any trouble over the gardens. There had been no-one, he thought sadly, to care about such matters since his wife's death thirteen years earlier, but he still remembered the riot of colour surrounding the house during her lifetime.

With a wary, sidelong glance, he seated himself rather more erectly opposite his son.

"You first." Seemingly casual, Stephen waved his hand in his father's direction. "I'm listening."

Another deep, calming breath. It was essential to Thomas that he remain in control of himself, not least for the state of his health. His boy, his only child and the light of his life, was on a runaway course bound for certain disaster; and he didn't know if he could steer him to safety. Blinded by the worst kind of hopeless, romantic infatuation as the boy was, Thomas was afraid there were no more arguments he could advance which had the slightest hope of impinging on the boy's damned, pigheaded determination; a trait inherited from himself, he acknowledged with a rueful shake of his head.

"I blame myself, you know," he began, honestly believing he deserved the lion's share of the blame for the perilous situation his son was in. "It was selfish of me to keep you here by my side. Instead of hiring a tutor, I should have sent you off to school, then university. I've denied you exposure to the wider world, leaving you far too inexperienced; too vulnerable. Most young men of our class leave home for a time to learn the ways of the world and sow their wild oats. Only I couldn't bear to be parted from you, Son. Following your mother's death, you were all I had in the world, and foolishly, I clung to you too long."

"Stop flagellating yourself, Dad."

A tiny hint of sympathy crept into Stephen's voice. His next words carried no such softer tones.

"Although really, no amount of worldly experience would have made any difference to my feelings for Isabella." Stephen was adamant on this point, and didn't miss his father's wince on hearing the unwelcome words.

Besides, he did have the kind of experience his father was surely referring to.

He had fond memories of several visits to a certain Newcastle house of ill repute in the company of his best friend, Adam Merton, who worked for an import company in the busy port. Since he was nine years old he had accompanied his father when he visited his friend and financial advisor, Peter Gordon, who lived in Morpeth, close to the busy port of Newcastle. In the last year or two he'd often gone alone with the men taking their produce down to the port to be shipped to Sydney, and had made the most of these excursions away from his father's watchful eye.

"That may be so," Thomas replied. "However, with wider experience you would have dealt with this situation more maturely."

Thomas caught a glimpse of Stephen's lips tightening, imminent mutiny once again casting a frowning darkness across his son's handsome countenance.

"But you're right; enough of pointless recriminations. Apart from all other considerations though, Stephen, predominant among them the marked difference in your ages, the unpalatable truth is, Isabella Cummings is a married woman! She's not for *you*, Son. How can she be? How can loving her hold any viable future? For either of you? In pursuing Isabella Cummings, you not only court disaster; you're doing her a great disservice. You will both earn the severest censure from society. Both of you will become outcasts, but the brunt of the blame will be visited upon her. Surely you don't want to expose her to such a damnably unpleasant fate."

Thomas had already had the disagreeable experience of overhearing the disturbing rumours circulating among their neighbours. What would happen when Isabella's husband became aware of them, as he undoubtedly would? At all costs, he must save his boy from ruin. Or worse.

Coming between a man and his wife was liable to attract greater danger than scandal. Thomas shuddered, remembering a duel fought for just such a reason, which had resulted in the death of a fellow officer during his army days. He redoubled his efforts to steer his beloved son onto safer ground.

"Do you imagine for one minute, that Archibald Cummings is going to step aside and condone his wife's having an affair?" Thomas continued.

"Absolutely not!" he thundered, bringing his fist down with a bang on the arm of his chair. Stephen flinched.

"You're fortunate he hasn't already become aware of what is going on behind his back. There's no future other than tragedy in a liaison such as yours, Stephen. It's always so when one takes liberties with another man's wife."

Stephen, squirming in his seat, hung his head.

His father's words were irrefutable.

There were a few more unpalatable truths; unsavoury truths; Thomas could tell about that damnable piranha of a woman; only the mood the boy was in he'd refuse to believe them. Instinctively, Thomas knew he would gain no advantage from trying to blacken Isabella's name. Quite the contrary. Such a move would serve only to drive Stephen further from him than he already had. Straight into the woman's arms.

He didn't know the full extent of the affair; feared knowing; although, as rumour would have it, he was already too late to nip it in the bud. He could only pray Stephen's infatuation proved to be as short lived as these affairs usually were. The woman would be bound to expose her true nature sooner or later, and surely Stephen would be disillusioned enough to break away when that day came. Thomas prayed it would come sooner.

"Isabella and I could go away together," Stephen began, somewhat tentatively. He saw his father shake his head, and spoke more urgently. "We could, Dad, I've been thinking. You and I have been discussing the potential benefits of acquiring another property in the new country being developed in Queensland. Why don't we go ahead with the plan? I'll persuade Isabella to go with me, and we'll say she's my wife. Nobody will know the difference."

Thomas cringed at the preposterous idea.

"Everyone would know," he ground out. "The colony isn't big enough to hide a scandal of such elephantine proportions. Think about it Son," He searched his mind, triumphantly pulling out the one unassailable argument his son had no option but to accept.

"Even if you could pull it off, do you really think Isabella would agree? She's a woman who enjoys her comforts. Somehow I can't see her in the role of a frontierswoman." Although, Thomas admitted to himself, as a last resort, the suggestion held considerable appeal; provided his son went north unaccompanied by his paramour.

Stephen stared blindly at his boots. Isabella had already shown herself to be recalcitrant in committing herself openly to their love. He hated to admit it, but his father had the right of it. His next words, born of hopeless desperation, came out tinged with unintended sarcasm. Not that he really expected a workable solution; he'd racked his brains for days over this very problem and had about given up hope.

"What do you suggest then, Dad?"

*****

"Stephen!" Isabella hissed her annoyance with her impetuous young lover when he pulled her into his arms in the middle of the morning. In the middle of her garden with the house full of spying, disapproving servants merely yards away. Tall for a woman, pale olive skin attractively flushed, albeit with annoyance, and eyes the deepest of velvety browns, now emitting a dagger-like glare, she pushed him from her and stepped back to a more circumspect distance. "What are you thinking of?" she hissed through perfect lips delicately enhanced with rouge. "With all the gossip doing the rounds we agreed to be more careful and not take unnecessary chances."

"It's alright my darling." Stephen reached for the sable-haired beauty only to be repulsed once again when she raised her fan as a barrier between them. A pulse throbbed at his temple and his lips thinned to an angry line. "I saw Archibald heading towards the timber-felling camp." Even to himself, he sounded petulant. Striving for a more mature tone he continued, "He'll be gone for hours, Darling. We're quite safe."

"It's not only him we need to beware of, my foolish pet." Isabella, ever observant, had noted his annoyance.

She moderated her tone to a seductive coo and risked giving her delightfully youthful lover's cheek a gentle pat. "This prison of a house is full of nasty, watching eyes and tattling tongues."

Instantly contrite, Stephen was quick with his apology. "Oh. Of course. I'm sorry my love, I forgot. I won't stay long, but we need to talk. You can pretend I really came with a message for Archibald. Dad knows about us Isabella, and we need to discuss what we should do. No. No, he doesn't know everything," he hastened to reassure a horror-struck Isabella. "He'd heard the rumours someone's been spreading about us, and taxed me with them." Defiance chased the melting glow of love from his eyes. Chin up, he added, "I couldn't lie to him, Darling; not about something so terribly important as our love for each other."

"But he'll go running to Archibald! I'll be ruined!" Why ever did the stupid boy have to be so open and honest? Didn't he understand how essential it is to be a good liar if you want to enjoy yourself in a way stuffy society frowns upon? If he wasn't so entirely satisfactory as a lover she'd give him his marching orders. She still might, if only there was someone half as entertaining to take his place. Going on and on about how much he loved her was undeniably gratifying, but after a while the constant repetitions became rather tedious. Especially since she didn't reciprocate his high-flown emotions.

Stephen claimed her fluttering hands.

"No. He won't," he assured her. "Dad abhors scandal. So much, he'd never do anything to precipitate one. Anyway, I stopped short of telling him we were lovers." Breathing in the heady scent of her musky perfume, he recalled the undreamt-of pleasures he'd recently discovered in Isabella's experienced arms. His heart raced anew as raw excitement flooded his veins.

The front of his trousers stretched tight, making movement awkward. How he wished they were totally alone at this very minute in their private bush hideaway. Better still, in Isabella's wide, comfortable bed, just a few short yards away. It was sheer torture to be so close and yet be denied even the most innocent of embraces. Not that their embraces ever remained innocent for long.

Isabella had taken over his heart and mind long before that magical night she had permitted him to claim her body. He was enslaved by her to the extent that when they were apart he could think of little beyond the next time he'd be making love to her. When they were together, there was time for nothing beyond themselves and the pleasure they gave each other.

Their hurried secret liaisons never allowed time for the usual social conventions, such as polite conversation. If only they could be together always, and live a normal life. Stephen's stomach knotted as his conscience lashed him. He absolutely hated all this deceitful sneaking around.

Now, desperate to appease Isabella, he continued his tale.

"All I admitted to Dad, was being in love with you."

He'd also claimed Isabella returned his love; though he thought that was more than she would appreciate hearing right now; even though he was certain it was the truth.

How could it not be, when she allowed him such intimacies? But she was rather peculiar when it came to admitting their love for each other, claiming it was bad luck to tempt the Devil, or some such female nonsense.

Isabella gently drew her hands from Stephen's clasp and sat on the rustic bench in the shade of the tall eucalypt sheltering them from the enervating heat. It was only Spring, and already so hot. How she longed for the cool breezes to be found in the homes overlooking Sydney's harbour, any one of which would suit her better than this isolated farm. Putting aside her discontent, she applied her fan with unwonted vigour, absent-mindedly sliding across to make a space for Stephen to sit by her side.

"What happened, then? I can't believe he had nothing to say to that." Isabella's lips assumed a bitter twist. Some months earlier, stiff-rumped Thomas Fortescue had spurned her advances, treating her no better than if she'd been filth beneath his highly polished, expensive English leather boots.

An insult she found impossible to forgive. One she had vowed to avenge.

Since her first lover had jilted her at the altar twelve years earlier, no man treated Isabella Johnson Cummings so disdainfully and got away with it. Thomas's uncompromising rejection had contributed hugely to her decision to relieve her deathly boredom with country life by corrupting his naïve pup of a son; an entertainment she had quickly found surprisingly satisfying. The boy had proved an adept pupil, fulfilling her needs in exemplary fashion. If only he hadn't got this dratted bee in his bonnet about *love*.

Better still if Archibald would take her to live in Sydney instead of incarcerating her on this stultifying back of beyond farm where she was forced daily into the company of ex-convicts and the like. Where the stuck-up local matrons looked down their noses at her.

What good was money if you couldn't flaunt your possession of it? A tiny frown flickered across her perfect visage as she contemplated the adoration in Stephen's rapt gaze.

There was no such thing as love. If anyone knew that, she should. Love was just a word people less honest than herself used to excuse baser motivations such as lust, or greed. For men and women alike, it was all about satisfying one's sexual needs, or acquiring influence or riches. Nothing more. Only Stephen was too young and idealistic to appreciate that fact. As if she was ever going to run off with him as he had begged her, thereby throwing away the hard-earned gains accruing from her recent marriage to Archibald Cummings.

Her husband might be a boring old goat, but he was rich; rich and malleable.

Except on the one issue of importance to her. However, she wasn't ready yet to give Stephen up. Not when dangling him on a string was such an enjoyable revenge on his father; not to mention the rest of this hide-bound rustic society. It was also the only entertainment available to her at present in this God-forsaken backwater! There wasn't even a decent shop, or a theatre, nearer than a journey taking several long, wearying days. Even longer if the road conditions were worse than usual. Merton's Store had nothing to offer beyond the most basic of general merchandise, and it took weeks for mail-order deliveries to arrive.

Isabella let her eyes rove possessively, savouring her lover's tall, rangy body. Lean, work-hardened muscles filled out a broad chest and shoulders topped by a shapely head covered in thick, springy, waves of sandy-blond hair.

His boyishly smooth skin, clear, periwinkle eyes and regular features were saved from prettiness by a strong, dimpled chin and an uncompromising, straight blade of a nose. He showed promise of one day becoming a man to be reckoned with.

For the present he was still an untried puppy, sufficient to amuse herself with, but not man enough to tempt her into an ill-considered elopement. Hiding a yawn behind her fan, she tuned back in to his tale of woe.

Stephen grimaced.

"Oh, Dad ranted and raved for a while. I'd never heard him shout and carry on like that before. He really lost control. Well, I got angry too, at being treated like a child. Next thing, I was yelling back at him. Things were getting nasty." He still felt sick in the stomach remembering how close he and his father had come to tearing an unbridgeable rift in their relationship. "I was about to walk away until he cooled down, when suddenly he backed off. Apologised for shouting at me, and suggested we sit down and discuss the situation, man to man." Isabella disguised an unladylike snort as a cough.

"Anyway," Stephen concluded impatiently, "I ended up asking Dad's advice, much good that did me."

Curious to know what that wily old fox, Thomas Fortescue, might be planning, Isabella asked, "Apart from ordering you to give me up, which I'm sure he tried, did he have any practical suggestions?" She acknowledged Thomas as her implacable enemy, and hoped to gain an advantage by learning how his thoughts were tending.

Too agitated to sit still any longer, Stephen sprang to his feet. After a few hurried steps to the other side of the tree, he swung back, bursting into angry speech.

"Oh, he had a suggestion alright. A couple of them, actually. Both totally out of the question. Giving you up was the very least of it! You don't want to know the rest!"

Intrigued to know what solutions Thomas could have arrived at to force her out of his son's life, Isabella clasped her hands coyly in her lap and turned an inviting smile in her lover's direction.

"Oh, but I do, Stephen Darling," she cooed, using her brilliant, dark eyes to sap his resistance. "I most certainly do."

At the intent gaze fixed upon him, Stephen's blood quickened in his veins, and his body stirred anew. He groaned, took a few hurried steps away, then returned, shaking his head as he reclaimed his seat. This time it was Isabella who reached for Stephen's hands, forgetful of watchers for the moment.

"Tell me Darling," she commanded, a thread of steel underlying her dulcet tones. "No secrets between the two of us, remember?"

Stephen, pressing an urgent kiss to Isabella's knuckles, took little persuasion. Maybe if he told her the whole of it, she would take his father's threats more seriously.

"First off, he suggested I should do what we've been discussing recently, and take a trip to Queensland to look into buying land there. He said it would give me the chance to study our situation from a distance and decide what I truly want out of life. Of course, he hopes I'll forget you if he separates us."

He shook his head at such absurdity.

"But there's no chance of that, Darling. I already know exactly what I want, so I told him I was perfectly willing to go, just as long as you come with me. Won't you Darling? Please?" Clutching at straws, he tried once more to persuade his lover to see things his way.

"You know Isabella, I've racked my brains and no matter which way I look at it, I can't see how we can be together unless you agree to leave Archibald? We could be so happy together, you and I."

He lifted pleading eyes to hers, unsurprised with Isabella's tiny, impatient shake of her head negating that idea. He sighed. There was no point going over old arguments yet again. Isabella was adamantly opposed to their running off together.

"I didn't think so," he muttered with another grimace, dropping his head into his hands.

"You said he had two suggestions. What was the other one?"

Once again Stephen was too agitated to sit. He stood, leaning his face against the smooth bark of the gum tree. Drawing in a deep breath, he turned, anger directed at his absent father radiating from every inch of his stiffened posture and flung himself back down at her side. Isabella reclaimed his hand.

"He said I should get married!" he burst out. "To someone else! As if I could! As if that would work! You know that if I can't marry you, my love, I'll not marry at all!"

He was totally unprepared for the full-throated laughter with which Isabella greeted his dramatic declaration. Affronted, he pulled away.

"How can you laugh, Isabella? I don't see anything at all funny in that idea."

"Sorry Darling. I know you would never look at another woman." Isabella reached out to draw him back to her. Clasping his hand in her lap, she gave it a mollifying pat.

"I'm quite surprised, I must say. Just who did he imagine you might marry, out here in the middle of nowhere? None of the local families have daughters who are old enough to marry. Even Rosie Mannering is only fifteen. He can't expect you to marry a servant girl, can he?" Suspicion sharpened her voice as she suddenly recalled the handsome, red-haired sisters who worked in the 'Eden Vale' homestead.

"No, of course not," he answered, mollified by her possessive tone. Isabella did love him. Really, she did, despite her refusal to elope with him.

"As you say, there's no-one local who would fit the bill. Dad suggested Lucy Gordon. We're old friends with Peter Gordon, our lawyer, and his family down in Morpeth. Mr Gordon was with the East India Company and Dad met him while he was serving in India. He steered Dad into some profitable business ventures and their friendship continued when they both came to settle in New South Wales. Anyway, Lucy Gordon is just eighteen. Dad's always cherished hopes of a match between us."

Not so long ago, before he met Isabella, Stephen would have been more than happy to marry Lucy Gordon.

He liked her well enough, and it was, after all, what he had always expected to do. Now it was totally out of the question. Despondent, his own eyes were fixed unseeing on the ground at his feet, otherwise he might have noticed the calculation gleaming in Isabella's tannin-dark eyes.

"Actually, his suggestion may have merit. Let me think a minute." She waved Stephen to silence when he opened his mouth to protest.

"Yes! Yes, Stephen, I do believe that's it. Listen. If you agree to his terms, agree to marry the chit, he'll stop pestering you, and everyone else will stop gossiping and spreading malicious rumours about us." Excited by the possibilities inherent in the idea, Isabella warmed to her theme. "Especially after the wedding. And since no untutored little schoolgirl has the power to come between us, we'll be completely free to pursue our love as we have been doing; just as long as we're careful how we go about it. Even Archibald will never suspect the truth. Oh, Stephen, it's a Godsend. Your father has played right into our hands."

His mouth twisted as anguish tore at Stephen's heart. He recoiled, yanking his hand from her grasp. How *could* the woman he loved find this preposterous idea a desirable solution to their problem? It was utterly inconceivable.

"But Isabella, how could you tolerate seeing me married to someone else? How could I bear to be married to another woman when you're the only one I want to be with; to make love to? I can't do it!"

"Certainly, you can, my dearest darling. You keep saying you'll do anything for me," she cajoled. "Surely you're not going to baulk at the first hurdle."

Her cool accusation rocked him. Her next words had him writhing with guilt.

"If I can suffer Archibald pawing at me, night after night, surely you can also make a tiny little sacrifice. It's either that or we part forever; and oh, my dearest love," Isabella brought all her histrionic talents to bear, "I simply couldn't survive if I couldn't be with you ever again. I need to feel your arms around me; your lips on mine."

She suited her actions to her words. Clasping him to her impressive bosom, she kissed him till he was in a mindless frenzy, then deliberately withdrew, reminding him primly of the nearby presence of hostile eyes.

If she could persuade him to follow her lead in this, what a delicious revenge it would be on all those backwoods upstarts who dared to look down their supercilious noses at her. A cruel feline smile curled her lips.

*****

Stephen didn't succumb to Isabella's urgings immediately; or even at their next, more heated, totally private assignation where Isabella was free to bring even more pressure to bear when she held him naked in her arms. He did succumb though. Eventually his lust for his paramour overcame his scruples.

Fathoms deep in love, Stephen could deny Isabella nothing she set her heart upon. Not when she employed every single one of her feminine wiles in the task.

His opposition worn down by constant pressure from both Isabella and his father, Stephen finally accepted defeat and agreed to ask Lucy Gordon to marry him, in spite of his deeply ingrained sense of honour telling him it was wrong.

Isabella's will had eventually proved stronger than his own, and while he would never give voice to such a disloyal thought, he felt less of a man for his complicity in such a dastardly scheme. And, deep down, he experienced a twinge of dismay at the duplicity of his dearest love. It was a side of her nature he had not previously encountered.

It was his unspoken prayer that either Lucy Gordon or her parents would deem him unworthy and refuse his suit. He rode slowly home, eyes blind to the brilliant displays of golden wattle blossom beside the path. When the cackling laughter of a pair of kookaburras jerked him out of his dark introspection, he cursed them to hell and back.

Even nature knew him for a weak fool.

How could he carry out such a momentous deception?

But he'd given his promise to Isabella. Somewhere he'd find the strength to follow through with the scheme, since the alternative, to give Isabella up, was utterly unthinkable.

Continued…….

Get

"Unto Death"

as soon as it's released – go to

www.lenawestauthor.com

and make sure that you are signed up for news and release notices!

About the Author

Born in tropical North Queensland, Lena loves living close to the sea, although she moved frequently during her early years, living everywhere from large cities to isolated farms. Her most recent home has a deck overlooking the ocean, which is her favourite room in the house, for reading, writing, art, craft or even birdwatching, when the local birds come to visit.

After working as a primary school teacher in both her native Queensland, and later in New South Wales where she met her own romantic hero, she took a very early retirement to travel Australia with him, in a motorhome. This idyllic lifestyle lasted several years, during which time she indulged in the creation of story plots and their settings, culminating in her taking steps to fulfil her lifelong ambition to write.

Storytelling came naturally - she had been making up stories for her own entertainment all her life, but it wasn't until she began traveling that she had time to write down some of her favourites. Now published, *Marrying Alan Morgan,* is the first in a series of rural romances set in the fictional town of Oxley Crossing.

It is followed by the soon to be released second in the series, *Saving Jonathon Armitage,* with several more in the series planned. She also writes standalone contemporary romances and Australian historical romances.

She has an addiction to happily-ever-afters, in both her reading and her own stories, so the romance genre was a natural fit, and the variety of places she has lived have all added to the settings in which she brings love to life.

You can find Lena on Facebook at:

https://www.facebook.com/LenaWestAuthor/

or sign up for her newsletter at :

www.lenawestauthor.com

Other Books by Lena West

Standalone Contemporary Romances

Loving Fenella

Bronwyn's Family (Coming soon)

Contemporary Series

The Wylde Flower Series (Coming soon)

Books in the
Love in Oxley Crossing Series

Marrying Alan Morgan

Saving Jonathon Armitage

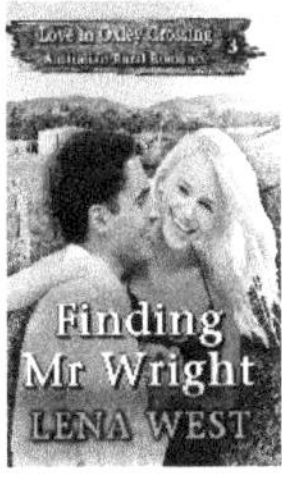

Finding Mr Wright (March, 2018)

Electing Robert Whitman (Coming soon)

Redeeming Josh Marten (Coming soon)

Historical Romances

Unto Death (May 2018)

Emily's baby (Coming soon)

Home is the Heart (Coming soon)

Blue Streak (Coming soon)

Love and War (Coming soon

Connect with Lena!

Be the first to know about it when Lena's next book is released!

Sign up to Lena's newsletter at

www.lenawestauthor.com